Though this novel is based in Hastings which is actually a real town on the south coast in East Sussex. None of the people or specific places actually exist. Neither are they based upon any person or place. They are what is known in the business as fictional.

At least, as far as I know they are.

However, if anybody should come across a hotel like the Prince Albert with a landlady and daughter as described in the novel, please let me know and I'll get their as soon as I can.

For anybody else who thinks that they recognise a person or place, well, tough. Look upon it as being free publicity. It's not intentional.

Now this twaddle is out of the way, please read on.......

Justice Prevails

By

Colin Lodder

colin.lodder.hastings@gmail.com

Chapter One

She entered my inner sanctum as she usually did, quickly without knocking, slamming the door behind her, eyes glaring, as though she expected to catch me doing something I shouldn't have been doing. She caught me sat back in my old, worn leather chair reading the sports section of an equally old newspaper I'd found at the bottom of a drawer in my second hand filing cabinet.

I looked up at her disapproving, glaring face. Melissa disapproved of everything and I wasn't an exception. I raised an eyebrow. Eyebrows can speak volumes and they do it quietly.

"You've got a customer," she told me, crimson lips barely moving. "A woman. Says she needs to see you urgently. She made the appointment a few days ago."
"You didn't tell me!" I don't know why I keep her on. Probably because I'm not totally sure how I got her in the first place. I think that maybe she came with the office. The rent's high enough. Maybe she's some sort of fixture or fitting.
"What's she want to see me about?"
Melissa shrugged. The secondary movement reminded me of a video I'd seen of undulating ground during an earthquake. "Didn't say," she said after the rippling had stopped.
"So what's she like?" I needed some preparation before I saw her.
"Fortyish, nice body, smartly dressed, must have money. An obvious slapper. Just your type. I'll send her in."

I sat back and folded my paper as I watched Melissa's rear cavort out of my office. She was replaced by my potential client. Introduced as Mrs Belinda Carter. She wore a charcoal grey business suit. Skirt a few inches shorter than was the norm for the style. It suited her white nylon clad legs and the high red stilettos. Fluffy red hair and significant make-up. Her alligator skin handbag looked expensive. She

2

carried herself with an air of confidence and haughtiness.

I gestured for her to take one of the two hard back chairs in front of my stained, leather topped desk. She looked a little nervous but I put that down to the fact the chair creaked and moved threateningly in several directions. I renewed my promise to myself to either get some more chairs or glue the joints of the ones I had. Then I waited patiently for her to open. It's the way I work. She did, but it took her awhile to begin. I think she was waiting for me to say something.

"I hope you can help me Mr Ree."
"Ree?" She had either said 'Ree', or she had some sort of weird lisp.
"Your name." She half turned in her seat and pointed to the outer office. "It's on your door." She was frowning, uncertain, and the wobbly chair wasn't helping.
"Name's Street," I told her. "Al Street. Somebody stole the 'T's'." Probably Melissa.
"Oh dear, I didn't realise." She put her hand to her mouth as if embarrassed. But I didn't figure her for being somebody who was ever embarrassed. Told me a lot about her. Figured her to be somebody who thought that she was better than most. Big tits can do that for a woman.
"Don't worry about it," I told her holding up both hands to placate her. I stared into her large green eyes that were surrounded by enormously long lashes; it was like a bird's eye view of two lakes in a forest, or something like that. "If you don't know my name, how'd you get here?"
"Private Eye."
I nodded. "Says something like that on the door. Only what it says doesn't have any 'T's' in it. Otherwise it'd say something different." Not sure why I told her that.
She shook her head and smiled nervously. No lipstick smudge on her brilliant white teeth. "No, I mean the magazine, 'Private Eye'. Your advert."
Advert in 'Private Eye'? First I'd heard of it. Melissa.

"Your advert doesn't give a name," she continued, "just a phone number which I rang on Tuesday and made an appointment with your secretary. It says that you're a private detective and an ex-Metropolitan

Police Detective. But now I've met you... Well..."

I sort of smiled. "You think that I'm a bit young for retirement?"

She nodded as her eyes quizzed me.

"You want to know why I quit the force?"

She nodded again.

"They sacked me," I told her before pausing for effect, "because I was caught shagging the Chief Constable's young wife." Sometimes these things just came out. Something like a verbal twitch.

She just stared at me, face moving as if various expressions were being tried to find the most suitable fit. Suddenly she snorted, threw her head back, opened her mouth and started baying like a donkey. At least, that's what it sounded like to me. Bet she went down a treat at a sophisticated dinner party.

Eventually, the donkey turned back into a woman who rummaged through her handbag to find something to dab her eyes with. It was good that her mascara appeared to be waterproof otherwise I'd have found myself sitting opposite a panda. Don't know how to communicate with pandas, a donkey is bad enough. Once she'd completed that delicate task I spoke again. "So why are you here?" I like getting to the point.

She hesitated, looking for the words that she must have rehearsed a thousand times. I patiently waited for them to form. "My husband," she said, "I want you to find out what happened to him."

I sat back and sighed quietly to myself, tempted to tell her that he probably traded her in for a more up to date model. But I desisted. I needed the work. Missing persons isn't hard, especially when you've got contacts who owe you a truck load of favours.

"Tell me about it," I said and wondered if I'd kept the expected boredom from my voice.

"They say he's dead," she said.

"Do they indeed." I sat up a little more. Not what I'd expected, but I shouldn't have been surprised; most things that happen to me aren't what I expect. "Who has been telling you stories like that?"

Her eyes narrowed slightly, but she answered. "I said everybody..."

"Everybody?" My words and eyebrows told her to be more specific.

"Lifeboat crew, coastguard, fishermen, police."

Pretty much everybody then, I conceded. "Lost at sea. No body." I caught on quickly. Well, I am supposed to be a detective.

She nodded and frowned. "But how...?" Her face relaxed and she flashed her teeth. "Obvious to somebody like you."

"You think that you're being lied to? Some sort of conspiracy?"

"No, no, nothing like that."

"What then?" I might be a detective, but I'm an impatient one and she was a woman and this was my own office so I wasn't in the position to give her a couple of slaps to make her get to the point.

"Okay, he was lost at sea, as you put it. But it's not straightforward. Look, Jim was an experienced... Well, he was with two experienced fishermen. The sea was totally calm. There was no radio call to the coastguard or anybody else saying that there was any problem. There was no rip-tide..."

"What's a rip-tide?" I asked her.

She shrugged. "No idea, but I understand that they can be especially dangerous when you're fishing around the Royal Sovereign Shoal...

I nodded. "I've heard that too." Sometimes I'm terribly tempted to punch myself. My mouth has always got me into trouble. Maybe that's why I keep Melissa on; self punishment.

Luckily, she ignored my comment and continued. "Anyway, Billy, he's a friend, was on the lifeboat that night and he told me there was no rip-tide. He can't understand what happened. It was a wooden boat, solid, well looked after. Apparently it's virtually impossible for it to sink without warning, without trace."

I saw her point, but preferred to keep an open mind. If the boat disappeared from the surface, it either went up or it went down. So it's either full of seawater and the fish got their revenge, or there are some aliens who fancied a fish and people supper. "Do these fishing boats have lights?" I asked her.

"Yes, they're well lit. But apparently, the Amy Grey's lights just disappeared."

I noticed she had said, 'disappeared' as opposed to 'went out'. In the past, I have found that little things like that have absolutely no relevance and are totally meaningless. But it's the sort of thing that detectives have been trained to pay attention to. Maybe that's why there are so many unsolved crimes.

"You implied earlier that there were other boats around. Were they close or just in the same part of the sea?"
"Fairly close. If you stand on the beach at night when they're out, you can see several."
"They're within sight of land?" I asked, unnecessarily.
"Yes," she said.
"So your husband's boat disappeared. When did anybody notice that it was missing? In the morning or whenever they returned to port?"
"There's no port," she told me, "they're dragged up onto the beach when they're done. But it was not noticed right away. It was that damned Arthur Gibson..."
"Arthur Gibson? Somebody you're not fond of?"
"I can't stand the man. Something fishy about him."
"Fishy? Is that a joke?"
"Joke?" She frowned. "I don't understand."

I wished I hadn't bothered. "Something fishy about a fisherman."
"Oh, I see what you mean." Not even a flicker of a smile from her.
"Arthur is not really a fisherman; he is, well, like Jim my husband, for them it's a sort of hobby."
"So let me get this right. Your husband, isn't or wasn't really a fisherman at all."
"No, not really. Sometimes he liked to think he was." She gave a little wistful smile. "He was really an estate agent. And a good one at that."

Good estate agent; not so good fisherman. "And this Arthur character is he an estate agent too?"
She shook her head, hair dancing like Medusa's snakes. "God no. To be honest, I don't know what he does. Jim and I have been to a few of his parties but I don't think either of us knew how he got his money. And he does seem to have lot of it."

"Ok," I said, "we'll get back to that if we have to. This disappearing

6

boat, I take it the incident is all logged; witnesses questioned by the police etc."

"Oh yes," she confirmed.

"Good. So tell me the best you can what happened, or at least what was reported. Don't leave anything out no matter how trivial you think it is." Standard detective spiel. I mean, let's face it, do I really need to hear all the trivial stuff? But I have to say it, makes the client think I'm able to find the hidden clue that nobody else has noticed.

She began:-

Ten o'clock:
Lights of several fishing boats visible from shore.
Later witnesses come forward with the following information:
Loud bangs out at sea attracted their attention. They saw a boat's lights go out. But came on again almost instantly. Then the lights started moving slowly as they continued to watch. Fishermen in other boats couldn't confirm events. They saw nothing and heard nothing. Possibly because of wind direction and distance between boats.

Coastguard had boats on radar but took little notice as nothing out of the ordinary attracted their attention.

When night's fishing was completed, boats returned on the tide. Arthur Gibson first to notice that the Amy Grey was missing. After a reasonable interval the authorities were notified. Lifeboat was launched from adjoining station. No trace found. Boat had completely vanished. Coastguard helicopter brought in but found nothing, no wreckage, bodies or debris. Nothing.

A local mystery. A tragedy. Three men lost. If there was a mention in the nationals I didn't see it. Probably too many bigger things were going on at the time.

"You want me to find out what really happened?" I asked her.

"Can you?" She looked hopeful.

I was tempted to tell her that there wasn't a hope in hell. Instead. "I can look into it."

"I'm willing to pay you generously," she said.

7

"I'll be expensive," I warned her, not really knowing what expensive meant. And not knowing how long I would choose to spend in searching for the undefinable. "And there's no guarantee," I added. "Maybe there's nothing to find out. Could be a simple accident."
She shook her head, "No, I know it's more than just an accident. Something happened that night. Divers have searched the area where the Amy Grey was last seen. They found nothing. That can't be right."

"Were they wearing life belts?" I asked. If they were, bodies should have floated. Probably should have floated anyway, unless they were all below deck when whatever happened, happened.
"They never bothered," she replied, "You know what men are like?"
"Got a rough idea," I said.
"So you'll take the case," she smiled.
"If you're paying."
"Good." She extracted a white envelope from the jaws of her alligator handbag and handed it to me. "A down payment."
I took it from her, opened it and gave it a rough count trying very hard to appear casual. "That will do for now," I told her. "If you see Melissa outside, she'll give you a receipt."
"I'll double that if you get a result."

I simply nodded and decided I needed a drink. "Right," I said, trying to appear professional, "it's time for places and people." I took a small black notebook out of my shirt pocket and opened it on a blank page. I wrote as she gave the minutiae.

Chapter Two

Thursday 4th June

Got a train to Hastings. Easier than driving, though not as quick. Took nearly two hours, stopping at every station along the way. Occasionally a passenger got off. One or two got on.

Two hours. Plenty of time to think and to plan. Instead, I picked up a discarded newspaper and amused myself with the crossword. Absolutely useless at crosswords but the time passed.

Eventually got to Hastings and easily found a cab to take me to the hotel Melissa had booked. It was on the seafront. An old Victorian house. Probably originally owned by a wealthy London rug maker or similar. A home by the seaside; somewhere to take his family and servants away from the dirt and noise of London. Some things never change. Some things do.

The house was now a hotel. The paintwork was probably original. Parts of it were still white. Inside wasn't a lot better, but it was clean in a shabby sort of way.

Some places can bring back memories even if you've never been there before. This place reminded me of Agatha Christie. I half expected to see Miss Marple pass by the end of the corridor. Pity she didn't. I could have used her. I certainly had no real idea why I was in Hastings. Looking for a missing fishing boat and a drowned fisherman it seemed. For the money I'd been given I'd have looked for a fisherman with three heads. And have the same degree of confidence in finding one.

I walked through the front door and along the worn out carpet. The reception consisted of a counter which basically sat in a wall. At some stage a large square hole had been put into an internal wall. The counter had on it a few scattered leaflets and bell.

I banged my hand down on the bell. I waited patiently. Two minutes later I repeated my action. Eventually a woman came into view. She wore a frown and not a lot else. At least, not to my eyes. Her tiny summer dress showed a lot of flesh, nicely tanned and shaped. Well, it was summer and this was the seaside. Nonetheless, if she was the hotel manager, she shouldn't have been advertising what wasn't on the menu. On the other hand...

"I heard you the first time," she said, frown staying put.
"Good." I gave her a big smile. "Must mean you heard the second time as well. Don't like wasting actions."
"Well?" she asked standing looking at me disapprovingly, hands on admirable hips, head to one side. Her expression was so familiar, I wondered if she was related to Melissa.
"Very well, thanks. You seem to be okay too. Anyway, enough of this chit-chat, I'm sure you've got more important things to do than to welcome your guests."

She took a deep breath and stood more upright sticking out her chest in the process. I didn't mind, it was a good distraction from her angry expression.
"Got a room booked," I told her before she could explode. "Name of Street. Al Street." I gave her one of my more endearing smiles. Had the same effect as if she'd just bitten into a really hot chilli pepper.

She stared at me, expression frozen. I could sense her mind racing. I continued to smile. It must have worked because even though her face was still doing the chilli pepper thing she snatched up a ledger from beneath the counter and slammed it down on top. She opened it and ran her finger down the names.

"Single room." She glared at me.
I nodded, smile intact.
"One week. Already paid."
I nodded, smile intact.
She looked at me and narrowed her eyes. "We have rules here."

"Really?" I let my smile fade. "I wasn't told about that. How annoying. Have you had them long?"

"Since we opened," she snapped. "No pets."

On cue there was a clatter of pans from behind her. She half turned. "Maria, do be careful." A little white dog trotted out from behind the wall and sat looking up at me.

She turned back to me. "Where was I?"

"You haven't moved. You were saying something about pets." I tried to look disappointed. I glanced down at the dog and back at her. I could see no resemblance whatsoever. Couldn't have been her dog.

"No pets. No guests. Especially of the opposite sex."

"Opposite to what?" A voice in my head told me to shut up, grab the key and leg it.

She pursed her lips. "Mr... Mr..." She looked down at the register. "Mr Street, I'm finding your attitude most unhelpful. We are very busy at this time of the year. I'm not certain that this hotel is at all suitable for the likes of you."

"Oh, but it is," I told her. "Most suitable. Wouldn't want to stay in a place without rules. Not at all."

I picked up my case from the floor and showed it to her. "Will you let me have the key and direct me to my room? I'm in a bit of a hurry. Need to freshen up. It is en suite? Good. Excellent. Have a meeting you know. All go isn't it? Never get any rest. Must be the same for you running a place like this. Ah well. Best to be busy they say."

She stared at me for a few moments, then rattled beneath the counter and came up with a key that had a large, red tag. 'Number 3'.

"Along there, to the right," she said pointing to where I hadn't seen Miss Marple. "There's a full list of the rules and what to do in the case of a fire, pinned to the door." She immediately turned her back on me and left. Seconds later, I heard a door slam.

With a shrug, I headed towards my room. Stopped. Listened. Certain I'd heard, just for an instant, squeals of laughter. I went to find my room.

The room was pretty much as I expected it to be. Clean but worn. The

11

bed was a little larger than an ordinary single, but smaller than a double. It was covered in a floral eiderdown. Top turned down showing a fat, white pillow. A small wardrobe, writing desk and a wooden backed chair completed the room's furnishings. A door led to the bathroom. Poking my head round I saw that it too was clean, with clean, white towels hanging from a rail.

There were several leaflets fanned out on the desk advertising local attractions. The one about Sea World caught my eye. Maybe if I popped along there I'd learn something about the sea. As things stood, all I knew about fishing boats, or any sort of boat for that matter, was that they floated. Or, at least, they did most of the time.

I put my suitcase on the bed to unpack but changed my mind. It could wait. I needed to get out and check my surroundings. It was late afternoon and I wasn't due to see Mrs Carter till the following morning to get the additional information that she'd failed to provide in her visit to my office.

I planned to take a stroll along the seafront and take a look at the fishing boats. I had no idea how big they were, or how they were built. Couldn't get a sense or a picture of what might have happened lacking that basic knowledge.

There was aloud rap on my door. I stared at for a few moments wondering if I'd inadvertently broken any of the rules that I just spotted pinned to the door. I walked over, opened it and stared into two large, blue eyes that were topped with short blonde hair. I stepped back. My gaze took in the pretty face with even prettier smile, and drifted downwards... Skin tight grey, halter top, stretched to its limit, tiny grey shorts stretched even more, and then legs. Legs that had the thighs and calves of a power-lifter.

"I work out a lot," she said, obviously reading my expression. "It makes me feel good. Makes me feel like a woman."
"Makes me feel like one too," I murmured. "Endorphins," I said more loudly.
"Probably. Anyway, I'm here about breakfast."
I glanced at my watch. "Bit late in the day for me."

She laughed at that. Gratifying. Not everybody has a sense of humour. Especially not like mine. Perhaps it was the sea air.

"The morning. Mother forgot to tell you. Breakfast is between 7.00 and 8.30. Any idea when you would like it?"

"Like it?" I was trying to prise my eyes from her beautifully moulded crotch.

"Breakfast." She wore a knowing smile.

"Right, breakfast," I said, finally managing to look her in the eye.

"Time you want to know. Eight. Yes, about eight. What happens if I'm late?"

She laughed, "Mother will probably spank you. She can be very strict, you know. She turned and walked off, shapely buttocks wrestling with each other.

I stared along the empty corridor and decided that a drink took precedence over fishing boats.

Chapter Three

On my way out I was stopped in what serves as Reception by daughter.

"Have you any idea what time you will be back?"

"What time am I allowed out to?"

"If you're going to be late, I'll give you a key."

"A key would be good," I said.

"We go to bed quite early," she told me as she handed me a key.

"Beauty sleep?" I grimaced inside. Much too corny.

Her smile broadened. "Sleep?"

I felt an urge to growl.

"One little thing," she said quietly, looking around to see if there was anybody listening and beckoning me to come closer, conspiratorially. I obliged.

"Mother," she whispered, "I must warn you. She's... Well, I'll come right out with it. My mother is a nymphomaniac. She can't help herself."

"She is? Thanks for the warning. I'll remember to keep my door unlocked." I turned and walked off.

The weather was warm and for a few minutes I relaxed and leant on the promenade railings and watched the holiday makers making their holiday on the beach. One or two were enjoying or maybe suffering a swim in the sea.

For some reason, Melissa slipped into my mind and I imagined her in a tiny bikini. This was actually somewhat overdressed from how I often imagined her. I wondered how buoyant boobs were. If they had any buoyancy to speak of, Melissa, if she tried to swim doing the crawl would surely keep flipping over onto her back.

I figuratively shook my head to clear away the sexual fantasies that were threatening to overcome me. I had got myself into such a state that every time I saw any attractive female go by in summer attire I wanted to howl like a sexually deprived wolf.

Fish and Chips, I told myself. I was at the seaside, I was hungry, and so Fish and Chips would do me fine.

I continued to stroll along the seafront. On the other side of the road were numerous places that I could have got fed in. However, I changed my mind and decided that seeing the fishing boats took precedence. I knew I was heading in the right direction to see them.

Small, sturdy and sometimes colourful. Couldn't see how one of them could suddenly fall apart and sink; even after a collision. If two had collided it would have been at low speed. Likely just bounced off each other. Minimal damage.

If the Amy Grey, the missing boat had been hit by something else; a speedboat, say. There would have been two damaged boats with the accompanying wreckage and debris. So, logically, if it didn't go down it either went up or somewhere else. I still didn't think it likely that some aliens fancied a fisherman supper. Which was just as well. I didn't see myself as an alien hunter. So I figured somewhere else is what happened. The questions, of course, were, where and why?

I found a fish and chip shop close to the fishing boats and ordered a large cod and chips with mushy peas. I knew how to eat well. As I sat and waited, I ran the case through my mind.

Where? Need to know how far a fishing boat can go. Need to know of anywhere where it could have been put without being found too easily. Could it have been painted a different colour, had a make-over and a name change and was now hidden in plain sight? Unlikely. People might notice if a strange fishing boat suddenly turns up somewhere.

But I wasn't exactly tasked with finding the fishing boat; I was tasked with finding the husband. And finding the boat isn't the same thing. Although it would mean some sort of progress.

So the where is still a mystery. How about the 'Why?' What reason could three people have for deciding to hide their boat and disappear? Now you hear of similar mysteries happening in the middle of the ocean, but a mile or two off shore isn't the middle of the ocean.

So what drove three men to decide to disappear? Chronic nagging might be an incentive for the husband to bugger off. And Belinda Carter does seem the sort that could produce such an incentive. There were several reasons why her husband might decide to disappear. Found himself a more up to date model? So called mid-life crisis? Money problems? Upset the wrong people? Amnesia? Breakdown? Any one of those reasons could account for one of them to disappear, but all three?

No, there was more to this than I previously thought. Now I felt something bad had happened. Though I had not the slightest idea what it was.

I finished my fish and chips and decided three things. The first was that fish and chips always tasted better at the seaside. The second was that I had done too much thinking for the day, but at least I had a few ideas to explore. The third decision was that I needed a drink. Tomorrow I'd make a phone call or two and visit Belinda Carter as arranged.

There were plenty of bars to choose from in Hastings Old Town where I had found myself. Most were real pubs whose purpose was to sell drinks in a convivial drinking atmosphere. Though there were also plenty of the other sort. Pubs where food was the priority. Not places that had once been real pubs but were now plastic caricatures serving pre-prepared pretentious dishes with fancy continental names. Most of which our continental cousins would turn their noses up in horror if they were served such 'delights.' But I suppose in this day and age, publicans have to make the best of whatever they've got.

I sat at the bar of a small pub down a side street. There were a few drinkers both at the bar and on surrounding tables. It was what I call a typical pub. Walls were adorned with various drawings, pictures and photos. They obviously meant something to somebody. Or had once.

I sat, drank watched and listened. Nobody seemed to notice me.
Maybe they thought I was a holiday maker and therefore somebody to
be ignored. The two girls behind the bar were friendly and efficient
and actually smiled when they served you. I felt good there. Relaxed.
Nobody seemed interested in who I was, or why I was there wearing a
suit on a warm summer's day. It was all so very relaxing. The San
Miguel went down far too easily as the windows darkened and the
street lights came on...

As I left, I said goodnight to the smiling girls and acknowledged the
nods of several other customers who had given no indication that I
even existed. My sort of pub. Hopefully I hadn't emptied the San
Miguel barrel though I'd had a good go at it.

Outside, I stood on the narrow pavement and wondered where the hell
I was. I knew I had to get back to the hotel by walking along the
seafront. If I turned left I'd go up hill. Right was down hill. Seemed to
me that downhill would more likely lead to the sea. I proved myself to
be right. It was satisfying that my years in the police force hadn't been
wasted after all.

Crept through the dimly lit, deserted reception area and to my room;
unlocked the door and went in. I decided not to lock it. Well, just in
case. Folded my trousers and put my jacket on the back of the chair.
The rest stayed where they fell. Then I took my bag of bits to the
bathroom to ablute.

I finished doing what I had to do and started to leave the bathroom.
Stopped. Something was different. Didn't take me long to figure it out.
My jacket neatly placed on the chair now had something small and
white draped over it. I looked closer. A pair of knickers, with the waist
carefully tucked under the collar. For a moment, I wondered if I had
been walking around all day with them tucked under the collar like
that. One of Melissa's little games.

Fortunately, the terror subsided when I saw the trail of clothes less
carefully placed. Then I saw a pixie on my bed. At least, that was my
first thought. Which didn't last long. When I focused and refocused the
pixie turned into a naked daughter sat on the bed, leaning forward,

17

elbows on knees and chin cradled in hands.

My eyes drifted down and stopped. Momentarily, I was reminded of
the wet, hanging lips of a boxer dog. A thought immediately banished
before I pictured myself licking the dog's nose.

"Does your mother know you're here on my bed?" Couldn't think of
anything else to say. Didn't really want to talk.
"Yes," she replied. "We tossed a coin."
"And you won."
She shook her head and grinned. "No actually. I lost."
"Right." What else could I say?

"Looks fit for purpose," she said. Does it work? Oh, yes it's waking up
quite quickly now." She looked up at the ceiling. Not being able to
help myself I did the same. Saw nothing, and looked back at her,
probably frowning.

"Just checking that there were no strings attached. Stood up quite
quickly once it had got going."
"Does that," I said as I walked towards her. "Never figured out why.
Tongue behave peculiarly too."
"So does mine."

She was gone when I awoke. Must find out what her name is.

Chapter Four

Friday 5th June

Woke up alone and started my day by wondering if I'd had a particularly vivid erotic dream. Then I realised that I could still smell her scent on my pillow, but it was probably just my imagination thinking that I could still detect an after-taste. Though I had had a good few drinks I could still remember in detail pretty much what had happened. Which, at that moment, was a bit unfortunate because I desperately needed to pee and as I stood up I found myself pointing the wrong way.

Overcoming all obstacles and getting my timing right, I showered, shaved, dressed and with some degree of trepidation decided that I needed breakfast. So I found the dining room and went in.

There were half a dozen tables set with the usual paraphernalia. Only one was occupied. By a sparsely haired, bespectacled, middle-aged man. Salesman type, sat with a fork in one hand with half a sausage on it. The other hand was busy typing away at the phone he almost had his nose on.

I sat down at another table with my back to him and waited, wondering if I should announce my arrival or maybe leg it to a local café where I'd feel safe from dragon fire. Not totally convinced that I wouldn't leave wearing a breakfast instead of eating one. Then, maybe, spending half the morning looking for somewhere else to stay, I decided to brave it out and sat quietly, certain that a low profile would be the best course of action. But I left myself the option to flee if necessary.

The kitchen noises in the adjoining kitchen eventually stopped and landlady emerged and came over to me. I smiled up at her, trying to make my expression as innocent as possible. It had no effect on her scowl. Such that I was now certain that she was related to Melissa.

"You can have sausage, egg, bacon, mushrooms, hash browns, beans or tomatoes."

"Yes please," I said.

She pursed her lips. "What! All of it?"

I nodded.

She shook her head in apparent disgust. Made her bra-less boobs wobble nicely. "Well you had better eat it all. I hate wastage. Tea or coffee?"

It was relief to get outside. I had managed to clean my plate, but it had been a struggle. I'm sure she'd given me extra just so that I would leave some. Which would have given her the opportunity to chastise me. But I wasn't going to give her the opportunity, even if it had meant leaving the hotel with a pocket full of sausage and egg.

I asked myself why didn't I just up and leave. Go to another hotel. Decided that it must be some sort of character flaw. Much the same as putting up with Melissa. Maybe I was being punished for something I did in some previous life and would suffer from Melissa's for the remainder of my days. Seemed to vaguely remember girls at school behaving in a similar way towards me.

I pulled myself together and read the directions that Belinda Carter had given me. Hopefully she'd got the information that I'd asked for. Once I had that, I might be able to make some progress. Or not. Anyway, I had plenty of time; it was a nice warm day so I decided to walk.

She opened the door in a short, thin, clingy mauve dressing gown, and stilettos. Stylish, perhaps, or perhaps not. Perspective is a personal thing. Was beginning to think that the sea air had an odd effect on people. Maybe the ozone affected the hormones or something.

"Ah, Mr Street, I've been expecting you. Please come in."

"Glad I was expected. We had an appointment."

She led me into her living room. It was furnished entirely in a modern style. No family heirlooms there. Could have been a show house. A show house that demonstrated the wonderful things you could do with money if you lacked any sense of style or class.

I went and sunk into the large armchair she had indicated, one of three. She sat on a matching settee across a coffee table that held carefully scattered pretentious magazines, which were likely to be unread. Probably demonstrating somebody's idea of what being posh was.

If her dressing gown fell open any more I'd likely start thinking about boxer dogs again.

"I've managed to scrape together everything you asked me for," she said. "It's not an awful lot, but I do so much hope it will help your investigation."
"Me too." I took the single sheet of paper from her and scanned the small meticulous handwriting. It told me where I could usually find Arthur Gibson; names, some addresses and phone numbers of others who were in some way involved. Lastly, she handed me a photograph. She said it was of both her missing husband and Gibson. Arms across each others' shoulders and grinning into the camera with the usual idiot grins you find in such photos.

"Can I get you anything? Coffee? Tea? Something stronger?"
"Coffee," I replied.

As she stood, her dressing gown fell completely open. "Oh dear," she smiled, looking into my eyes. She slowly, very slowly refastened it.

What I had seen had tempted me along a path I didn't need to tread. It would have been unprofessional. On the other hand, there was a time and a place for professionalism.

It was almost lunch time when I left after having my second shower of the day. I stood outside her front door and considered what had just happened. I was starting to like being in Hastings. It had something going for it. I figured that I had just been tempted by the devil. That is, the red devil tattoo she had on her belly. The devil whose tail wound downwards, arrow head pointing to where I had no option but to go.

The sea air, I told myself.

A seagull flew over and laughed at me.

Chapter Five

I had been told that nearly every afternoon Gibson held court in a pub in Hastings Old Town. The King's Head. I found it easily enough. On a corner marginally off the sea front. Another real pub. Old but well looked after. It had a couple of garden tables outside populated by a few punters who obviously preferred the beer to the beach.

I went through the old fashioned, glass panelled door and immediately saw my target. He was seated at the far end of the bar, back to a pillar and facing the door. He was huge. True he was overweight and age hadn't helped. Heavy features, several chins but he still carried himself well as he sat upright on his suffering bar stool. Yet his eyes, penetrating as they were, held a sense of humour, of irony.

Though I knew nothing about him, my instincts told me he was what I would call an old fashioned villain. Crime was a business to be conducted like any other sort of business. You had your customers and your suppliers. You had company rules. You had your employees. Though one of the differences being that being sacked from a normal company you got your cards. Being sacked from a business like Gibson's probably meant getting a certificate.

Of course, the above thoughts I knew, were just conjecture, gut. Yet, there tends to be something about villains and coppers. Mutual recognition. He saw a copper just walk into his pub. I saw a villain sat at the back of the bar on a bar stool. I might have an 'ex-' before my profession but the principle was the same.

After the initial recognition, we both made a point of ignoring each other. I ordered a pint. No San Miguel so I had some weaker Australian substitute and took it to a table. I preferred to sit at the bar. But if I had, I would have either been too close to Gibson or unable to observe without being obvious. And I was merely there to look, to get a feeling, not to have a cosy, or not so cosy, chat.

As I sat at my chosen table, I scanned the rest of the pub. Usual sort of clientele you'd find in a seaside pub on a warm, sunny afternoon. Except, that is, for the two heavies seated by the door trying hard to be inconspicuous.

To me that proved my instinct to be right. Gibson was into something. If he need minders there had to be a reason.

Observing is easy. You just look. Observing without looking isn't so easy. But I'd had a lot of practice. So whilst apparently checking my emails on my smart phone, in my peripheral vision I saw Gibson catch the eye of his heavies and with those same eyes draw their attention to me. The message had been, "He's the Bill; keep your eye on him." We can communicate so much without words.

I had nearly finished my first pint when Gibson had a visitor. A kid. Early 20's, scruffy, torn t-shirt and equally torn jeans, arms full of tattoos and a ring in his nose. I saw the barmaids' look of disgust as he approached Gibson. A look of disgust that Gibson himself seemed to share. The kid pulled a barstool closer to Gibson and it sat on it facing the large man. Its sullen, narrow, spotty face was topped in a hairstyle that was half Mohican, half idiot. Though sullen, I could tell that he was also cocky and arrogant. And being that way with Gibson also meant that he was also stupid.

Gibson simply smiled down at him. I say smiled down, because that is exactly what it was, and it had nothing to do with physical size.

They were too far away, and there was background music playing so I could hear nothing of what was being said but the kid's face became animated when he spoke. Gibson simply listened and smiled. Eventually the kid finished whatever it was he had to say. Gibson stopped smiling and shook his head slightly. That resulted in a sneer from the kid. A sneer which caused Gibson's smile to return more broadly.

It resulted in the kid reaching down into his pocket. A movement which caused Gibson's smile to disappear to be replaced with annoyance. He leant forward and said something into the kid's ear, and as he spoke his eyes fell upon me. He sat back and nodded towards the door. At that moment one of the two heavies got up and went outside.

After the kid had sloped out, shoulders hunched, feet dragging, Gibson immediately turned, smile back, and stared at me. I simply held his stare. When you're watching somebody it's important to act naturally. It wouldn't have been natural not to observe the interaction between such a mismatched pair.

I picked up my now empty glass and went to the bar. The heavy returned from outside. I waited for the barmaid to finish serving an obvious holiday maker. Naturally, I glanced sideways at Gibson. As I half expected, it gave him the opportunity to speak to me. The Gibsons of this world like to talk. Partly because they like the sound of their own voice, partly because they are forever delving for information. A bit like a typical policeman, actually.

"Do I know you?" he asked. "I'm sure I've seen you before. Or somebody like you."
"Probably somebody like me. We haven't met before."
"You must have a double. You live around here, or just visiting?"
"Visiting." I turned to the barmaid who had arrived and ordered another pint.
"You're not dressed as a tourist," he observed.
I paid for my drink and then turned my attention fully to Gibson.
"We're all different," I said. I had to make up my mind quickly. I could return to my table or talk. I leant on the bar after checking that I wasn't about to put my elbow into a beer puddle, but the bar was clean. "How about you?" I asked.
"You live around here? You're not dressed as a tourist. We must be the only two people in town wearing suits on a day like this."
He laughed, but I wasn't convinced it was genuine; I detected an undercurrent of suspicion. I would have been surprised otherwise.
"Lived here for ten years now," he told me. "I like the sea air. Are you working down here?"
"Relaxing."

"It is good to relax. Staying somewhere interesting?"

"Not particularly." I hesitated. Do I give him unnecessary information? "Prince Albert."

"I know of it. Is it any good?"

"They do a decent breakfast." And other things.

"How long are you down for?

"Until I've relaxed. Tell me, what do you do? Are you some sort of social worker, or was that kid your son?"

He laughed again. Strangely this time it sounded genuine. "I like you. You've got a sense of humour."

Then he casually pointed a finger at me. I was tempted to reach out and break it. But that would have resulted in a local version of Ragnarok. It was a nice pub. Hate to see it wrecked. So instead I ignored his finger and listened calmly to his words. The finger I was ignoring moved to the beat of his words.

"You're wasting your time, you know. I've retired. I'm clean. The sooner you lot realise that the less annoying you will become and the more time you'll have to look for criminals."

With the back of my hand I gently moved his finger aside. "Two things. I'm not on the job any more. I don't give a toss about what you do or did. And whatever it was, you're still at it or something similar."

"That is more than two things," he smiled.

"That's why the bill sacked me," I said. "I couldn't count."

He laughed again. "I like your attitude. Refreshing. Most refreshing. Let me buy you another drink."

I turn down drinks as often as I turn down attractive women.

Chapter Six

Last night I got back to my hotel room and found it empty. Not sure if I was disappointed or relieved. It had been a hard day and I needed a rest. Still, the freshly made bed did seem a little empty.

I got into bed alone and lay back to review the day's progress.

Outside, the seagulls were laughing when I woke up.

Another breakfast without sign of daughter. Breakfast room was empty, though there were signs that others had been down before, so I wasn't the only guest. Managed to eat everything again, so I didn't need the toilet tissue I'd put in my pocket as a precaution.

Went back to my room and made a phone call. Got through the insults that came from the other end and with threats and pleas in equal measure, managed to get what I wanted. Luckily my contact said he had an hour free. Though it was likely he had the whole day off. In any event, we arranged a meeting around lunchtime. Twelve o'clock. That gave me enough time for the first visit on my limited schedule.

I sat in her living room with a cup of tea in the bone china cups obviously reserved for visitors. I put it down on the coffee table in front of me. I hadn't ringed ahead, so I suppose I was lucky to find somebody at home. I supposed it helped being a Saturday.

I was in a small, two bedroom terraced house. The interior was clean and well kept, but cluttered with cheap furniture and ornaments. A line of various sized family photographs were displayed in different styled frames on top of the 50's style sideboard.

Across from me, seated in an armchair that was covered in what seemed to be an old candlewick bedspread was Mrs White, mother of Timothy White, one of the missing crew members of the Amy Grey. She gripped her teacup tightly, a look of hope in her bespectacled eyes.

That had always been the worst part of the job; questioning the recently bereaved. Not quite as bad as having to spring on somebody, or a family, that somebody they loved wouldn't be coming home any more. But it was nonetheless unpleasant. Especially if you had only questions, when they wanted answers. One of the few situations that I actually cared about what I said, or carefully framed questions.

So I spent the next half hour asking the really stupid typical questions that one is expected to ask. "Have you heard from him? Was he behaving any differently last time you saw him? Had anything like this happened before? Did he ever say anything about Jim Carter that might be important? Did he ever say anything about Dick Tweedy, the other crew member that might be important? Did he ever say anything about anybody that might be important?" And on and on.

I finished both my tea and my questions and was about to stand and leave having got precisely what I expected to get, which was nothing, when she spoke again.
"There is one little thing," she said slowly, thoughtfully, frowning as if trying to remember. "Tim used to joke about how, sometimes; Jim ordered both him and Dick into the cabin and not look at what he was doing. It apparently didn't happen often but when it did Mr Carter became very stern. They thought it quite funny, because being stern was so unlike him. They tried to peek but it was always dark, and all they could see was him bent over the back of the boat. Do you think that could be important? I only mentioned it because..."
"Didn't they ever question the order?"
She shook her head and smiled wistfully. "Tim wouldn't do that. He was a kind, gentle boy. Perhaps a little too much so. He always went along with things. Always doing what was asked of him. I often told him that he was too easy going. He used to grin at me and tell me that life was easier that way."
"Some are like that," I said gently, noticing the tears welling up. It was time for me to go.

As I walked down the hill towards Hastings Old Town, I tried to picture the scene. Fishing boat out at sea in the middle of the night. The two lads, the real fishermen, forced to go into the little cabin at the front end of the boat whilst Carter did something outside at the back of the boat.

What? What could he possibly be doing that required privacy, secrecy? Throw something overboard? I would have had to have been small otherwise the two lads would have seen it, known what it was. And it happened more than once! Possible, I suppose, but extremely unlikely. Could he have been bringing something on board? Maybe. But again it would have to have been smallish otherwise... Or maybe... I couldn't think of a third option.

It was a mystery. But a mystery, I felt, that had significance. Well, now I had a mystery to solve. All I needed was an accompanying miracle. Without one I couldn't see myself getting a lot further. But he was friends with Arthur Gibson. Arthur Gibson appears to be dodgy. How dodgy I hoped to find out soon. So maybe there was a pattern. Carter and Gibson doing something dodgy that involved a boat. Something went wrong? Possibly. Gibson's here and Carter isn't. So whatever went wrong was heavy.

Maybe Carter's wife wasn't living in a fantasy world where some sort of conspiracy concerning her husband was going on. Though I can personally attest to the fact that she was quite willing to express her fantasies in other directions. And that indicates that her desire to find out what had happened to her husband wasn't motivated by love. No, more likely money. Which is nearly always the case.

The Dolphin was a pub near that part of the beach where the fishing boats were kept when ashore. I sat outside on the veranda, sunning myself as I watched the people stroll by along the narrow street. A street that also contained the Sea World tourist venue, a small museum and several shops related to the local fishing industry.

I was waiting for my visitor. Somebody who I hadn't seen for a few years; somebody I had worked with for several. Once he had almost been friend. But a friendship ultimately lost through circumstance. We'd been a team. But things change and people move on.

He eventually arrived looking exactly as I remembered him. Shabby, wrinkled suit, still stooping as if his untrimmed moustache was terribly heavy; an acne scarred face topped by thinning, black plastered down hair. Always thinning but never seeming to get any thinner. Ten years older than me. Once resentful, but later accepting with, almost, good grace.

It was Detective Sergeant Joe Able, nicknamed Notso. He spotted me. Came over and sat down. He stared into my face with his piggy eyes. "Arsehole," he eventually said.
"Same as usual?" I replied. I stood and left to get him a drink and me a refill.

"Good to see you too," I said after I'd sat back down.
"Yeah. For the last time." He got a couple of sheets of paper out of his coat pocket and handed them to me. "It's all there. Everything I could find out. Everything on the computer."
"How am I supposed to read this?" The writing looked like that of a child who'd used their wrong hand. Notso was never very good with a pen or pencil and wasn't a lot better with a keyboard.
"Buy yourself some glasses."
"Just tell me. Then I might be able to decipher later."
He leant back, crossed his legs and picked at his teeth with a thumbnail. A 'tell' in a poker game. He was thinking, weighing up the pros and cons. After a minute or two of contemplation, he made up his mind, uncrossed his legs and leant forward.
"Interesting character is your Arthur Gibson. First came to the attention of the Met in the early 70's when he was a kid. He was a gopher for one of the gangs that worked the Krugerrand scam. Remember that?"
"Before my time," I said. "Though I've got some vague memory. Something to do with VAT wasn't it?"
He nodded. "Got it in one. Back then you could buy Krugerrands without paying VAT. An ounce of gold turned into a coin. So what they did was to buy VAT free Krugerrands, melt them down and turn them into ingots and sell the ingots to bullion houses. Then they

pocketed the VAT paid on the sale. They made millions before the Treasury caught on and put VAT on the Kruger and sales.

"So when that came to an end Gibson moved on, a little bit older, a little bit wiser and a little bit richer. The next step in his climb up his particular ladder is uncertain. But several of his associates, colleagues in the Krugerrand business were eventually sent down for armed robbery and similar pleasant activities. Gibson was suspected but after investigation he came out squeaky.

"He was next suspected of being involved in nicked cars. You know the scene. Nick a luxury car, put in into a container and ship it off to east Europe. Got arrested, got away with it. Too little evidence. So once it got too hot he moved on.

"Started running illegal betting houses. Weren't many betting shops in those days. In any event, he paid better odds, it was tax free and you could get credit. Of course, when you couldn't pay your debts it weren't the bailiffs who came around, and it weren't your tele that got taken away. Rumour is, he's still involved in that sort of thing.

"So we move on to the next step. Beer and fags. Thanks to our continental cousins who chose to sell them at a fraction of the cost we did here. These days, there's not a lot of difference in the price of fags, in France that is. But you can still get beer cheap.

"Anyway, where was I? Right. At one point he had up to thirty half trucks going to Calais daily. Each one coming back loaded with beer. Back then, there were dozens of 24 hour beer warehouses in Calais. So it was a run all hours business.

"That's a lot of beer and after paying expenses he made thousands, probably millions. Profit was around a couple of quid a can. Might not sound a lot but it soon adds up.

"Add onto that the convoys that went regularly to Luxembourg for fags and spirits and you can figure that Gibson is a very wealthy man. Especially when you factor in the fact that he got away with it for several years.

"Customs and later Border Control finally got their act together and shut most of it down. However, it still goes on to some extent. But instead of sending over loads of cars and vans they send a lorry. It brings the beer back where it's distributed for local supply. But, as you know, none of that has anything to do with the police. It's down to Customs or Border Control or whatever. So we let them get on with it. It's basically their problem not ours. But, intelligence wise, we still have to keep tabs on things.

"The money he's made is kept well hidden. He owns a couple of pubs and a nightclub. All that income goes through the books and no doubt some of his other income is laundered through his accounts. But so far nothing is showing up."

"What's he up to now?" I asked.
Notso shrugged. "Moved down here from Essex and immediately slipped under the radar. Coincided with a big increase in all the other shit we have to deal with. Intelligence is stretched and so are we. Sussex keep half an eye on him but nothing pops out. Maybe he's retired."
"Retired to Hastings? Wouldn't have Spain suited better?"
"You'll have to ask him that," Notso said. "I take it that all this isn't just about you being curious."

I told him the whole story.

"Interesting," he said. "There's nothing on file about him being a fisherman." He looked thoughtful. Thumbnail picking at teeth. "Any idea what he's up to? No you wouldn't have. So, a missing boat? Could be something to do with a couple of bad guys falling out over some dodgy deal. Smuggling of some sort? Drugs? That's what I think of when I think of boats.

"This Carter. Jim Carter you say. I'll have a look at him when I can get a chance. See if he's got history."

"That'll be useful," I told him. "Smuggling. Boats. They go together. And one of the missing kids reported that Carter got them out of the way while he did something at the back of the boat. Maybe dragging on board a shipment dropped off by another boat. Something that couldn't be found on the other boat?"

"Fits."

"It works. Pity we can't get the times and dates when he needed to be alone at the back of the boat. We might have been able to find a pattern between Carter's behaviour and the docking of ships or yachts.
"

I suddenly had an idea, or rather a need. Slim, but possible. It meant seeing Belinda Carter again. Ah well. As they say, a man's got to do what a man has to do. And I was getting paid for it.

"I think I might activate Gibson's file," Notso said. "Poke around a bit."

"We share?" I asked, knowing I'd only share if it helped me.

"We share," he agreed, knowing he'd only share if it suited him.

He left and I rang Belinda Carter and told her I had a question or two.

Chapter Seven

After getting the pointless information I said I needed from my employer, I had to have another shower. So it was worth the visit. As I put my clothes back on I wondered if she'd seen through my ruse, and if she had, had she cared? Apparently not. Maybe tomorrow I could think up another reason to visit.

Dressed again, I headed to my next port of call. The home of Dick Tweedy, the third member of the crew. A visit I was certain would bring no useful information to light. But it was something that had to be done. I didn't expect to have any light shed upon the missing boat, or anything, but you have to look under every stone so to speak. And after that, a visit to the person who Belinda Carter insisted I visit.

I walked up a garden path that was bordered by small garden where weeds were flourishing, to the front door of a small terraced house, an almost identical house, but considerably shabbier, to that of the Whites'. I rang the doorbell and faintly heard the chimes from inside.

The door partly opened and a harassed looking middle-aged woman peered out.
"He's not here," she told me as she began to close the door.
"Who isn't?" I asked quickly.
"Ray. You've come about the money, haven't you?"
"No. Don't know anything about money; I'm here to talk to you about your son, Dick. You are his mother, aren't you?"
"Was," she said. "Bloody little idiot. He wasn't insured, you know, if that's what you're hoping."
"Right," I said. That must be a relief to you.
"What do you mean, a relief?"
I gave her my most disarming smile. "Well if he had been insured they wouldn't have paid out until they knew what happened to him."

She frowned at me thoughtfully and then nodded. "Bastards. They're happy to take your money, but when it comes to paying out what they owe; well that's a different story, isn't it?"

"Exactly, would you spare me a few minutes of you valuable time? I'm trying to find out what happened to your son."

"Somebody paying you? Police have already asked a lot of stupid questions."

"That's the police for you. You'd think that with the money they earn, they'd be able to ask more sensible questions."

"Better come in," she said, obviously reluctantly. "Not got time for tea and biscuits if that's what you're hoping for."

She led me into a room that looked as harassed as she did. Everything seemed to be in a state of almost. That is, almost tidy, almost clean. The smell of recent cooking hung in the air. But the old, worn, armchairs weren't so forbidding as to opt to stand. But at first, we stood in the middle of the small, living room facing each other.

"Well?" she wore suspicion naturally.

"Did Timothy ever tell you anything about Jim Carter?"

Jim Carter? Scum-bag. I kept telling Timmy but he wouldn't listen. They never listen to their mother. Just because he's got money, I told him, doesn't mean he's alright. Means you can't trust him, not with all that money."

"Scum-bag.?" I questioned. "Why did you call him that?"

She raised her eyes throughout her arms in a gesture of apparent hopelessness, as though I'd asked her to explain the obvious.

"Right," I said quickly. I wanted to get out before she started to charge me. "Did Timothy ever tell you about any strange happenings on the boat?"

"Stupid little bugger hardly ever spoke to me. Ungrateful he was. All I'd done for him. Too busy keeping out of my way he was. Guilty about the way he behaved I suppose. Treated this place like a doss house. Always tried to avoid paying his keep he was. Seemed to think food grew on trees."

I almost squealed but it wasn't manly, so I also avoided a deep chuckle. "One final question," I managed to say. "The Amy Grey, the fishing boat..."

"I know the name of it," she said. "God knows how much it cost to run a boat like that. But none of them made any money out of it. Especially Timmy. Told him to get a real job. Bring some decent money home. A proper wage. But he never listened. They never listen to their mother."

"A tragedy," I nodded. "Now, when that Scum-bag, Jim Carter wasn't running the boat, wasting all that money, I understand it still went out but was captained by somebody else. The original owner. Can you confirm his address? Mrs Carter knew it was this road but wasn't sure of the number. I was told you'd have it."

She thumbed towards the wall.

I frowned at her gesture. Not sure what she meant. Maybe some quaint Hastings way of asking for money?

"Tight wad next door," she said.

"Ah!" I replied inanely.

"I call him tosspot."

"Not sure he'd take kindly to me knocking on his door and saying, 'Hello tosspot, would you mind answering a few questions?'"

She looked thoughtful for a second or two. "Suppose not. But the old fart deserves it."

"Probably does. Probably never listened to his mother. But the old fart's parents probably didn't know that in the beginning so they likely gave him a name."

"Wilson. Tay Wilson. What sort of name is that?"

"Wilson? Quite a common name is that. Especially in London."

She sneered. "London? Can't stand the place. It's..."

"Thank you very much for your time," I said, backing away.

"You're wasting your time," she told me as she saw me out. "Don't know how much they're paying you but you'll never find the little bugger. Crab food that's what he is. After all that time down there. Crab food. I told him something like that would happen, but he wouldn't listen. They never listen to their mother."

Chapter Eight

I stood on the pavement outside of Tay Wilson's house and tried to focus. I needed a different mindset to the one I'd just found myself in. I needed to sit down and relax for a few moments. To focus. I couldn't afford to knock on Wilson's door and say something like, "Hello tosspot, mind answering a few questions." I stood and took a couple of deep breaths, pictured a cool, refreshing pint of San Miguel and composed myself. As soon as I considered myself to be in control and my last encounter and accompanying attitude to be consigned to where it should be, I knocked on Tay Wilson's door.

He was a tall man, with thinning grey hair, a well worn face and pale blue eyes. Perhaps in his late 60's, but still looking fit, standing without any sign of a stoop.

We were seated across from each other in his functionally decorated living room. I'd given him a brief outline of who I was and who I was working for and he seemed to be willing to co-operate.

"Yes," he said, "I am, or was, the part owner of the Amy Grey. So I'm surprised that nobody has bothered to come and speak to me about it." "So you've not had a visit from the police?"

I too was almost surprised, but not totally. From what I understood the police weren't that interested. An accident at sea, No suspicion or indication of a crime. They'd look at it but not spend too much time at it. No gain. Probably went through the formalities. Visiting relatives of the missing crew members to see if they were actually missing; interviewing other fisher folk to see if they could shed any light on what had happened but took it no further. Not even bothering to ascertain the fundamentals of the ownership of the boat. Just taking it for granted that Jim Carter was the owner. Probably means that any insurance issues haven't been checked. Well there are so many more serious crimes that the police have to avoid dealing with thoroughly.

"So you're happy to answer a few questions?" I confirmed.
He nodded. "Gladly. I've heard so much nonsense about the Amy's disappearance; it'll do me good to get it off my chest." He seemed to be most eager to speak. Refreshing. Not as refreshing as a beer but still good.
"Firstly, what can you tell me about the crew? Timothy White and Dick Tweedy/"
"Chalk and Cheese. But both lovely boys. Tim wasn't the brightest but he was keen and willing. Bit of a mother's boy really. Barbara doted on him. The light of her life he was. She's still hoping that somehow he'll show up. I think when she's at home; she sits and listens for the key to turn in the lock and for Tim to walk in with his sheepish grin."
"Yes, I met her. A nice lady. It's very sad," I said, meaning every word. Some things are hard to take lightly.
"Barbara is a nice lady. He nodded towards the adjoining wall. "I can't quite say the same thing about her next door. And her husband's just the same. Benefits Ray they call him down the club. Not done a day's work in his life and you've met Mouthy, Money Mad Mary."
"An alliteration," I said, pointlessly.
He frowned for a moment before continuing. "Dick was totally different to them, his parents. How parents like that can produce a kid like Dick is beyond me. He was bright, hard working, and keen to learn. If he'd had a different upbringing he would have made something of himself. Instead, well..." He paused, stood up, went over to his sideboard, opened a drawer and took out an envelope which he handed to me. I opened it and looked inside. There were several £20 notes.

"They're Dick's," he said. "Poor kid had to hide them with me. His mother often went through his pockets and stole money from him. She thought he was as thick as she was and would never know she was doing it." He took the envelope back from me and dropped it onto the coffee table. "Not sure I know what to do with it now. But I sure as hell don't want those next door to get their hands on it. Don't think he'd want that."

I shrugged. "Can't advise on that. Ask yourself what Dick would want.

You knew him.

He nodded, apparently resigned to having to figure it out for himself.

I'd got the drift with respect to the missing kids. "Can we move onto Jim Carter? How'd you get together with him? An estate agent wanting to be a fisherman."

He leant back and arched his long narrow fingers, closed his eyes for a few moments and then began. "You know, sometimes lots of little things stack up on top of each other and you suddenly find yourself somewhere where you never expected to be, That's basically what happened.

"Conversations down the club. You know the sort of thing. What's it like fishing? He'd like to try it. Eventually, I took him out one night and one thing led to another. I was reaching that point in life when you start thinking about retiring. I used to ponder about how I could get young Dick more involved. Let him take over Amy. But I knew that in reality it wouldn't work. No matter how it was dressed up. You see, Mary would've been a problem. She'd have forced him to sell it so she could get her hands on the money. At least, that's what I figured.

"Anyway, getting back to the point. I worked out a way with Carter for him to buy half the boat which gave me enough money to semi-retire. Part of the deal was for him to keep on Dick and Tim. He was happy with that.

"It was a good deal all round. He took her out some nights. Or rather, Dick took her out pretending that Carter was running things. Although, in fairness, he did learn the fundamentals pretty quickly. Anyway, where was I?"

"Jim Carter took the boat out some nights," I reminded.

"Right. Yes. He took it out some nights and I did the rest."

"Do you keep a record of that? The nights he took the boat out."

He smiled. "I've heard of the rumours too. The lads often chatted to me about it. Sending the kids into the cabin while he fiddled with something aft. And yes, I kept a log. Everything's written down. I'll get it for you before you go. But I need to have it back when you're done."

"Of course, I'll get it back to you as soon as I've finished. Probably as early as tomorrow once I've extracted all the dates and times where

Carter played at being fisherman."

"Looking for a pattern?" he asked.

"Something like that Mr Wilson."

"Tay," he amended.

"Tay," I obliged. I paused. "What do you think happened to the Amy Grey?"

He smiled broadly. "I hoped you'd ask me that. You've no idea how long I've thought about it. Thought about it from every possible angle. Over and over again. And always coming to the same conclusion."

He looked at me. Waiting for a reaction. Instead. "Aliens?" I suggested. Another one of those instances when I wanted to punch myself in the mouth.

He sighed loudly and shook his head. An expression of uncertainty briefly passed across his face. "Now that's an angle I never considered. Just goes to show. You think you've covered every possibility, then you find out you've missed the most obvious. Aliens..." He shook his head. "Never thought of that."

"These things just slip out," I explained.

"Can't help yourself, hey? Tension got to you, had to break it."

"Probably. You don't think it sank then?"

"Sank?" 'course it didn't bloody well sink. Don't care what those clowns with their bloody theories say. It didn't sink and they should know it didn't."

"How can you be so sure?" Was I finally getting somewhere? I hoped so. I had an intuition that I was about to get an answer I'd be happy with.

"A fishing boat is littered with, what you might call, clutter. Most of that clutter floats. Buoys, life belts, even empty or half full bottles of water. If the Amy Grey had gone down the sea would have been littered with traces, and a few bodies come to that. But what did they find? Nothing."

I raised a finger to interrupt. "I was told that it was most likely scenario. A loud bang was heard. The lights went out. An explosion perhaps?"

"Explosion?" he scoffed. "It's a wooden boat. If it somehow blew up there'd be even more debris."

"Bottom ripped out on undersea rocks?" I suggested.

"Another idiotic idea, if you don't mind me saying. We're not talking speedboat here. If the Amy bottomed it might cause some minor damage. Worst case, might even hole her. But it wouldn't tear the hull apart causing to sink so fast that everything on board forgets to float."
"Nicely put," I smiled.
"I know. Told you. I've thought about it."
"What then?"

He sat back and clasped his hands together. A slightly smug expression on his face. Waited for effect. And then...
"Well, if it didn't sink there aren't a lot of options left, are there."
I shrugged. "It's hidden somewhere?"
"Exactly." He nodded in agreement with himself.
"How can you hide a boat the size and shape of the Amy Grey for this long?" I asked. I'd thought about it too.
"Ah, now that is the problem isn't it."
"And you've solved it?"
"I have a solution, yes."
"And it is?" I was beginning to get frustrated but I managed to control my more violent impulses.

"Many, many years ago," he began, "when I was a kid, I went to stay with some friends up the coast in Hythe. Early one morning we hired a canoe, or row boat. Can't remember which. And we went out on the river. At least, I thought it was a river. Found out later that is actually a canal."

"And?" I had no idea what canoeing had to do with anything.
"I remember it clearly," he continued as if I hadn't spoken. "Quiet river, or canal. We were the only people on it. Kids. Early in the morning. Yes, I can picture it now."

My impatience was getting harder to control. "Tell me!" I wanted to scream. "Tell me! Get to the bloody point!" But I managed to stay silent as he floated along the river years ago.

"Picture it now," he repeated. "Thick trees on either side. Through the tree you could just about see the riverside houses. Occasionally, a lawned garden that ran to the water's edge. Now and then a small, private quay. And even more infrequently... Boathouses."

"Boathouses?" Something was beginning to gel.

He nodded, face full of satisfaction "Yes, boathouses. Garages for boats if you like. I remember some of them being quite big. Big enough to take the Amy Grey."

"And she could have got to this river, this canal easily?" I needed to be certain I was onto something.

He nodded. "Dead easy. Couldn't guarantee she wouldn't have been seen, especially in the early hours as she was reaching her destination. But the trip would have been easy. The Amy just needed to sail along the coast a bit, to the River Rother. Gone up it a short way and then onto The Royal Military Canal where I spotted the boathouses as a kid."

I had the desire to jump up and kiss him on the nose. Fortunately, I have a lot of willpower when I need it.

Chapter Nine

I sat in my hotel room and thought long and hard. Not an ideal state to be in but sometimes it had to be done. I had to put things into order. Figure out what I knew, what I didn't know and what I needed to know.

The Amy Grey had disappeared along with three crew members. It hadn't sunk. Wilson had convinced me of that. Though, in reality, I wasn't at all certain about him. Appeared to be too good to be true. Something wasn't quite right. I put my doubts to one side and continued.

No evidence of Aliens. Which was a pity, but you can't have everything. Therefore if it hadn't sunk and aliens weren't involved it had to have been taken somewhere. Tay Wilson had suggested a boathouse along the coast at Hythe. Was close enough so there was enough time to make it disappear before too many people could witness it.

And that was the first problem. Who made it disappear? Couldn't have been Gibson in person, because, conveniently, he was the first to point out that it was missing. That is, he had an unbreakable alibi. I still had trouble visualising the big bugger play acting the fisherman. Couldn't see how there could be any room left on the boat for the fish. But with respect to that, why? Did he actually enjoy it, or, more likely, was there an ulterior motive? If so, what?

Yet Belinda Carter was convinced that he was responsible. Now Gibson would obviously have the resources to put a couple of guys on the Amy Grey and force Carter to drive, or sail, or whatever to Hythe. But how do you get a couple of heavies onto a boat without anybody seeing? It was far too small to hide in.

I thought back to Belinda Carter's original statement. There was loud bang, maybe two and the lights went out. Gunshots and then a struggle? Could be. So maybe a dinghy or something pulled alongside. There was a struggle, a gun was fired. Carter and the two boys were subdued and the boat disappeared.

That scenario worked for me. There were two, probably related questions. Why had Gibson decided to get rid of Carter, and what dodgy activity was Carter up to when he made the boys go into the cabin?

It doesn't require a lot of imagination, which is fortunate because I know my limitations, to figure out that Carter and Gibson were partners in some criminal activity. The sea and boats go hand in hand with smuggling. Okay, so what was being brought in?

Whatever, it was had to be damned lucrative to warrant such a complicated process. One that involved a lot more people than just Gibson and Carter. Drugs were the obvious candidate for that. Especially when you factor in the incident in the pub with Gibson and the scruffy kid who seemed to want to buy something from him.

So how would the pieces fit together? Process first. A passing ship drops the payload with some sort of electronic beacon. Carter detects it and pulls it on board. Passing ship docks clean. Nobody is going to check a fishing boat for drugs when it barely gets out of the sight of the beach. Yet, can a passing ship get close enough to land to drop a payload? I decided to leave that question to later.

So what went wrong between Gibson and Carter? Carter tries to double-cross him by hauling in a load and then pretending it hadn't been left? An extra large payload that Gibson didn't want to share? Or maybe something more mundane like Gibson having an obsession about getting into Belinda Carter's knickers; if she ever wore any, that is.

So where did that leave me? Firstly, all those theories were one thing. What my job is, is to find Jim Carter. Or at least, prove what happened to him. It isn't about bringing his killer to justice. Others, such as my mate Notso, can do that. If I found him in some boathouse I would have done my job. Whatever state he was found in. Having done it, I could bugger off back home with the rest of my money and settle back to reading old newspapers.

But first, I had to find his body, or some trace of it. Because now I was convinced he was dead. Easy option would be to get Notso to do the grafting. But that would be extra complicated. Notso would have to go through the Kent Police. For me, that was too long a chain. And Belinda Carter might renege on her contact with me by saying that it was the police that sorted things. In any event, it was always more satisfying seeing things through. Especially when you could get one up on the police.

Therefore I figured that it was down to me to sort it. I knew exactly how to make it so. I had the photo of Carter I got from his wife. Carter and Gibson standing side by side, arms on each other's shoulders. Little and large, grinning inanely into the lens.

Secondly, I had somebody to do the leg work for me. And there were no better legs I could think of to do the job I had in mind. Melissa. It was time for her to earn whatever it was she had decided that I should pay her.

I sat back feeling satisfied. I'd had what might be termed 'a good think.' I didn't think it would take long to sort out now I'd found all the pieces. It all seemed to fit nicely together. What, at first, seemed to be impossibly complicated turned out to be rather simple. This was often the way in this business. Mind you, the opposite was also true. Cases which, at first glance, seemed simple and straightforward, could turn out to be almost impossible to solve. But, luckily for me, the Carter case wasn't one of those.

I picked up Tay Wilson's log book and wondered what I should do with it. Give it back? I didn't need it now. Or give it to Notso and hope it would complicate his life by forcing him to do some real detective work.

I opened it out of curiosity and noticed the precise, neat handwriting; the details of sailings, the entries for Carter's trips. A quick perusal showed up what appeared to be a pattern. Bursts of activity by Carter, then none for several weeks. That was good. It fitted my theory. Ship drops a load but obviously can't guarantee exactly when. Today or tomorrow, sort of thing. So Carter keeps having to go out until he picks up the signal and retrieves the load.

So, If I gave the log to Notso all he would have to do was to find a ship that docked somewhere regularly around the time of Carter's outings. Then, having tracked it down, wait and watch until it passes again, that way maybe cracking a major drug smuggling case.

Having thought about Notso, I remembered the scraps of paper he gave me outlining police intelligence on Gibson. I glanced over the scrawl and when I saw it I couldn't help thrusting out and up a clenched fist as if I'd just scored a winning goal. After leaving Essex and before moving to Hastings, Gibson had spent some time in Hythe.

Chapter Ten

It had been a profitable day. Light at the end of the tunnel. Hopefully it wasn't the light of a train coming the other way. In any event, I reckoned that I'd earned the few pints I treated myself to. Though, in reality, I've never actually denied myself a drink because I hadn't deserved it.

I was back in the hotel relatively early because I planned on an early start. For ruining Melissa's day, the earlier the better. Especially it being a Sunday.

I took my clothes off and tidied them as usual, feeling quite at ease with myself, almost content. And the feeling was due to more than the mellowing effect of alcohol. Unfortunately, the almost contentment evaporated at the sound of loud, aggressive banging on my door.

"What?" I called as I walked naked towards the cause of the unwelcome noise. The door opened, it hadn't been locked due to optimism.

The landlady stormed in. "I've had a complaint..." She stopped and stared.
"I hope you're better now," I said.
She stared down at my hangings and then up into my smiling face. She reddened slightly. "Sorry. I didn't mean..." she said quietly, hesitantly.
"Can happen to anyone. What's been wrong with you?"
"Wrong with me?" she frowned. "Nothing is wrong with me.
"Yes, I can see that now," I agreed, pointedly looking her up and down taking in the well filled, low cut dress, which revealed much at both ends. "Nothing wrong at all." Slowly, my hangings were becoming less so.
"Your music..." she began, stopped as she slowly looked around the

room.

"Am I? Very kind of you. Not been called that before."

"No! No! No!" She shook her head as if trying to concentrate; eyes looking down to that part of me still on its upward journey but was currently pointed at her.

"Oh my god," she breathed. "You've been playing your music too loudly." She took her eyes away from the single eye that was staring at her and glanced at the door. "Oh my god," she said again. "Wrong room. It's just that... Well, if I had a complaint about anybody I expected it to be you. It's the second floor I wanted. And stop that thing from staring at me."

She crossed the room, sat down heavily on the bed and held her head in her hands. "I'm going mad," she muttered.

"Can happen to anybody," I told her as I shut the door.

"I've had a terrible day. I'm just not thinking right. It's been one thing after another. On top of it all, Maria has been whining at me all day."

"Wanting more food?"

"She's always wanting more food. For some reason, today she's been wanting my continual attention."

"I hear they can get like that. Moods."

She nodded.

"Could it be worms?" I suggested. "I seem to remember something about that."

"Worms?" Her face took on several expressions in quick succession.

"Yeah. Apparently it's easily cured. Something you stick up her bottom."

"I... I couldn't do that."

"If you want, get the stuff, bring her here, plonk her on my lap and I'll do it for you. I've seen how it's done. Pretty simple really."

"I can just picture the look on her face if you were to do that." For some reason she appeared to becoming upset at the prospect. At least she was shaking and I could see tears forming in her eyes.

"In a few minutes when it's done, she'll forget all about it and be back to normal."

"I don't think so," she managed to say. "She might object to you poking something into her bottom."

"I'll take her by surprise. Pat her on the head or something to distract her."

"Please," she said. "No more. I can't take it anymore."

"Okay. But you'll have to do something if she starts chewing the carpets."

She made a strange squealing noise, stood up and said, "Okay. Okay, Enough."

It nearly always surprises me how quickly a woman can rid herself of clothes when she's in a hurry. Especially when you consider how long it takes them to put them on.

Sunday 7th June

She was gone when I awoke to the now familiar sound of seagulls laughing and frolicking. I stretched and lay back."Must be the sea air," I said aloud.

Got up, showered, shaved and dressed. I was just about to go down to breakfast when there was a light tap on the door. I opened it.

A little white dog trotted in followed by a not so little daughter. "Have you met Gloria?" she asked.

"Right," I said, mind racing along an ever decreasing spiral that threatened an explosion when it reached the centre.

Maria looked into my eyes. "I understand you are quite happy to stick something up my bottom. Distract me by tapping me on the head and taking me by surprise."

I simply stared. Probably with a glazed look in my eye.

"Ah well, got to go. Come along Gloria." As she walked away, she turned and grinned. "Got a carpet to chew."

That morning, I skipped breakfast. I wasn't even a tiny bit hungry anyway.

Chapter Eleven

I left the hotel. Didn't feel too comfortable there that morning, for some reason. I hoped it would be a feeling that would soon pass. I found a nearby park bench and sat. For a few moments I simply surveyed the scene. Calm sea, gentle cool breeze. Though it was warm for that time of the year. Especially when stacked up against recent summers. Plenty of cars and buses passing by, but few people were wandering about. The occasional dog walker passed me by. I decided I don't like dogs.

I first rang the office phone wondering if Melissa went in on a Sunday. Never really knew when or what time she got there. She was always there when I got there; always there when I left. But the phone rang for awhile without being answered. So she didn't go in on a Sunday.

I rang her mobile. It was answered after a few rings.

"What do you want," she asked, voice as brisk as I expected it to be.
"It's Sunday."
"It's good to hear from you too. And I'm glad you've got a calendar."
"What do you want?"
"I need you to do something for me."
"What?"

She had the skill to turn the simplest of things into a huge effort. She made me want to scream at her, throw insults and generally vent. But I managed to control myself; stay calm. I took a deep breath and continued. A little nervous about the response I was about to get. "I need you down here. I've got a little..."
"When?"

"Now. It might take a couple of days. I just need something confirmed and I can't do it myself."

"I'll ring you when I arrive," she told me.

For a few moments I was stunned into silence. No arguments; no refusal; no insults. Was she ill or something? I pulled myself together.

"Wait! Before you hang up."

"What?"

"Wear something, or bring something smart. Business like."

"Such as?"

"I don't know," I think I might have shouted. "How about a pink crotchless Batman suit." I hung up on her. Regretted my temper tantrum and hoped she would still come.

I sat shaking my head. Melissa! Office furniture with attitude. I still had no idea how I came to employ her. Maybe I was suffering from concussion at the time. Though half the time I felt as though she was employing me.

And what did she do all day? Type! What did she type? I hadn't a clue about that either. Countless times I've tried to sneak out of my office and find out. Each time I found the screen locked and needing a password to get in. Her damned computer seemed to know when I was around.

Time I sacked her. Thought about doing so often. But never tried. Wouldn't know how to cope when she ignored me. I know I get so angry with her. I overreact. Though when I think about it, my overreaction is probably down to unrequited lust.

I stood up and went in search of a café. Soon found a little one. Its window boasted several fancy types of coffee. Looking in I could see that it was of these trendy places, a dive trying to look sophisticated. A bit like some working class women who put on airs trying to sound 'posh' by putting an 'aitch' in front of every vowel. It was empty inside. So the world isn't totally without justice. But my immediate need for coffee outweighed any principles I might have had.

I went to the counter. The young guy behind the counter looked as trendy as his café or Bar de Cafés as he preferred to call it. His

50

expression when he saw me read something like, 'Oh dear, not a damned customer. Certainly not the right sort.'

I felt like grabbing him by his white, continental chef's jacked and introducing his nose to my forehead. But I wasn't a police officer any more so I desisted. So I thought I'd be difficult instead.

"A mug of tea and an egg and bacon sandwich. White bread." I ordered. I glared at him. I was in that sort of mood. The Melissa effect. And the still vivid memory of last night's little discussion in my room. A bit like kicking the cat, or bloody dog for that matter.

"A mug of tea..." he began in a high supercilious voice.
"Want me to write it down for you?" I said, glare hardening. "Or maybe you want it tattooed on your face. I can do mirror writing."

He took two steps backwards holding up his hands as if trying to ward off something he'd preferred not to have met. "We... We don't do egg and bacon," he stuttered. "This is a vegetarian establishment."
"Vegetarian?"
He nodded, and with a shaky finger pointed to the window. "It says it quite clearly, there."
"Why didn't you tell me before? It would've saved a lot of time?" I turned and walked out. Under my breath I was cursing myself. Cursing everybody else. Especially women; the two at the hotel, Melissa, Belinda Carter. The effect they were having on me was dangerous.

I needed to calm down. Relax. Breathe slowly, deeply. Relax. Feel positive. Be at ease. Then I thought, 'Fuck all that, I'll feel better after I've eaten.'

I soon found another café. One that catered for carnivores and tea drinkers. When I finished I looked at my watch. It was time to visit the last of the names on my list. One Sam Samuels the lifeboat man. Hoped he'd be more imaginative than his parents had been when they named him.

Samuels was a butcher in Hastings Old Town, that was, like all the shops there, open on a Sunday. A tall, thin man in his 40's who, as he

51

served, kept up a continual banter with his customers, who obviously loved it. They all left happy, with a smile on their faces.

I waited in-line until I was at the counter and then introduced myself, telling him I was working for Belinda Carter who wanted to find out what had happened to her husband.

"Ah," he said beaming at me. "It's time that affair was treated seriously. Pity the authorities didn't do it in the first place. And now you're here to do it. Good. Good."

He wiped his hands on a cloth and took his apron off. "We'll pop across the road and have a coffee. Things will quieten down now. We always get a bit of a rush on this time on a Sunday." He turned to his two co-workers. "Take over lads, I won't be long."

One of the 'lads' was at least twenty years older than him.

"So you want to know what happened that night," he said when we were seated in the coffee house. This one wasn't at all trendy and it was busy.
"That's right. You can give me a more or less official version of things."
"Don't know about official," he laughed, "but I was on the lifeboat that morning, that's true. Do you want me to start at the beginning and run through the sequence of events?"
"That would be good."

"Okay," he began, "Do you need exact times and that sort of thing?"
"Not really. Just the sequence will be fine."
"Okay. Well we launched as soon as we heard the Amy Grey was missing. No sign of her anywhere. Understand, we weren't looking for the boat itself. If it was around we would have been able to see it from shore. It was clear and light. In other words, visibility was excellent.

"So we were basically looking for survivors of what appeared to be an unknown catastrophic event. So we went full ahead towards the Amy Grey's last known position. We reached it in a few minutes and saw nothing. Nothing at all." He paused thoughtfully. "It's a mystery to this day.

"But back to the sequence of events. We did what we could. The sea was flat and calm. If there'd been anything to find, we would have found it. However, we followed procedure and called in ASR, Air Sea Rescue. We waited for them to turn up and hung around while they circled looking." He gave a gesture of hopelessness and sat back in his chair. "The upshot is, there was nothing to find. And nothing has ever turned up either. No flotsam, no wreckage. And no bodies. It's a mystery. Probably will always be a mystery. But you can't help but hope that something, someday..." He didn't bother to finish his sentence,

"Any theories?" I asked.
He shrugged. "None. None at all."
"You've never thought about it?"
"Of course I have," he said. "Jim, Tim and Dick, nice people, gone."
"Gone where," I pushed.

Samuels gave me an expression of hopelessness. Nice guy. Helpful, but as imaginative as his parents had been when they named him. I wondered if, if he had a son he'd call him Sam.

"The other thing that's a bit of a mystery..." he began.
I stopped my mind from wandering inanely.
"... is the press coverage."
"I didn't think there was much," I said.
"Exactly my point. You'd think a story like that would have generated pages of speculation. Yet it somehow failed to raise anybody's interest. Weird."
"Weird all round," I agreed. "One last thing. I want your opinion."
"Fire away."
"I believe you know Arthur Gibson."
"Arthur? I know Arthur."
"I've met him. Doesn't seem much like a fisherman to me. Yet I understand he is."
He laughed. "He doesn't seem much like one to me either..."
"Yet he goes out fishing."
"It's just a bit of fun to him. As far as I know, he's only ever been out a

handful of times. Just wanted to have the experience he told me. In fact it was me who introduced him to Willy."

"Willy?"

"Yes, Willy Brown. He's got the Normandy Beach. The boat that Arthur goes out on."

"So Arthur Gibson doesn't actually own his own boat?"

"No, no, no. Why would he want to own a boat?"

I couldn't answer that one. At least, I couldn't suggest a possibility to Sam. They appeared to be friends.

"How about Jim Carter? I understand he owned the Amy Grey."

"Half owned it," he corrected.

"What was your opinion of him as a fisherman? "

"He had Dick Tweedy to look after him," he replied tactfully.

"Why'd you think Jim Carter took up fishing? An estate agent."

He shrugged. "Who knows? I didn't know Jim all that well. We didn't talk much. Maybe it was something to do with what they call a mid-life crisis. He chose a fishing boat instead of a motor bike. Maybe he was just copying Arthur. Who knows what goes on in people's heads?"

"Who knows indeed," I agreed.

Sam Samuels said goodbye. I thanked him and he returned to his butcher's shop and I ordered another black coffee. It was time for another review. Clarify things while they were still fresh.

I was fairly confident I knew broadly what had gone on that night. The Amy Grey was taken over, sailed to and hidden in Hythe. Jim Carter was disposed of. Tim White and Dick Tweedy were collateral damage. The motive being revenge or maybe a warning to others, or both. Carter double-crossed Gibson and paid for it. Paid for it out at sea where there were no witnesses.

It's true that details of how the boat was taken over were unclear. As was why they decided to do things the way they did. Surely it would have been far easier to just get rid of Carter by an easier method that didn't require killing two innocent kids. Assuming that they were innocent. Even if the decision had been made to take them out on the boat, why not just kill them and throw them overboard? Why go to the lengths they did. The longer a process goes on, the greater become the chances of things going wrong. More actions, more things can foul up.

Though, I suppose that I've had enough experience of villains who overcomplicate things. Generally they're those who confuse simplicity with the actions of simpletons. So the more complicated they make things, the cleverer they feel that they are... Ironically, reality is the reverse.

Yet Gibson doesn't seem to be that sort. Judging by both my personal experience of him and by his history. He probably is clever. He doesn't need to complicate things. So maybe he just ordered the hit using an outside contractor. And, of course, being at sea at the same time with countless witnesses is a pretty good alibi.

Chapter Twelve

Early afternoon. Sunday. Had no idea whether Gibson did on a Sunday what he did most days of the week. That is, to hold court in the pub. If he was there today I would see him. I needed to somehow get to know him. To really know him. I didn't have a specific reason, but I'd run out of other people to speak to. I might have the main gist of what went down but I couldn't move forward until Melissa arrived. Assuming she would, that is. With a bit of luck, I should have the whole thing sewn up in a couple of days. Gibson was icing on the cake, so to speak.

Déjà vu. Gibson sitting in his usual place. Tweedledum and Tweedledee in their usual seats by the door. Probably with the same half drunk pints in front of them. The same two barmaids behind the bar. The only difference was that it was considerably busier than it usually was. At least, when I'd been there before. Fortunately, though people were stood and sat at the bar, the area around Gibson was kept clear. They must instinctively keep away from him.

Gibson watched me approach, a half smile on his large face. I nodded to him and turned to the now waiting barmaid.

"I'll get this," Gibson intervened as I stood with my mouth in the process of ordering. The barmaid looked at me expectantly. I shrugged my acceptance and said, "San Miguel. Pint. Please."
"Sit down. Sit down," Gibson told me, patting the empty barstool beside him.
I obliged.

Neither of us said a word until the barmaid had returned with my drink and put it down on the bar. As I adjusted the barstool I watched her go to the till and write something down on a notepad beside it. Obviously Gibson had a tab.

"You've got a tab," I said. Well, it was something to say.

He nodded. "Indeed. Indeed. Least effort. I firmly believe that the least effort produces the best results."

Looking at his build I could see that his philosophy had paid dividends over the years.

"Does that extend to everything you do?" I asked.

"Everything," he said. "Absolutely everything. Wouldn't have it any other way. Why take two steps when one will suffice?"

"Why indeed? Some might say that you've got to put a bit of effort into staying fit."

"Fit for what?" he chuckled. "Do I look like the sort of chap who has a need to go to the gym every day in order to feel good?"

"You most certainly don't," I agreed. "If you did, I suggest you get yourself a new personal trainer."

He laughed, whole body shaking along with his many chins. "You're a fine fellow. A fine fellow." He paused and looked at me, eyes suddenly serious, but mouth still full of humour. "Yes, a fine fellow. Even if you do have a somewhat dubious past."

"I have?"

He looked at me, still smiling and slowly nodded as if he had had a question answered. Then I realised that I was dealing with a very clever man and I might have made a serious mistake. Too much emphasis on the 'I' in 'I have', inferring that I knew that he too had a somewhat dubious past. Well, how would I know that if I was just a casual customer who met him in a pub? He was supposed to be a bloke who I came across whilst having a drink. In certain circles, and this might be one of them, silly slips like that could get you into serious shit. I felt somewhat contaminated as it was. I needed to recover. And quickly.

"I was curious about you," I told him. "Why was a bloke like you sitting in a little pub in Hastings, You obviously had money. You've got a couple of minders sat by the door. And you don't look like a priest. I made a phone call."

"A good answer." He chuckled. "Interesting how you knew my name."

"I was a detective. A good one."

"Indeed. Indeed. Are you still a detective?"

"Old habits die hard."

"Quite a truthful cliché. But you didn't really answer my question."

"The short answer is yes. The longer answer is no. At least I'm not employed by the state. What I now do is take on mundane private cases. Hence, I suppose I'm called a private detective."

"Private detective," he mused. "I take it that you're here working on a case."

I nodded.

"And am I part of your investigation? Have I perhaps upset somebody? Left them dissatisfied with some past transaction."

"I know nothing of any transaction you've done, past or present. No interest. Apart from curiosity. And I'm not a cat."

"That's good. Excellent in fact," he said beaming. "So tell me Mr..."

"Street. Al Street."

"So tell me Mr Street, why are you here, in sunny Hastings?"

"Not something I want to discuss with you. All I'll say is that it's a husband and wife thing."

He nodded vigorously, chins wobbling. "The answer I expected. Hoped you would give me. Confidentiality. Most important in your line of business."

"And in yours," I said and wished I hadn't.

He laughed. "Indeed it is."

He sat back and we looked at each other in silence for a short while. He was obviously thinking. I was treading water.

A few pints later and after a casual grilling as to my experiences as a policeman, I left the King's Head, walking out into blinding sunlight. The sun still bright even though it was low in the sky.

Chapter Thirteen

I walked into the hotel lobby and stopped. If they hadn't noticed my entry I would have turned round and legged it. Unfortunately, they had seen me, so I attempted to put a socially acceptable expression on my face.

They were standing there, the three of them. My entry had obviously stopped the conversation they'd been having before they had spotted me. Mother and daughter with a knowing smile on their faces and Melissa, now with a knowing scowl. Yet she'd been showing her teeth before she saw me. At least I was having some sort of effect on her.

As I hesitated, torn between the need to escape, with mind searching for a reasonable excuse to do so, and the need to appear cool, I was suddenly poked in the back. I looked around, and then down. A little old lady's bespectacled face beamed up at me.
"Excuse me young man."

I stepped to the side as she walked into the hotel. As she went by, both mother and daughter said in harmony, "Good afternoon, Miss Turnbull."

Miss Turnbull appraised Melissa as she went by. I hoped she wasn't impressed.

Perhaps Miss Marple was staying at the hotel after all.

As I advanced towards the three I was reminded of a scene from Macbeth. *"Fair is foul and foul is fair."* Though it wasn't them saying it, it was me.

"What are you doing here?" I asked Melissa.

"You sent for me. Have you forgotten?"

"Why stay here? There's better places for you to stay." I knew I was being irrational but I couldn't help myself. This was the first time I'd seen her outside of the office. At least, in the office, the familiar bare, shabby walls offered some sort of security. If not physical, at least of habit.

Here, outside of the office, in public, I felt vulnerable. Not a feeling I'm used to. There was something about her. Maybe it was her perfume. Perhaps I was allergic to it. And it caused me to feel paranoid, psychotic. See too much of her and I'd likely be committing murders, not solving them.

"Why should I consider staying somewhere else?" she snapped.

"Comfort. You ought to book into somewhere more suitable."

"Do you want my help or not? If you do, tell me what you want and I'll consider doing it. Otherwise I'll be on my way in the morning."

"Okay. Okay," I said, holding up my hands, "Calm down."

At that point, mother and daughter nodded farewell to Melissa. But only after giving me a glare that Medusa would have been proud of. That left us alone.

"Well," she asked, "what do you want?"

"This isn't the right place to discuss that sort of thing," I told her in my most professional voice.

She tossed her head in an even more professional show of exasperation. "The walls have ears! There are listening devices planted everywhere. Why not just say what you want me do and have done with? I've not come all this way to play silly games."

"Listen. We need to talk about this seriously. Because it is deadly serious. Literally. There are things I need to tell you. Standing in a hotel lobby isn't the best place to do it. Come to my room and we can discuss it."

She leant her head to one side and a half smile appeared on her face."You want me to come to your room with you. Is that why you've got me down here? Run out of local talent already? Want to make some sort of record?" Her almost smile became real. "I have heard you know."

"Heard what?" I didn't really want to know, but I could guess. Some women like to talk.

"I know you had a reputation before I had the misfortune to meet you. Now I've had it confirmed."

"What do you mean misfortune to meet me?" I was now angry, but even more defensive. "What have I ever done to you?"

"Nothing," she snapped. "And I plan to keep it that way. So I won't be coming to your room and you won't be coming to mine. So if you can't think of anywhere else for you to tell me what you want from me, why you've sent for me, we'll just have to do it here."

I forced myself to calm down. Couldn't understand why she'd got so irate with me. She was always offish, but I couldn't remember her being particularly angry. But I needed her. If she didn't co-operate it would have to be me doing the leg work. Something I really hated. I needed to back down. Humble myself if I had to. Pride wasn't something I usually burdened myself with.

"You're right," I told her, fingers metaphorically crossed. "We'll talk about it in the lounge. It's next door to the breakfast room." I pointed its direction along the corridor." Down there and left. You can't miss it. It's got 'Lounge' written on the door."

That got me a filthy look.

"It's usually empty," I said. "Go on ahead. I've just got to pop to my room to get something. I won't be a moment."

She followed my directions and I went to my room to get the photo of Gibson. When I got to the lounge, Melissa was sat back in one of the large, randomly scattered, large comfortable armchairs, dark stockinged legs stretched out, posing almost. She had made no attempt to pull down the already short skirt that had ridden up as she sat down. Probably winding me up. But I managed to avoid drooling and sat down opposite her.

"Right," I said. "I'll fill you in with everything I've found."

"Wouldn't somebody have noticed a strange fishing boat, obviously out of place, on the river or canal?" she asked, after I'd given her the run down.

"It went along in the early hours. Not a lot of people around to notice. And what's so strange about a boat on a river?"

She had a point. A strong point. Reports of a missing fishing boat. Similar boat seen on the canal. Even the locals could have worked that out for themselves. But there hadn't been any such report. That left three possibilities. It had been seen but not reported. It hadn't been seen even though it had been there, or it hadn't been there at all. If it hadn't been there, where was it?

"Okay," she said. "So where do I come into your little scheme?"

I ignored her sarcastic tone. "Go to Hythe. Trawl the estate agents. See if Gibson or anybody has recently rented property with a boathouse attached. Show them this picture." I handed her the photo of Gibson and Carter. "Gibson is the big geezer on the left."

"And the other one?"

"Carter, our suspected victim. Maybe you could ask around. See if anybody's seen him floating in the canal."

Melissa simply stared at me coldly. No sense of humour. She even missed the bit about trawling the estate agents.

"You're going to have to put your hand in your pocket," she told me. "Hythe isn't that easy to get to. And I didn't drive down here. So I'll either have to get a cab or hire a car."

"Hire one for a few days. If you find the property, we might just go along and have a look at the boathouse."

"You might."

"There's not a lot we can do today. Let me take you out for a meal.

"You sober enough?"

"Totally. Well, mainly."

She stared at me for a few moments, obviously in the process of making a monumental decision. Then she nodded. "I'll have a quick shower and get changed. Wait for me here."

I obeyed. I wondered what she was going to get changed into. She looked perfectly alright to me as she was.

Chapter Fourteen

"I believe she likes you really," a voice said.

I turned to find the source of the voice. The little old lady who'd poked me in the back was peering at me from over the rim of her glasses. She was in an armchair, one of two whose backs were turned to where I was sitting. Obviously placed so that the occupants could sit and look out of the bay window that faced the sea. Currently, she was leant, looking back at me from over the arm of the chair.

Curious, I got up and plonked myself down in the chair next to her.

"She does like you," she repeated. "She reminds me so much of Lauren Bacall."
I responded with a short humourless laugh... "If she does like me, she shows it in a pretty strange way."

Miss Turnbull folded the newspaper that she had been reading and put it down on her tweed covered lap. She held her head to one side, thoughtful as if trying to read my mind. "I hope you don't feel as if I am intruding," she said. "But I did overhear what you and the young lady were discussing. May I ask, are you by any chance a private detective?"
I nodded.
She smiled with satisfaction. "I thought that you were. You're not quite right to be a real policeman."
"Others have thought that too."
"As soon as I saw you in the lobby I thought you might be. You look so much like Humphrey Bogart."
"Humphrey Bogart?"
"Yes, an actor. Before your time, perhaps."
"Casablanca."

"Yes. Yes. And to think, or to imagine, that I'm sharing a hotel with both Humphrey Bogart and Lauren Bacall. Perhaps I'm becoming a little wacky in my old age."

"You seem perfectly alright to me."

"Well, Humphrey Bogart often played the private detective, so it all fitted together."

"So you thought that because I look like Humphrey Bogart, I must be a private detective?"

"Yes. Silly isn't it?"

I shrugged. "Certainly different."

"And, of course," she continued, "the man who followed you home the other day, and the day before that, I think, told me that you were... How do you say...? Into something."

I leant forward, suddenly interested. Or rather, more interested. She didn't strike me as being delusional. On the contrary. "What man?"

"Rather a large gentleman in a dark suit."

"He reminded of young Jamie Rushton, the butcher's son. Terrorised the smaller children. But he met his match when he was silly enough to pick on little Tim." She smiled wistfully as she remembered. "Spent two weeks in hospital young Jamie did. He was never the same afterwards. He had a furtive look about him. Always looking over his shoulder and he used to run everywhere." She paused, thoughtfully. "I wonder what happened to him."

"So how do you know this man was following me?"

"Shadowing you, I think they call it. Well, what other reason would he have to follow you a little way behind, and then stop and wait for awhile after you entered the hotel and then turn around and go back the way he came? And to do it more than once.

"I think that he might have been checking up on you. Seeing that you were actually staying here. Had you told somebody that you were? Somebody who had reason not to entirely trust you?"

I found myself smiling. Maybe I had found Miss Marple after all. I nodded in response to her questions.

"I am so pleased" she said clasping her hands together. "Sometimes an old woman's imagination can get the better of her. We have enough time on our hands to tell ourselves little stories about people we don't know. It is so satisfying when they turn about to be true."

"I suppose it must be," I said, still smiling. "And most disappointing when you are wrong."

She frowned thoughtfully. "Yes," she said slowly. "I would imagine being wrong would be deeply distressing.

Then her face brightened again. The latter possibility obviously being dismissed. She leant forward "You know what it means, don't you?"

I shook my head. Hadn't a clue what she was talking about.

She explained.

"This man. The one who doesn't trust you. He is going to ask you for something. He wants something from you."

"He does? What?"

She sat back.

"I have no idea. But he must have a reason for being sure he can trust you." Her expression slightly changed and she took hold of her newspaper. "Your young lady has just arrived."

I looked around the chair and saw Melissa standing in doorway. I turned back to Miss Turnbull, my face questioning.

She smiled.

"Scent," she replied to my unasked question. She unfolded her newspaper.

Chapter Fifteen

Monday 8ᵗʰ June

The next morning I ate breakfast, thankful that I could fit it all in without having to put some of it in my pocket, and grateful that Melissa had already left for Hythe. The night before we had shared a curry. Or rather, we had shared a table.

Now, for me curry is best eaten when somewhat inebriated and happy. A meal eaten in an atmosphere of laughter and banter. It is not a meal to be eaten in stony silence being glared at; it is not a meal to be eaten whilst being scared that you might accidentally dribble something down your chin or make some other trivial mistake that would cause the person opposite you glare and make you feel worse.

I realised, and I hate to admit this, there was something about Melissa that frightened me. Not so much physical fear, but mental. Until I met her, I can't remember ever experiencing that type of fear. She made me feel like some poor Dickensian child under the power of a harsh and cruel mistress. I think that if Melissa had produced a cane from somewhere and laid it on the table threateningly in the curry house; I wouldn't have batted an eyelid.

I finished my breakfast, which had started out as hot but soon cooled in the atmosphere of the breakfast room. That morning I was the only occupant, so maybe the other guests knew something I didn't. Apart from ordering, I managed to avoid meeting the eyes of both landlady and daughter and as soon as possible escaped back to my room to plan the rest of my day.

The planning didn't take long. I had bugger all to do until lunchtime when I planned to revisit the pub and the acquaintance of Gibson. Apart from the obvious reasons, I was curious to discover whether or not Miss Marple's predictions would turn out true.

After a fairly relaxing morning of listening to the mischievous laughter of seagulls and children enjoying themselves; strolling in the sun, and as usual, too much coffee, I arrived at the bar where I expected to find Gibson sat and lording the place.

I was not wrong. He greeted me like an old friend, patting the bar stool beside him. A pint of beer miraculously arrived in front of me. The afternoon session had begun.

We passed brief niceties for several minutes before I decided to get down to the heavy stuff. And hoped that the old lady's perception had been correct. Otherwise, it might be time to leave Hastings. I would have added Gibson to the list of those who looked at me in strange ways.

"Did you have a good reason for having me followed," I asked him as calmly and lay back as I could.

He raised an eyebrow, obviously momentarily surprised, but his recovery was almost instant. His smile had wavered, now it broadened. "Good. Very good in fact. I like a man who gets down to things right away. Straightforward. A man after my own heart. Like to think of myself as a straightforward type of man."
"The reason?" I interrupted.
He wasn't fazed. He simply continued in the same way. "Impatient too. Time is precious to you. Always a good sign."
"The reason?" I felt like strangling him. I might have done if my fingers had been a lot longer.
"The reason? Quite simple, Mr Street. Quite simple. Look at it from my point of view. Learnt to be very careful of my dealings with others. Learnt not to accept everything as being as it first appears. Saves much heartache in the long run." He nodded in agreement with himself.

"What I've learnt from you, Arthur," I said, "is that brevity isn't one of your strongest suits. Why say something in ten words when you can use a thousand?"

He laughed. "Indeed. Indeed. You are right, of course, sir. Brevity is a thing I feel should be avoided at all cost. Clarity is the key. A thing well described is rarely a thing that can be misunderstood. And I'm most certain that you will agree, misunderstandings can often achieve the most unfortunate of consequences."

Although his smile was constant, his last words might easily have been taken as an underlying threat. But maybe my recent experiences, especially with Melissa were causing me to be a little paranoid. I let it pass and allowed him to continue in his own way. I just hoped I wouldn't doze before he got to the point. I'd hate to have to ask him to repeat himself.

"I have met you just a few days ago. A stranger come to town."
"Sounds rather dramatic that," I couldn't refrain from saying.

He continued, ignoring my comment.
"In such a short time we appear to have become friends."
"Friendly," I said.
"Indeed. Indeed. Friendly. Both of us here in Hastings together. Men here for different reasons. Men with somewhat different pasts. Would you not agree?" He nodded in acceptance of my agreement even though I hadn't moved a muscle. "Now, the question I forced myself to ask, Mr Street, was this. Was our meeting a chance encounter, or was there something somewhat less salubrious behind it?

"A man in my position, Mr Street, cannot afford to simply take a situation as it may appear." He leant forward slightly, his huge bulk moving as if in slow motion. "A man in my position, Mr Street, cannot afford to trust anybody. *'Take care of yourself, young Arthur. And make sure you get the buggers before they get you.'* That is what my Grandmother used to tell me. It is advice that I follow to this day."

He sat back quickly, barstool creaking and jowls quivering. He obviously felt that he had given me an explanation.

"Not quite the whole story though, is it," I said.

He raised an eyebrow and cocked his head to one side slightly. "No?"

"No! You're right. We met in a pub and we've chatted. You know my background, or at least, you have a fair idea. You tell me what you want to tell me knowing that. You've no reason to check out where I'm staying. What would it matter to you if I was still on the job? You're not going to suddenly unload your dirty laundry on me having found out that I'm really not the Bill anymore."

"Continue, sir. Continue. I'm enjoying your argument. Makes perfect sense when you put things that way."

I found myself laughing at the ridiculousness of his argument. I managed to control myself and continued. "So there has to be another reason. The only one I can think of is that you're going to want something from me. So you need to check me out. Make sure I am who I say I am."

He smile broadly and clapped his hands together.

"Excellent deduction. Excellent. You are right of course. I do have need of somebody such as yourself, with the connections you have."

He saw that I was about to speak and held up his hand to stop me. I complied.

"A moment more. The small job I have in mind for you is perfectly legal. No question about that. No question at all. Legal and above board, I can assure you. And I'm also sure that you have the capabilities to succeed...

"And of course, there is also the promise of a generous monetary incentive should you achieve the objective."

"Sounds interesting," I said.

Miss Marple had been right. He did want something from me. But I hadn't a clue what it was.

"So what do you want?"

"Not now, sir. Not now. This is not the right time or place to go into detail."

"You've got my attention. "When will be the right time?"

"The ideal time Mr Street will be in a couple of nights from now. Yes, ideal. I am having a little get together with some of my closest friends and associates. If you are willing to come along, I will introduce you to somebody I am sure you will find interesting. When you have met this person, then I will outline my request."

"All very mysterious. Are you sure you're not being a little dramatic?"

"Ah. Mystery and drama. Are they not both wonderful to experience, Mr Street. The richness of life." He smiled. "Wouldn't life be so much poorer without them?"

"It would be simpler."

"You will come then?" he asked.

I nodded.

Not at all sure what I was committing myself to.

"Can I bring somebody?" I had briefly considered Miss Marple, but decided that that would be too weird even for me. Instead I opted for Melissa. Insurance, as it were.

"Of course. Of Course. Bring anybody you like."

His look told me that he fully understood why I should want to bring somebody. If you're about to enter the lion's den it's handy to have some sort of protection or insurance against possible harm.

"Details?" I asked.

"Before you go. One more thing, Mr Street."

"Which is?"

"Discretion. You are an old friend from my past. If anybody should have the audacity to ask."

"Maybe I've met some of them professionally. Now wouldn't that be interesting."

He looked thoughtful for an instant and then laughed. "Highly unlikely, sir. Highly unlikely. But I always say that life is so much more interesting when the unexpected does occur."

"That it is. But I suppose that you'd come up with a solution if it did."

"Creativity, sir. Would be a wonderful opportunity to be creative."

Chapter Sixteen

I'd never asked Melissa if she was any good at rowing a boat. Not a thing that usually comes up in most people's conversations. Certainly not a chat up line I'd heard. Though anything's worth a go, I suppose. Though, in reality, I can't remember ever speaking to Melissa about anything that wasn't to do with work. She might be married with three kids for all I knew. Though I doubted the existence of any kids. And if she had been married she was probably a widow. Suicide or despair being the reason.

Rowing was my 'Plan B'. Hiring a boat and going up and down the canal looking into boathouses to see if I could spot an out of place fishing boat. In truth, I thought I was being just a bit too hopeful with my 'Plan A'. In my experience the only way you could get an estate agent to admit to being an estate agent was to hand him a few hundred quid. But then, I wasn't built like Melissa.

When I'd met up with her late afternoon, I decided to take control. I had met her outside of the hotel. I'd been on my way back from my latest chat with Gibson, and she was back from Hythe. At the time I was dying for a wee. We arranged to meet in a side street pub in St Leonards, one I'd passed by earlier that looked reasonably attractive.

The pub turned out to be a busy little place full of 'Real Ale' drinkers whose only interest in life seemed to be discussing the merits or demerits of what particular ale they were drinking, or had drunk in the long distant past. Any mention of murder or dead bodies would not in any way distract them from their more serious discussion.

I sat at a table facing the door, as far away from the crowd as I could get. Which wasn't very far, but it would suffice. In front of me was a half drunk pint of lager. She was five minutes late when she came in. Now it's a contradiction to say that somebody could both glide and sort of bounce as they walked but Melissa managed it.

My third reaction had been to down the remainder of my drink in one. My first reaction had been to throw back my head and howl like a wolf; my second, to fight the impulse.

I'd never seen her in jeans before. A few weeks earlier I'd read something about a very attractive girl who'd walked around a city centre naked from the waist down and nobody had noticed. They hadn't noticed because her lower body had had a pair of jeans cleverly painted onto her skin. Melissa's jeans were no looser than the imaginary ones.

Around me, even the ongoing droning about 'Real Ale' seemed to lessen, but in reality it was probably just my ears popping because of a build up of pressure in my head.

She undulated over and sat down opposite me. "Wipe your chin," she ordered.

I felt my chin and wiped the dripping lager from it. So much for being in control. "A drink?" I asked.

"It's a pub isn't it?" She looked around slowly as if to confirm her first impression.
"What do you want?" I tried to sound curt, but it came out a little too high pitched. I coughed to get my throat back in order.
"G and T, ice and lemon."

I picked up my empty glass and went to the bar. My head was still full of the after image of a black, satin top; buttons tastefully undone to the extent that at first glance they seemed to reveal everything but, in fact, revealed nothing. Nothing, that is, except for a great deal of smooth, silky flesh.

A barmaid eventually rescued me from my less savoury thoughts. I
happened to glance at the guy standing next to me at the bar. He raised
his pint glass. ""Great stuff," he told me. "Looks good as well."
I nodded, still thinking of Melissa, or rather to be absolutely honest,
her body.
"You ought to try it," he continued.
"I would if I could."
"Leaves a wonderful after-taste,"
"I bet it does."
"Dragon's Tits," he informed me.
I turned to him. At times, the brain can move super fast. Thankfully, it
did then and I realised he was speaking about the beer and not Melissa.
I calmed down. "You're right there, sunshine," I said to him as I
collected the drinks.

I sat across from Melissa again. "Dragon's Tits."
Her face remained expression free. "A real ale. 4.8% ABV."
I sat back in my chair. Sometimes attempted jokes just don't backfire,
they explode in your face.
"It's written up on the board behind you. Now are you ready to hear?
Or do you want to continue doing whatever it is you're trying to do?"
"I'm ready."

"I'll keep it as brief as I can," she began. "The third agent I went to
was a rat. He never once looked me in the eye. Reminded me a little of
you." She paused until I raised my eyes and looked into the green,
bottomless lakes that were hers.

"I handed him my card," she continued."
"Card? What card?"

She sighed impatiently, delved into her small hand bag and eventually
extracted a business card and handed it to me. I read it quickly. Had
the address of my office on it, a web site and a phone number. Both of
which I'd never heard of. But it was the name that got to me.

"Melissa Jan Stoikov. LLB?" I stared at her.

"My father was Russian."

"You have a law degree?"

"I have many things."

"Why are you working for me?"

"Do you want to know what happened?"

I nodded, feeling quite numb and bemused.

"I handed the slimy, little rat my card. Told him I was acting for Gibson's uncle and needed to get hold of him urgently. Then I showed him the picture. It jogged his memory. He went to his filing cabinet and found a file.

"I read it. Is this Gibson a total idiot?" she asked me.

"Far from it. Why do you ask?"

"Well, if this whole thing was planned, it would have been rather stupid of him to use his own name."

"That it would," I concurred. "Maybe it wasn't planned."

"He lives in Hastings. Why would he want to rent a furnished house in Hythe?"

I simply shrugged. "Can't answer that right now. How long ago did he rent it?"

"Three months. A year long lease.

"Does it have a boathouse?"

"An extra large boathouse according to the advertising literature that was in the file. A detached, four bedroom property. Long rear garden leading down to the canal."

"Just as well," I said, "seeing that it has a boathouse."

She ignored my attempt at sarcasm and took out her phone. She pressed and swiped the screen a few times and handed it over to me. As I started to look at it, the picture flipped from portrait to landscape. I turned the phone to landscape and it flipped back to portrait. We eventually caught up with each other.

The image showed a detached house as viewed between two open gates. Ivy clad high brick walls extending either side of the gateway. A driveway led up to the house. By the side of the house was a double garage. A thick hedge divided the property from the adjoining one on the garage side. I could not see the other side. There was quite a gap between the garage and the hedge. It suggested a way into the rear garden, and the boathouse beyond, that didn't involve going through the house.

I could feel a new adventure coming along.

"Another?" I asked Melissa, pointing to her glass that had the lemon, unaccompanied by any liquid, resting on the melting ice.

I returned with the drinks.

"The slimy, little rat of an estate agent actually asked me out," she said out of the blue. "Asked me if I'd like to join him for lunch and then he could pop us along to the property."
"Did you go?"
The green depths of her eyes frosted over. "Smiled at him as sweetly as I could manage and told him I'd much prefer to chew sawdust as to have a meal with him."
"Good," I said. Immediately, I wished I hadn't.

"Mr Street," she said, leaning slightly forward, folded her arms. It had the effect of making the already adequate even larger. I pleaded silently, for the seams of her top to give way, or a button or two to pop off. Her voice quieter than usual, "our relationship is purely business. I work for you and..."
"Sometimes, I think I'm working for you," I told her. And meant it.
"That's exactly how it should be. Our relationship is not going to change. You just aren't my type."
"What is your type?" I asked. "Just curious," I added quickly.
"My type?" she stared into my eyes as she spoke. "Small, chubby, bald men. Preferably somebody like a computer geek. Inexperienced, so that I can teach them all sorts of wonderful things. And get them to do things to me. There is nothing like lying naked across a little, innocent, fat man's lap and having your bottom smacked hard. And little fat men really appreciate you when you sit on their face."

I should not have pictured her naked lying across my lap. I was in agony. I need to readjust myself before it snapped. I couldn't get up and rush to the toilet. I'd be sticking out too much. I didn't want to give her the satisfaction.

"Interesting," I said through gritted teeth.

She finished her drink and stood. "Let me know how you intend to move forward." She leant over me. For a moment, I thought that she was about to kiss me. Instead, she whispered sexily, her warm breath apparent, into my ear. "All this talk of sex. It's made me feel quite randy. I'll see if any of the girls back at the hotel want to play. Perhaps both of them. That would be fun. Otherwise, I'll just have to fly solo. Enjoy your drink."

She went. I quickly flicked myself up and sighed with relief. "Bloody sea air," I muttered to myself. "Little fat men; sitting on their faces; wanting to see if the girls were willing to play; going to play with herself." Whatever happened to the cold Melissa who I knew so well? Or not

Chapter Seventeen

After getting a message to Melissa not to dispose of the hire car, and letting her know what I had planned, I spent the day in preparation. Preparation involved buying some cheap items from a local army surplus store; drinking lots of coffee; strolling along the seafront and spending a few quid trying to win a cuddly toy buy hoisting it out of a glass cabinet by means of a crane. Needless to say, the crane always managed to drop it before it reached the opening. But it helped pass the time and take my mind off the spot of illegality I had planned.

Though the most difficult part of the day was avoiding bars. Bars and waiting make good bedfellows. However, I was waiting for dusk, and I needed to be sober.

It was almost completely dark by the time Melissa had driven me to Hythe. I wanted the darkness for more than one reason. It hid my very ill fitting freshly purchased army surplus camouflage trousers and shirt. For that I was grateful. It had been a terrifying ordeal escaping the hotel without being seen in my ridiculous outfit. The expression on Melissa's face when I leapt into the car is still engraved in my mind.

We drove to Hythe in silence. She in a skin-tight, black outfit and me in too tight, too short trousers that ended way above my ankles. It matched my shirtsleeves which ended halfway up my forearms and had to remain undone. The store had had nothing in my size but I had to get something.

She pulled the car into a lay-by. "That's it," she said pointing.

There were no lights showing in the upper floor, but the view of the lower floor was blocked by the wall.

"No point in hanging about," I said as I unbuckled my seatbelt and extracted myself from the car. "Time I went. Shouldn't be long."
"Wait just a second."

I turned and saw her leaning across the car's passenger seat, there was a simultaneous click and flash. I was momentarily blinded. When my vision returned she was looking at her phone with a big smile on her face.

"Wonderful," she laughed. "I must get this framed for the office. Albert Street. Man of action."

As I slammed the car door, she climbed out of the other side. "Quiet might be a good tactic," she said as she closed her door almost silently. "This might be useful." She handed me a flash-light.

I took it from her sullenly, suddenly feeling terribly stupid. How could I have forgotten to bring something as basic as that?

"Are you coming?" I asked her. My plan was for her to sit in the car and wait. Maybe blow the horn if anybody showed up. "You sure you'll be alright?"
"Come on," was her response, "Let's see what's in that boathouse."
"Might have to wait until they go to bed."
"Why? If anybody's in they'll likely be watching television or playing music. That might drown out any noise that you're likely to make."

We reached the gateway which gave us a view of the whole house. There were no lights on or other signs of occupation. We moved forward slowly. My ears straining as I listened for the dreaded growl in the dark. Dogs in daylight were one thing. Dogs at night, something else. I wish I'd invested in a cricketer's box.

Using the flash-light intermittently, we made our way down the side of the house and to the rear. There were no lights showing at the back of the house. However, I could see through gaps in the hedge that the house next door was occupied. There were lights in several rooms. Luckily, we were protected from view by the hedge.

79

Still using the flash-light sparingly, concerned that a nosy neighbour might spot trespassers and take appropriate action; we made our way down the garden.

We soon reached the boathouse without incident. Constructed of wood, it was nothing more than a big shed with a single door in the rear. First look showed it was padlocked, but on closer inspection I was thankful to find that the padlock was just hooked on and not locked. A relief because not only had I forgot to bring a flash-light but I'd also neglected to bring any tools. Hadn't even thought about them. If I had, I'd have bought some basic implements. I hate to think what some of my burglar 'friends' would have said about that. Perhaps the sea air was rotting my brain.

The door creaked as I pulled it open. Melissa went in first and I followed pulling the door to, behind me. Now I could use the light properly. I turned the light away from the door. And there it sat. A fishing boat, just like the ones I saw pulled up on the beach in Hastings. The wooden nameplate spelt 'Amy Grey'. I'd found it!

Beside me, Melissa turned on another flash-light. She'd come well prepared. And at that moment I didn't care how big a bill she'd put in for getting them.

"Perhaps, you're not quite as dim as I thought you were," she said.

I ignored her as I walked along the planking beside the boat. Shining my torch around, I saw nothing broken, nothing out of place. I climbed on board and Melissa followed.

We moved towards the central wheelhouse at the front of the boat. That's when I saw it. Along the edges, both sides. Now closer, I could also see it on the windows.

I pointed. "Blood spatter. High velocity. Somebody... No two people have been shot. High calibre. Powerful to have gone straight through them, but tumbling on the way. Hence the amount of blood. And down there, on the deck." I shone my torch downwards and over the dark reddy, brown stains on the deck.

There's more over here," Melissa said.

I went to her at the back of the boat, saw where she was shining her flash-light. It was illuminating a number of blood drops of various sizes on the deck, and on the edge of the boat right along the back. "These are different," I told her. "They're circular. Gravity drops. Whoever was bleeding was just standing here. Maybe not for long, but long enough to deposit those drops. Could have been drops from the entry wound."
"Three killed?"

I nodded, feeling satisfied. Wasn't any point in mourning for the victims. "It's what I expected. Carter gets shot, and the other two, too scared to move get it next."
"The killer, or killers, dump the bodies overboard and bring the boat here," she added.
"It fits."
"But why leave all this evidence? There's been plenty of time to clean up."
"Can't answer that," I admitted. "Though it's not easy to clean up thoroughly and not leave a trace."
"They could have least have done something. Somebody was going to find this boat sometime. If it had have been me, I would have used petrol."
"Petrol?"
"Set fire to the boat and boathouse," she suggested. "Got rid of all the evidence. It would have gone up in flames long before anybody could get here."

She was right of course. It didn't make sense leaving everything just like it was. "Maybe that was planned for the future," I said, knowing I was clutching at straws. "Maybe Gibson thinks he's got plenty of time to get round to it. People have made that sort of mistake in the past."
"So, now the police?"
I shook my head. "No, not yet."
"Why?"
"Well, firstly, I want the rest of my fee from Belinda Carter. Secondly, curiosity."

"Curiosity?"

"Been invited to a party at Gibson's. He say he's got a job for me. I'm interested in knowing what that's about." I looked at her in the torchlight for a few seconds. "Hope you've got something suitable to wear. It's tomorrow night."

Chapter Eighteen

Tuesday 9th June

It was about 8.00 pm. I was standing outside the front door of Gibson's place. A house that fitted him perfectly; large with considerable grounds at the front. Already several cars were parked in seemingly haphazard positions. Each one saying, 'how much space can I take up to inconvenience others?' But there was a lot of space to take up.

I'd gone to bed the night before still thinking of Melissa's successful attempt at winding me up. Something that left me with an ache that wouldn't easily go away. Not without some outside assistance. And since she'd been at the hotel, I had no opportunity to seek out that assistance.

At the same time, I was terribly pleased with myself for so easily sorting out the case of the missing boat and its crew. I might not know who actually did it. But I had a fair idea who was behind it. I couldn't prove it. But I'd done enough to earn the rest of my fee.

Yet, I didn't sleep too well. And it had nothing to do with my ache. Kept waking and thinking. Obsessed even. Same thoughts going through my head over and over. Never really getting anywhere. I continued to get the imagery of being on the Amy Grey, shining my torch over the blood spatter and drops. Everything fitted into place so easily.

Too easily. That was part of the problem. Something was wrong about the whole thing. Had no idea what it was, but something was nagging at me. So I had decided that I had a need for Notso. Or rather, a need to get at the police records. I wanted somebody checked up on.

Notso had never been the easiest person to get on with. He wasn't the brightest button on a blazer but he wasn't a total idiot. What he was, was in the main, difficult. My task was to convince him that if he got me the information he could solve, or be seen to solve, a triple murder. At the same time I could not afford yet, to tell him anything. It had been hard but I succeeded.

Now I was waiting for Melissa.

Two cars pulled into the driveway.

"Mr Street, isn't it?"
I looked around and into the face of Barbara White. Timothy White's grieving mother.
"Mrs White," I said. "I didn't know you'd be here."
She shook her head. "I'm not going to the party. I'm just off home."
I frowned.
"I work for Mr Gibson. Keep house and other jobs. Part time, of course. I'm a little late home today. I had to help with the preparation."
"Right..."

The cars pulled up together. I could see by the stickers on the doors that they were both cabs, but different companies. Then I spotted the passengers in each. In the first was Belinda Carter. The second held Melissa. The gods certainly know how to play games.

When she spotted me, Belinda Carter's expression changed. She approached, uncertainty written on her face.

"Tonight, you don't know me," I told her quickly before she could speak. "It's important. You've never seen me before in your life. Keep walking by me and listen."
"But..."
"You don't know me," I repeated with more urgency. "I've nearly got the answers you want. I'll come and see you in the morning. If Gibson finds out I'm working for you, everything will go down the pan. Do you understand?"
She nodded as she brushed by me. "Okay. I don't know you," she said without turning her head. I watched her enter the open front door. And

considered, by the side, the possibilities of the following morning.

I just hoped that the wheels wouldn't fall off after a few glasses of champagne.

Then I nearly choked. In concentrating on Belinda, I'd failed to see Melissa's approach. I had no idea where she'd got the dress from that she was wearing. I only wished she hadn't. My ache was threatening to turn into chronic pain.

Black. Open at the front, almost down to the waist. Yet still, somehow, holding everything in place. From the waist down to a few inches above the knee it was light fitting but clingy. On one side there was a split that seemed to go up to the hip. I made up my mind there and then. As soon as this case was over and we'd got back to London I was going to sack her. No matter the cost. But before then I needed a drink badly.

Together, we entered a tasteful decorated, long hallway and headed towards the murmur of voices and the occasional laughter. At the far end of the hallway, one of Gibson's minders quietly stood, hands behind his back.

There were about a dozen people inside. All ages, all types. Some sophisticated, others a little rough around the edges, even a punk girl festooned with tattoos. It was as though Arthur Gibson had managed to get together for his little soirée, as he called it, a sample from every walk of life.

As we stood in the entrance I saw that Belinda Carter was not looking entirely at ease. She was stood by large table full of champagne bottles, glasses and a variety of expensive looking snacks. But no bowl of crisps or sausage rolls as far as I could see.

"Let's get a drink," I said to Melissa. "And you've never seen Mrs Carter before," I warned her, quietly.

She turned to me and gave me a big smile. Then mouthed the word, 'Idiot'. Whereupon I followed her to the drinks' table unable to keep

85

my eyes off her rhythmic, undulating backside.

Ignoring Belinda Carter, and the food we each poured ourselves a
glass of champagne and moved from the table. That's when Arthur
Gibson, currently holding court with a few obvious lackeys, who
appeared to cling to his every word, spotted us. He cut short his
conversation, pushed through a couple who were partially in his way
and approached us.

Sat down, Arthur Gibson looked big. Stood up he was even bigger.
Many huge men waddle when   they walk. Arthur Gibson walked
with the purpose of an Abram's Tank. I'm sure that if anybody had
really got in his way they would have been flattened. And Gibson's
stride would not have faltered. I'm over six foot, yet I had to look up to
him as he stood there, beaming down at us.

"Wonderful that you should come," he said. "Wonderful."

I simply nodded. Not a lot I could say.

He pointedly stared at Melissa and then turned to me. "Remarkable.
You are a remarkable man, Mr Street. You have given me so much
pleasure in bringing into my home one of the most beautiful women
that I have ever had the good fortune to lay eyes upon. You are a very
lucky man, Mr Street. Very lucky."

I didn't feel lucky when it came to the person on question. "This is
Melissa. She's my personal assistant."
"Of course, of course. I understand," he chuckled, multiple chins
wobbling.
"It's true, Mr Gibson," Melissa said. "We just work together, nothing
more."

He stared down at us for a few moments. Then he put a hand on our
shoulders. "I am a man of many, many experiences. But let me tell you
a little secret. I have been blessed, and I really do believe that it is a
blessing, that I have never had any interest in sex. No. Do not get me
wrong. I can, and do get immense pleasure from experiencing beauty,
but I have no desire to personally get pleasure from experiencing it

86

physically. If you understand my meaning."

He smiled, and it seemed to be a genuine smile. Almost wistful. And I think that in that moment my feelings about him changed.

"However," he continued, "in the course of my work and other occurrences I have had the need to see how sex and relationships affect others. Indeed, I admit to taking advantage of such needs in others,

"The point I am making, is that over the years I have learnt to spot many signs in the way people behave towards each other. I see the way you two behave. I saw you enter, come into my room. I saw your body language. I saw your unspeakable desire for each other."

"Nonsense," Melissa snapped, shrugging his hand from her shoulder.

Before removing his hand from my shoulder, Gibson gave it a gentle squeeze. And he chuckled. Obviously quietly satisfied about something.

He looked directly at me. "Now I must get down to the reason I invited you here. Apart from, of course, the fact that I enjoy your company. But business is business, so everybody seems to say." He glanced at the angry looking Melissa. "Am I free to speak?" he asked me.
"Go ahead."
"Good, good. I told you that I had a little job for you."
"You did, I'm curious to know what it is."
"And you will. You will. But first, and this is most certainly to do with that job, there is a rather attractive woman standing on her own by the table, keeping close to the drinks as is her way at such do's as this."
Belinda Carter! "I see her," I said

He addressed Melissa. "If that's alright with you, of course."
She gestured that she didn't give a damn.
He nodded. "I would like you to make her acquaintance. Speak to her. Befriend her. Get to know her."
"Why?" This wasn't going in any direction I had imagined. Was it some sort of trap? I'm not often thrown by events. I was then.
"Later, later. Bear with me Mr Street. Soon I will tell you exactly what

87

all this is about. But first, I need you to do this little thing for me. Something that I'm sure you will not find at all distasteful."

"You're right there," Melissa said in a sarcastic tone.

I looked at her.

"Go ahead," she said. "There's a guy over there I'd like to meet." She pointed.

I looked to where her finger led. There was a little, fat, balding, middle-aged man in a crumpled suit.

Gibson looked momentarily bemused. Then brightened as if had just suddenly completely understood what was taking place between us. Maybe he had!

"Don Prior," he told her. "My accountant, or one of them. Mind like a razor when it comes to money. Unfortunately for him, a tongue like a rubber ball when it comes to women. Please be gentle with him otherwise he will never forgive me for inviting him tonight."

"I will," she promised as she smiled at Gibson and then more lingeringly at me.

She turned and walked away, as did Gibson who was laughing and shaking his head.

What had she said in the bar? Small, fat, chubby men. Really appreciate it when you sit on their face.

Bitch!

Chapter Nineteen

I turned to her after pouring myself, what I hoped would be many, another glass of champagne. "You're on your own," I said, knowing it was corny, but not caring.

"You're observant," Belinda Carter replied. "Are you some sort of policeman?"

"Some sort," I answered. "Saw you were on your own, thought I'd come over and say hello."

"Have we met before?"

"Never. We're just two people meeting and chatting at a party."

"How long have you known Arthur?"

"Not long."

"Does your partner mind you speaking to me?" Her smile was a message. Something to do with morning showers, I thought.

"She's my personal assistant," I said, glancing over at Melissa, seeing that she seemed to be having fun with the little, fat idiot. "It doesn't matter what she thinks."

"She does look familiar. I'm sure I've seen her before."

"Probably got one of those faces."

"Probably."

"How come you're here alone?" I asked, continuing to play the game.

"Because I am alone, at the moment."

"Surprising. You don't look the sort to be alone."

"I'm not the type. Circumstances. It's a long story."

"I've got time," I said, knowing that somewhere in the room, Gibson would be keeping half an eye on us.

"You really don't want to..." she began, but stopped as her phone began to ring. "Excuse me." She delved into her spacious handbag and extracted her phone. She looked at the incoming number and frowned. Answering it, she nodded to me, turned and walked away.

After a short time she appeared agitated, using her hand to emphasise some point. Agitation grew and her expression turned to anger. Immediately, phone still at her ear, she strode towards the open door and left the room.

"That didn't look as if it went to plan."

I turned and looked down at the heavily made up but pretty face of the girl with the punk, spiky hair. Her choice in clothes seemed to be no style, yet every style all rolled into one. Perhaps purposely designed to displease everybody except for her own kind, whatever that was. Though I couldn't help noticing her legs which descended from her tiny mini-skirt. They were something else, so to speak. I immediately had this desire to slowly stroke my face and lips along them, upwards.

"She got a call," I told her, trying to rid my mind of my less salubrious desires. It was an unnecessary statement, but I couldn't think of anything else to say.

"Not seen you before at one of Uncle's little do's," she said, staring up at me as if trying to work out what sort of animal I was.
"Not been before. You're Arthur's niece?"
"Tina."
"Right. I'm Al."
"An old friend of Uncle?"
"A new friend."

We carried on the small talk for awhile. She looked like a punk, but didn't speak like a punk or at least, she didn't speak like I imagined one would speak like. For some reason, I'd never encountered any whilst on the job. Maybe they didn't go in for murder that much.

As we chatted, I had difficulty in stopping myself from frequently glancing in Melissa's direction to see how she was getting on with her little, fat arsehole. I succeeded most of the time. It was especially painful when I saw her laughing. Didn't know she could. Never seen it before. Didn't suit her somehow; laughing.

Then I spotted one of Gibson's minders enter the party room. He had an even more serious look on his face than he normally had. An expression he managed to transfer to Gibson after whispering something in his ear, without a word that I could see, to any of the guests that he had been speaking to, Gibson turned and followed his minder out of the room. The latter having to move quickly to avoid being trampled by Gibson's tank like stride.

I turned back to Tina. She was in her twenty's. Slim, but well shaped. My eyes couldn't help but travel down to her legs. And couldn't help but wonder about the sexual behaviour of punks. Were they different in some way?

However, my sexual musings and fantasies, and my ongoing chatting were interrupted a few minutes after Gibson had bulldozed out of the room looking so serious.

His minder suddenly materialised by my side and whispered into my ear. "Boss needs to see you now." Without waiting for a response, he turned and strode away. He was obviously used to people complying with his boss's wishes.

I shrugged at Tina. "Seems I have to go."
She gave me a sweet smile, sort of knowingly, and I followed after the minder, making sure that my attitude was casual.

He strode along the hallway, passing by doors on either side before stopping and rapping his knuckles on one. He opened it and stood aside for me to enter. I complied and he immediately closed the door behind me.

That was an instant impression that collided with all the other impressions that hit me as I stood just inside of the room.

A library. Bookshelves. A large desk. A few scattered leather armchairs. Arthur Gibson seated, unmoving on one of them, staring up at me. And the body on the parquet floor.

Belinda Carter. A knife sticking out of her chest.

I wouldn't be having any more morning showers at her place.

After my irreverent first thought, what was left of the policeman inside me clicked in. I went to the body and squatted down beside it. She couldn't be more dead. The handle of the blade suggested kitchen knife. Plunged straight into the heart from a slightly upwards direction. Very little blood. A mere staining around the wound.

I turned my attention to the handbag lying beside her. A few items scattered in its fall. Disturbing it as little as possible, I looked inside. Then I decided to disturb it lot more and started rummaging. I eventually found a phone. Not the one I had been looking for. But an old style one. Not the phone she'd received the call on. That had been a newer smart-phone in a turquoise leather case.

I moved her body and then let it fall back to how she had fallen. The phone she had received the call upon was missing.

"Have you touched her phone?" I asked Gibson.
"I have touched nothing."

So first impression was that somebody at the party had rang her, lured her into the library and killed her. They then removed her phone to stop the incoming call from being traced. Fortunately, phone companies keep records. Assuming that both she and the killer had registered phones, that is.

I stood up and looked around a little more, noticing one of the French Windows ajar. That complicated things. An open door can be an open door to the whole world. Anybody could have come in from the outside. On the other hand, the murder weapon was a kitchen knife, presumably from Gibson's kitchen. This suggested that the killer was somebody already in the house. It was a little unlikely that somebody would come in from the outside planning to kill somebody, but would first have to go to the kitchen to get a murder weapon. Yet...

"We need to talk, Mr Street. Gibson interrupted my mental rambling.

I turned to him. "Have you rung the police, yet?"

"Not yet." he pointed to a nearby chair. "Please sit. We need to talk."

Chapter Twenty

It was surreal.

For what seemed an age, we simply sat and stared at what was left of Belinda Carter. To this day, I can't figure out what went through my mind during those few minutes. Everything? Money; who could have done it; reliving recent experiences; my last minutes with her; sex and showers; first time I met her; her donkey laugh? At the same time I remember being temporarily mentally numb.

It was surreal.

"Before I involve the police, Mr Street," Gibson began. "I have a need to tell you a little story. It is to do with that woman." He nodded towards the body.
"I'm listening."
"I asked you here tonight because I wanted you to find somebody for me. That is the reason I asked you to get to know Belinda. If anybody had any information, she surely had.

"But I need to go back in time a little. Back in time." He settled himself back in his chair and clasped his hands together upon his enormous stomach. "Where to begin. Where to begin."

He paused for an age. I didn't prod him on. With him, one had to be patient.

"A good deal of my business activities, Mr Street are not what one might term as Kosher."

I smiled knowingly.

"I have done many, many different things, Mr Street. I admit to being ashamed of some. Freely admit it. However, I like to think that most, if not all, of my ventures have been without victims. Except, of course, for those victims who have arisen from, shall we say, disagreement. I have never robbed a bank or a person. I have never harmed another in pursuit of profit.

"I admit, that in the early days some of my confederates were less scrupulous than I. For example, some found it advantageous to offer personal insurance to local pubs and clubs whereby it was almost guaranteed that they would be free of trouble. The cost being only a small and reasonable fee.

"But I myself moved on. Eventually I decided that it was time to retire. Not entirely, I admit. I still retain a small interest in one thing and another. A steady income if you like. The reason I moved away from the centre of activity down here to Hastings was to remove myself from temptation. However, I still have one major scheme that I have an interest in. One that, unfortunately, is nearing its conclusion due to the current political climate."

He stopped and looked at me intently. "How far can I trust you, Mr Street? Can I reveal certain details that might get me into a little trouble if you were to relay them to your ex-colleagues?"

"Maybe. Don't like drugs too much. Sexual exploitation. Don't like kidnapping as a means of making money. Not all that keen on murder or anything to do with kids. In the main, I don't like innocent people getting hurt."

"Well said. Highly commendable, I must say," he beamed at me. "Glad to say that I too do not like hurting innocent people." He paused and stared at me again before gesturing towards Belinda Carter. "Desperate times, Mr Street. Desperate times. So I have to take a chance with you. But what is life without a little risk?

"Retired. Mostly. Moved down to this part of the world. Travelled around some before I decided upon Hastings. In so doing, I met many people. Old friends as well as new. One night I was in a little hotel in

Southsea. Pleasant bar. Most of its customers were non-residents. Met a chap who worked on the docks in Portsmouth. Heard from him about a Russian seaman trying to sell diamonds. And that is how my current venture began, Mr Street. Pure luck. Being in the right place at the right time, and speaking to the right person.

"Do you have any knowledge of diamonds, Mr Street?"
I shook my head. "Not really."
"I will tell you. It is quite astounding. Quite astounding. Well, there are basically only two main sources for diamonds. One legitimate. The other not so."
"The other being blood diamonds." I hoped I sounded a little knowledgeable.
"One of many names, Mr Street. But you are basically correct. I will continue. The Russian seaman with his little bag of uncut diamonds led me along a path which proved to be somewhat profitable.

"It works like this. To you it might sound somewhat dramatic. But, as complicated as it is, or was. I'm not currently sure which. It did reduce risk somewhat.

"A Russian cargo ship carrying various commodities from Africa to Europe. Specifically Holland as a rule. Not an easy place to attempt to unload uncut diamonds, Mr Street. The authorities are very hot on that sort of thing. Trust me on that.

"To continue. Somewhere out on the horizon our slow moving Russian cargo ship lowers a high powered inflatable which runs under the cover of darkness and is too small to be noticed by any coastguard radar. This little, fast boat runs towards Hastings in the cover of night. The occupant drops a package tied to a small buoy with a simple transmitter. He then returns to the cargo ship and the inflatable is hoisted back on board and it continues on its way.

"The following night, a fishing boat with a suitable receiver finds the package and brings it home. You understand what I am saying?" he asked me.
"Totally," I replied. "Clever, but complicated."
"Indeed. Indeed," he smiled.

"And what does that have to do with her? I thumbed towards our silent witness. The body in the library.

"Patience," he said. "I am about to tell you that very thing." He thought for a few moments then continued. "A colleague of mine. One Jim Carter. Her husband in fact. He and I had some mutual acquaintances in London. Our paths had crossed quite a few times over the years. He, back then, was not really somebody who I would willingly choose to get involved with. He had his good side, I must admit. Unfortunately, he also had his weaknesses. One of his strengths was that with the right direction he could be relied upon to get a job done. He did not mind taking risks. Especially if the reward was there at the end. And he was able to keep his mouth shut. Except when it came to Belinda, who had to know everything. But she too could be closed lipped if it meant more money in her ample pockets.

"It was serendipity again, Mr Street. Pure coincidence. Having decided to move away from the epicentre of my somewhat dubious past activities, I should first come across the Russian seaman desperate to sell his diamonds at a good price. Then, not long later, when my plans were still in an embryonic state, I should bump into Jim Cater, now playing at being an estate agent.

"Back in London, Cater had been an avid boater. Owning his own cruiser and no doubt using it to get up to nefarious activities. Now, with his background taken into account, plans and personnel soon fell into place. He had been here few years. I was a newcomer. Well, Carter arranged to get control of a couple of fishing boats using inducements that I provided.

"When the drop happened, Cater went looking. While I, shall we say, fished nearby ready to intervene if something unexpected were to occur.

"Pleasant nights mainly. The stars, the sea and a large flask of Scotch. Pleasant, I say, until the night that Carter slipped away and disappeared. Vanished under my very nose. Vanished with around two million pounds sterling of uncut diamonds. My biggest import by far!"

He sat even further back into his chair and was breathing heavily, fighting the intense anger he so obviously felt. His almost perpetual smile had left him. Replaced with an expression of determination that spelt great problems for anybody who crossed his path in that matter.

Unfortunately for me, the strength of his emotions told me that his story must have been more or less true. In which case, who had killed Jim Carter? Seemed obvious really. Somebody who'd known about the diamond pick-up and had decided to hi-jack the shipment.

Gibson got control of his feelings and continued. His heavy breathing had subsided. He continued. "I am not used to being double-crossed, Mr Street. It is not a pleasant feeling. Not only does it impact upon my finances it also affects my reputation. I cannot have either damaged. I hope you understand my strength of feeling with regard to that, Mr Street."

I nodded. I certainly did.

"Good," he said. "I need to find Carter and put this matter right. I need both him and my diamonds. That is why I asked you here. I wanted you to get to know Belinda Carter. Let you experience what you are likely to be up against. I planned to bring you in here to my library at around this time and offer you the job of finding my diamonds and the man who took them from me.

"I am totally certain that she knew where he is. Had full knowledge of the whole affair. She and he were close, Mr Street. Very close. I do not believe that he ever did anything without her knowledge. Indeed, without her guidance as well."

I had no 'Plan B'. No other ideas. Everything had fitted so well. I needed to review the evidence. Had I missed something? Got something wrong? I need a drink and I needed sex. But mostly I needed to be somewhere else. I felt as if my head was going to explode. I get like that sometimes. Too much information. All conflicting.

"The offer still stands, Mr Street."

"Offer?"

"Use your resources to find Cater for me. Will you do it? You will be well rewarded when you succeed. I have every confidence in you."

I nodded slowly. Very slowly, mind racing but failing to keep up. A little fearful that if I nodded my head too quickly, it might fall off.

His smile returned. "Good. Excellent. We can go into details later. Now, and I'm sure you will agree, it is time to get your ex-colleagues involved."

"Yes, I agree. Best make sure that nobody leaves. It'll keep them happy when they arrive."

"Already sorted, sir. Already sorted. One of my first instructions to Toby." He seemed to be back to his jolly, confident self.

Unfortunately, I was about to change that.

The police were going to complicate things. Especially if they were any good. I was going to be questioned like everybody else. I was the last person to be seen speaking to Belinda Carter. If they dug deep, my chances of keeping my previous involvement with her were slim. I needed to stay ahead of the curve. Which meant that I had to tell Gibson that I hadn't been strictly straight with him

"Something you should know," I said to Gibson who was in the process of raising his bulk from the comfort of his chair. He sat back down again, expression curious, expectant.

"Not been entirely straight with you," I said, not knowing or being able to even guess what the eventual outcome of my confession would be. The two minders didn't immediately bother me. Lying in bed at night listening out for creaking floorboards did.

"The job you've just given me. Find Carter. Well, that's why I'm here."

"Indeed," he said quietly, head leant slightly to one side as if intent on hearing and understanding my every word.

"I mean, that's why I'm here in Hastings."

"Indeed," he repeated.

His response was unnerving but I continued. "Belinda Carter came to

99

me several days ago and offered me the job of finding out what had happened to her husband. Paid well, so I took it on.

Thing is, she put the finger on you for doing away with him."

He raised an eyebrow and smiled.

"That's how I came to meet you," I added.

He didn't react.

"Thought you ought to know."

"Have you discovered anything?" Calm voice.

I shrugged. "Haven't found him or his body."

How much should I tell him? I needed time to think and I wasn't getting it. In such situations, mistakes are easily made. My well imagined scenarios had withered away in front of my eyes. Why would Belinda Carter pay me to find out what had happened to her husband if she knew he was still alive? Why would Gibson offer me the job of finding Carter who he had murdered?

With respect to the slaying of Belinda Carter, in my mind the 'Why?' screamed at me louder than the 'Whom?'

"Have I discovered anything," I said. "Yes, but I need to think about it before I tell you. And if I tell you what I know, you might decide not to pay me anything."

"You assume, Mr Street, that after your confession that I still want to employ you. You know, another man might take what you have just told me very badly indeed. Very badly.

"Desire all sorts of retribution for your rather devious actions. Your deceit and dishonesty. Your abuse of the offer of friendship. And believe me, sir that if I were such a man the retribution would not be half-hearted."

"So what happens now?"

"I consider myself to be an understanding sort of person. I like to think things through. So my current view of this matter is that you had a job to do, Mr Street, a job to do. The fact that you are now here, sitting across from me, implies that you have done your job very well indeed."

He paused. "On the other hand, it is possible that you have been a little naïve."

"Naive?" I repeated pointlessly.

"Indeed, sir. Indeed. I have a personal question, Mr Street. Perhaps a little delicate, but I must ask it anyway." He pointed a finger towards the cooling, or cold body. "Were you ever intimate with her?"

That made me sit up. "Why'd you ask that?"

"Good reason, Mr Street. Good reason. Known the Carters for a good while. Knew of Belinda Carter a lot longer. Never met her. But knew of her before she became Mrs Carter. She went around in, shall we say, neighbouring circles. Belinda Strickland she was then. She had a certain reputation. Used her, not unattractive body in the same way as a writer uses a pen. Not to put too finer point on it."

"Not sure I understand the significance."

"To make it plain, Mr Street. She used her body to manipulate. As far as I understand, she did not change her ways after she married Carter. Indeed, Mr Street, rumour has it that Carter encouraged her to continue. Much can be learnt whilst resting your head upon the right pillow.

"It is unfortunate for her, that when I eventually did get to meet her, her considerable talents were wasted when she attempted to apply them in my direction. Instead, it provided me with information. That being I should keep a close and watchful eye on the pair of them. Which I did successfully until several weeks ago.

"My point, and I do realise it has taken a while to get to, is that if you had been intimate with that woman it is extremely likely that she was trying to manipulate you."

"And I thought it was just my charm," I joked. Though I didn't feel even a tiny bit humorous. "So what do you think the manipulation could have been about? I was doing what I was getting paid to do."

He shrugged. "I do think that you really have to work that one out for yourself. I am not a detective, Mr Street. But if I were, I might well wonder why a woman would employ somebody to find evidence of her husband's murder knowing the said husband was still alive. And I might also consider the possibility that intimacy might over-ride, to some extent, one's critical faculties."

Chapter Twenty-One

A police car turned up about fifteen minutes after Gibson rang them. By then, I had managed to get Melissa away from her little arsehole and tell her about Belinda Carter. The rest of the party were still unaware of the murder. Any announcement would likely instigate an attempt at a rapid exodus. Something that Gibson, and me, wanted to avoid. For many obvious reasons, he wanted the investigation to go as smoothly as possible.

Though, I must admit that the devil inside of me tried to get me to announce the murder simply to watch the rush to the door and to wind up Gibson's minders who would have the job of preventing departure. But I desisted.

I knew for certainty that Gibson wasn't directly involved. I knew that I wasn't and neither was Melissa and her little, bald turd. I knew that Tina the punk had nothing to do with it. And I doubted if either of the two minders were responsible.

The rest of the guests, were, as far as I was aware, unaccounted for. The door to the party room was open. The toilet was just along the corridor. Guests would likely regularly pop out to relieve themselves. Something which isn't generally timed by others. It takes awhile to realise somebody isn't where they are supposed to be. They were therefore all suspects. And, of course, there was the open French Windows. However, one mustn't forget the phone call that caused the victim to leave the party room. Had anybody been seen making that call?

Two uniformed officers arrived. Male and female. The latter stayed by the front door to make sure nobody tried to leave. The other accompanied one of Gibson's boys to view the body.

"So what happens now?" Melissa asked as I was pouring myself another glass of champagne.

"We wait. We get questioned. We bugger off."

"I mean, what happens about the case? Your client is dead."

"Very."

"You're not going to get the rest of your fee. I can't see any point in going on. Are you going to tell the police about the fishing boat and call it a day?"

I shook my head. "No! We don't tell them anything other than the truth. But the truth doesn't extend to going to Hythe for any reason."

"So, I ask again. What happens now?"

"We carry on as before," I told her. "Same job, new client. Gibson has asked me to track Carter down. He's convinced that he's still alive and his disappearance is down to the fact that he ripped him off for a lot of money. And by a lot I mean a lot."

"But..."

"Indeed, but," I interrupted. "We need to take another look at the boat. See if we can paint another picture of what might have happened. Gibson intimated that I might have suffered from a form of penile deception when I last looked."

"Penile deception?"

"Yeah, don't worry about it. I'll explain when you're not sober. Anyway I take it that you're on for another visit. Unless, of course you've got something better to do." I nodded in the direction of her little turd who was watching us, or rather her, over the rim of his champagne glass.

She smiled at me in her own special, sardonic way. "Oh, I can think of lots of things that I'd prefer to be doing. But I'll come along. I admit to being curious as to how you might find a new reason to explain the evidence of the blood on the boat. Three lots of blood. Three missing people. Seems most straightforward to me. Yes, I'm curious to find out where this goes. If anywhere."

She paused, a tiny frown disrupting her usually smooth, perfect forehead. "Who do you think did away with Mrs Carter?"

I shrugged as I often did. Tried to stop doing it. Never succeeded.

"Who knows? I know a few who didn't. And that includes me. And, I hate so say this, you. Somebody here." I gestured around me. "Somebody from the outside. If Carter really is still alive maybe it was him. Seems like a good candidate to me. Cutting off the last string, so to speak."
She nodded slowly, thoughtfully.

"Can I have everyone's attention, please?"

We turned and saw the two police officers standing in the doorway. You could tell that they were trying very hard to be authoritative and strong. But they were young, inexperienced and would have looked more at home holding hands.

The male officer continued after he'd got the attention he'd asked for. The expression on the guest's faces ranged from curiosity to anger. What's going on? Why are the police interfering? Somebody committed a minor motoring transgression on the way here? But nobody looked particularly guilty. A little surprising seeing that they were Gibson's friends. I would have thought that most of them would have been guilty of something or other.

"As some of you may be aware," PC whoever, continued, "there has been a tragic occurrence here tonight. I must ask you to remain calm. Some senior officers will be arriving shortly. They might want to ask you some questions. Thank you for your co-operation."

"What tragic occurrence?" a voice called out. It was a guy who looked like a pugilistic bricklayer. Bling around his neck in the way of multiple gold chains; cropped hair, broken nose, pink, short sleeved shirt that revealed arms full of cheap looking tattoos.

"There has been a death," the policeman replied reluctantly.
"Death? Who? Not Arthur is it?" The bricklayer looked concerned.
"No sir. Mr Gibson is still in the room with the body." He took his notebook out. "The deceased is one..." He obviously struggled to read his own handwriting. He'd probably written it whilst avoiding looking at the corpse and with a shaky hand. Poor little bugger. "Er... One Belinda Carter," he finished.

Murmuring among the guests. The bricklayer looked relieved but otherwise unconcerned. Melissa's little. Fat friend looked shocked, as did Tina. The rest of the guests were either too stunned to react or they weren't particularly bothered. Obvious that Belinda Carter hadn't been either the life or soul of the gathering or a great favourite of the other guests. Evidenced by the fact that she had stood on her own and not mixing.

"How did she die?" A middle-aged woman asked. Probably once pretty, but now using excessive make-up to cover up that faded prettiness. Sad. But, of all the guests, she did show some concern.

"Er... Suspicious circumstances," was the officer's response. Hopefully, he probably realised the stupidity of his response, yet having to sustain a position ingrained by the mindless training of political correctness.

"She was stabbed through the heart with a kitchen knife," I said loudly. Couldn't help myself. Faces turned towards me. Some wore expressions of disbelief, others shock, others mere curiosity. But again, a quick scan revealed no sign of guilt.

"Suppose that is bloody suspicious," the bricklayer said.

I added him to my list of those who hadn't done it, and he gained a few notches in my esteem.

The two police officers still standing in the doorway were both staring at me. Maybe wondering how I knew. Maybe fantasising about how they caught a murderer. How else could I have known? They were probably also trying to make up their minds as to whether to be relieved at my revelation, thereby curtailing any more questions, or to be annoyed that I had made it. In any event, they were temporally forgotten as Belinda Carter's murder became a noisy topic for hot discussion and no doubt the generation of countless theories and nonsensical speculation.

The bricklayer, glass in hand, approached. "Don't know you," he said.

The sort who used his bulk and his nose to intimidate.

"Could be because we've never met," I replied.

He nodded, grinning. "Could be that." He offered me a large hand. "Bill Crane."

I took his hand and for a few seconds we tested each other's grip. "Al Street."

He glanced at Melissa. "And who is wonderful example of womanhood?"

"You can speak to me directly," Melissa snapped. "I do understand English."

Bill Crane raised a hand. "Sorry. No offence meant. What I call habit talk. One gets to talk in a certain way. Acceptable in some circles. Not in others. I apologise gain." He smiled at her broadly, revealing unexpectedly perfect white teeth. "Forgive me?"

He didn't speak like a bricklayer. Or at least, my probably prejudiced, view of how a bricklayer should speak. Don't think I'd ever met one, to be honest. But stereotypes are useful. Some of the time.

Melissa didn't respond. But Melissa wouldn't. I think that with her, first impressions are all important. If you don't start off on the right foot, you're never given a second chance. Which meant. That when we first met I must have done something wrong. Probably why her knickers are off limits to me.

"So how do you know Arthur?" Crane asked. "Not seen you at one of his little gatherings before. Then we haven't had a murder before. Any connection?"

I held up my hands. "Okay. You've got me. How did you mange to work it out so quickly?"

He laughed. Melissa's expression continued to show disapproval.

"Not been here before," I told him. I saw no reason in giving any unnecessary information. But there was always the chance I might get some.

"Do you work for Arthur?" he prompted.

"Why do you ask?"

He gestured around the room. "You could say that this is more of a company get together than a purely social one. Pretty much everybody here has a business connection with Arthur. Even Belinda Carter. Or at least her husband does, or did. Thought you might fit in."

"He asked me to do a little job for him. A confidential one," I replied.

"Understand," he nodded.

"How about you?" It was my turn to delve. It was as good as any way to spend the time before the more senior plods arrived.

"I do work for him," he replied.

I didn't ask him if he had built Gibson's wall or put people's heads through them. Instead I kept my questions more civilised. "What sort of work? Or is that confidential?"

"Not really. The details are though. But the job itself isn't."

"What sort of work?"

"I'm into diamonds."

"What? Stealing them?" I couldn't help myself. Out of the corner of my eye, I saw Melissa grimace. Didn't blame her. Wanted to do it myself.

Fortunately for me, after a few seconds hesitation, Crane took it good-humouredly and laughed. "I know what I look like. But no, I don't steal them. I own a diamond business. Wholesaling and cutting. Though I do a little setting occasionally."

"And that's what you do for Arthur?"

He nodded but I spotted a sudden wariness in his eyes.

"I wondered how he got that done," I said quickly, letting him know that I was aware of Gibson's connection with diamonds and at the same time implying that I was one of the 'in' people in his organisation.

"Then you can guess how things work," he said.

"More or less."

"So what do you think of this business?" he asked, changing the subject. "Belinda, I mean. Saw you talking to her earlier."

"Not sure what to think." And I meant it.

"Can't think of anybody here wanting her dead," he said. "I admit she wasn't all that popular. Or rather, Jim wasn't. But he rubbed off on her.

And most of the women here hated her. Thought that she was a threat. She had a reputation you know. Rumoured that Jim encouraged it. He'd try to make a profit out of anything. Still, I don't think anybody hated her enough to want her dead. At least, hated her enough to kill her.

"Even if somebody here did have a motive," I added. "It's insane to lure her into the next room to stab her. Why do it when you can be pretty damned certain that you're going to be on the list of suspects and there's nowhere to hide."
"An impulsive act?" he suggested.
"Doubt it. You've got to be damned angry to suddenly lash out and stab somebody. And if you're that angry, and do lash out with a knife you just happen to have in your hand, temper makes for multiple stab wounds. Not one single well aimed one."
"Always?"
"No, not always," I conceded. "But look at things logically. Somebody lures her into another room. Why? To kill her? To have something out with her? If it was just to have something out with her where does the knife come in? If it was to kill her. That would be premeditation. Moreover, if you planned to kill her, doing it here would be crazy. You have the whole world out there. Here, you're an instant suspect."
"What sort of knife was it?" Crane asked.
"A kitchen knife. And that makes the whole thing even more difficult. The killer first had to go into the kitchen and find a suitable knife and confront the victim. That takes time. Arthur's boys are wandering around keeping their eye on things. Too great a risk. Now, I know hardly anybody in this room but the fact that they are here suggests that nobody is thick enough to take such a risk when there are so many other options."
"So it was somebody from outside." Melissa, speaking for the first time, suggested.
"That seems the best bet," Crane agreed.
"Similar problems. If somebody came here to kill her wouldn't they have brought their own weapon? If the killer rang her and arranged to meet her in the library and things got out of hand and she ended up dead, then where did the kitchen knife come from?"

Melissa spoke again. I enjoyed her interventions. She often made a lot of sense. "Perhaps it was Belinda Carter who got the knife from the kitchen as protection and the killer took it from her and stabbed her."

"I hadn't thought of that," I admitted. "Yet there was no sign of a struggle. I'm sure she would have screamed or something if she'd had time. Yet... No. Best idea so far and I need to think about it. But it doesn't fit with my gut feeling. I'm not seeing something. Or maybe, just maybe, I have seen something that's lurking just outside of my consciousness."

"How dramatic," Melissa scoffed. "The great detective..."

"Detective?" Crane looked wary.

I glared at Melissa. She didn't actually say 'Whoops', but her face did. "I was," I told Crane. "That's why Arthur has employed me. I've still got contacts. But I was what you might say, dishonourably discharged."

"Right," Crane said slowly, thoughtfully. But he managed to continue the conversation. "So basically, it's not likely to have been anybody here. On the other hand, it's unlikely to have been anybody from the outside. A mystery."

"Bloody right, a mystery," I said. "Look who's arrived."

Two men in suits stood in the doorway beside the two uniforms. They ran their eye over the guests.

"Let's see if they can solve our mystery," I said, smiling.

Chapter Twenty-Two

Time flowed, as did the champagne and I was beginning to feel as though I was approaching the point where being irresponsible would be a good course of action. The unexpected death of Belinda Carter was still there in the back of my mind. But it was too soon to attempt to work out what had happened. I needed to remove the murder from my consciousness. Let my unconscious get to work. In other words, currently I wasn't able to search for a solution.

My ongoing conversation with Melissa, Crane and Tina was brought to an end by the interruption of a uniform who informed me that my presence was wanted elsewhere.

I followed him out of the room, along the corridor past the library to another door. The library doorway was now festooned with yellow tape as was another, which I assumed to be the entrance to the kitchen. Obviously waiting the attention of the crime scene incompetents. I hoped that Gibson had a good local takeaway, Because of the speed that the forensics went, he'd need one. They always claim that they're being thorough. But most of us think that they're so slow because they're looking up in a book what to do next.

I entered what was the dining room. Seated at the end of a large, oak, twelve seater, oblong dining table was one of the plain clothes police officers. His partner was seated beside him. Probably a Detective Inspector and a Sergeant.

The one at the head of table, the older of the two, wore a dark blue suit under which was a blue and white striped suit with light blue tie. He was either colour blind or had no imagination. His narrow face was topped with a trendy, slightly spiky, head of hair. Obviously greased to hold the spikes carefully in place. His eyes followed me, staring, as I casually strolled towards him, champagne glass in hand.

He gestured for me to sit. I complied, seating myself opposite his eager looking, baby faced companion, who sat notepad and police issue pencil at the ready.

The one in charge introduced himself as Detective Inspector Chandler and his buddy as Constable Montrose. He probably had trouble working with sergeants. Maybe they didn't nod and agree so readily. I took Chandler to be one of those politically correct policemen who believed that rules were everything no matter what the circumstances were or how inappropriate they could be in certain situations.

I considered asking to see their warrant cards, but resisted.

The questions began with the usual name and address, and then moved on.

"I understand that you were speaking to Mrs Carter, the deceased, before she left the room to go to the library," Chandler said.
I nodded and took a sip. "She wasn't deceased then."
His eyes hardened. I suppressed a giggle.
"Will you tell me what happened?" he asked.
"I was speaking to her. She got a phone call. She left."
"Any idea who called her?"
"None at all."
"Did you know the deceased?"
"I'd been talking to her. Probably means I knew her."
"Before the party!" he almost shouted.
The constable winced.
"Yes," I replied.
"Will you elaborate on that?"
"I knew her. Not known her for long," I elaborated. "Perhaps a couple of weeks."
"And your relationship was?"
"Business."
"Business? What sort of business would that be?"

"It would be the looking for a missing husband sort of business."

He leant forward, his interest perked up. His mate stopped scribbling and stared at me.
"Please elaborate."
"Her husband went missing on a fishing trip," I elaborated. "Both he, two crew members and the fishing boat disappeared."
"Disappeared?"
"Disappeared. Vanished," I gestured wildly, narrowly avoiding knocking my glass over. "You've got it all on record. Check it out. Now's your chance. You lot failed to do it properly before."

He visibly took a few deep breaths, coughed and continued, in a voice of forced calmness. "When, exactly, did that occur?"
I took another sip. "It occurred exactly a few months ago."
"Did she invite you to the party tonight?"
"No."
"Then how did you get here."
"Taxi."
"I mean who invited you?" He was having trouble containing himself. But political correctness came out on top.

If our roles had been reversed, by now I'd have made him stand up so I could whack him in the guts. Sat him down again and saw how the conversation went from then on. No bruise, my word against his.
"I was invited by Arthur Gibson."
"Have you known Mr Gibson for long?"
"About a week?"
"About a week." I took another sip. There wasn't a lot of champagne left in the glass. I might have to interrupt proceedings to go and get another.
"About a week?" he repeated. "Mr Gibson told me that all the guests were either close friends or business associates. How could you become a close friend in just a week?"
"Incredible isn't it. Of course, there's the other option."
"Other option?"

The fumes of the champagne must have been getting to him. Either that or he was as thick as he looked.

"Yes. Other option. Friends or business associates. Take away the friends bit and what are you left with? I'll tell you because it is so obviously difficult. Business!"

The constable covered his mouth as if wiping it, but his eyes looked a little moist and his body shook slightly. Chandler reverted to deep breaths again. "What sort of business associate of Mr Gibson are you?
"The investigation sort of business. It's what I do."
"So Mr Gibson is one of your employers?" He looked somewhat dubious. "What are you investigating for Mr Gibson?"
"The disappearance of Belinda Carter's husband."

That shut him up for quite awhile. When he did speak, some of the confidence had ebbed from his voice.
"So two people are employing you to do the same job?"
"Yes, good isn't it? Or it would have been if she hadn't been murdered. Now I'm not going to get any fee from her when I find out what happened to her husband."

His already disapproving frown deepened. "A human being has just had her life taken from her and all you seemed to care about is not getting your money."
"Not true," I said in my most indignant voice. "Not true at all. I'm going to miss the sex as well."

For a moment his face went completely blank. Any expression he had had vanished. I thought his eyes were about to roll up and he'd drop dead on the spot. But I wasn't that lucky it's possible that Constable Montrose's little squeal helped him recover.
"So you were intimate with her?"
"Find being intimate is a damn good way to have sex."

Constable Montrose's cough earned him an angry look. He reddened and bent over his notepad as if short-sighted.
"This isn't a laughing matter, Mr Street."
"Who's laughing? She might be dead but I've got to live with my losses."
Wind the bugger up some more, I decided.

114

He stared at me, eyes narrowed. I smiled back, tempted to put my thumb on my nose and waggle my fingers. Looking back I regret not doing it then. The timing would have been perfect.

"Let's move on," he said after a few more exercises in self-control. "Have you got far in your investigation? It could well be that Mrs Carter's death and her husband's disappearance are related."
"Really? Never thought of that. Well..." I shook my head. Before he could speak, I said, "Questioned a few people. Got a few ideas. But no, I've not made much progress. But early days."
"Did Mrs Carter believe him to be still alive?"
"Belinda Carter was convinced that he was dead."
"Her evidence was?"
"Husband went missing. Two crew members went missing with him. Fishing boat went missing. You really should check your records on this."
"So what else can you tell me?"
"Nothing pertinent to Belinda Carter's murder."

He leant forward, intent on making a point. He said slowly, "We will decide, Mr Street, what is or is not pertinent. You simply give us any information you have."
"So you want any information I have. Even though I can't see how it could possibly be connected with this case?"
He nodded slowly. "Just provide us with the information, Mr Street. We will do the thinking."
"Right then. Where should I begin?"
"At the beginning," DC Montrose suggested, glanced at his boss and wished he hadn't.

"Right. Start at the beginning." I picked up my now empty glass and stared into it as if I was composing myself; to get my story organised; things in the right order and all that.

"Maternity ward. Hospital. West London. I distinctly remember a trolley being pushed by a black lady. It had a tray of jam tarts on it."
"Jam tarts!" Chandler breathed.
"Yes. Small disc like things." I demonstrated with finger and thumb.

"They've got jam in the middle. I don't remember being offered any. Probably because I had no teeth at the time. But I've always had a soft spot for tarts ever since. Strange but..."

"Mr Street," Chandler shouted. Finally losing his cool. "What do bloody jam tarts have to do with anything?"

"Buggered if I know. Hoped you might tell me. You told me to tell you everything from the beginning. You said just do it and you'd do the thinking. I've done exactly what you wanted" I leant towards him. "Are you okay? You look a little poorly to me. If you ask Arthur, he might let you have a lie down somewhere."

DC Montrose jerked, spluttered, dropped his pencil and held his mouth with both hands. I quite liked him.

Thereafter the remainder of the interview was a little strained, but fortunately brief. Probably because Chandler had difficulty speaking because his teeth were pressed together so tightly.

I returned to the party, noticing the look the others gave me as I entered. To most of them I was a stranger. A stranger comes to the party. There's a murder. I would imagine they thought that as I was escorted out, the next time they saw me I'd be in handcuffs.

I took Melissa to one side and reminded her to tell the truth, but not the whole truth and certainly nothing but the truth.

What seemed like hours late, thankfully, champagne notwithstanding, we were free to go. I ordered a cab and after a brief word with Gibson, we departed.

Chapter Twenty-Three

Wednesday 10th June

I saw Melissa the following morning as I was having a quiet, thoughtful coffee in what passed for a lounge. She sat herself in a chair facing me and we stared at each other in silence until the hotel landlady had deposited another coffee on the small table between us. A table that barely had room for two cups and the untidy pile of out of date magazines.

"Well?" she opened, tone as friendly as usual.
"Well what?" I wasn't in the mood to be cowed by my so-called assistant.
"Have you figured out what's going on yet? You are supposed to be detective?
"And you're supposed to be an assistant, secretary or something," I replied just as snappily as she spoke.
"I'm assisting you, aren't I?"
"I suppose," I reluctantly admitted. "But you attitude could be a lot better." I didn't want to lose the battle that easily.

She waved a dismissive hand as if to say her attitude was irrelevant.
"So do you, or do you not have any ideas what is going on?"
"Motive."
"Motive?"
"Yes, the key seems to be motive. Think about it." I'd been thinking about it since I'd woken up early. Much too early.
"Explain."
I complied. Talking is often good for me. It helps the arrangement of

my thoughts.

"Belinda Carter employed us to find out what had happened to her husband. Information led us to a boat-house where we found evidence of three murders.

"It seemed that Belinda Carter's theory of Gibson having her husband killed was well founded. Especially since she managed to get herself killed at the main suspects' party. All rather neat, isn't it?

"Except, that at that same party, Gibson employs me, or us, to also find Carter, who he is sure is still alive."

"That's what he claims," Melissa interrupted.

"Exactly. And this is where the problem of motive comes into it. We'll start at the beginning. Three men in a boat. All killed. Bodies disposed of. Probably dumped overboard. Why? Why would Gibson, an intelligent man and most unlikely prone to making quick, rash decisions go to the trouble of killing Carter on the boat when he could have more easily done it at another time and place without the need for collateral damage in the form of the two murdered kids? Why would he feel the need to hi-jack his own illicit cargo?"

"Cargo?"

Melissa hadn't known about the diamonds. At least I had no recollection of telling her.

"I'll explain that later," I promised her. "My point is that I can see no motive at all for the killing of Carter and the other two. There's no reason for it. Not if we stay on the path we've been.

"The only possibility is an unknown third party. Somehow, somebody got the information that
Carter was about to make a pick up and hi-jacked the shipment.

"But that means there was another, unknown boat in the sea, waiting," I continued, trying to sort things as I went along, Thinking out loud, "Possible, maybe... Yet, if that was the case, why not just take the haul? Why go to the trouble of killing Carter and the crew. Maybe Carter knew the hi-jacker. That would be a motive."

It still didn't ring true. "But then, why go and hide the boat? That would have to be pre-planned. If it was planned in such detail, couldn't they have thought of something better? I know I could have. And they not only hid the boat, but hid it in a boathouse rented by Gibson. That would mean the killer was somebody close to Gibson. Knew he had a place in Hythe. None of it fits."

"Perhaps it was done in that way to get Gibson off his back. Framing him," Melissa suggested.

I stared at her. Pieces of the puzzle began to ease together. Maybe... "You're wonderful," I found myself saying.

Her mouth formed as if she wanted to say something, but nothing came out. That made a pleasant change.

"I need to take another look at that boat," I told her. "This evening. Think you're up to it? You've might just have solved half the problem."
"I have? Half?" She seemed a little confused. The day was going well.
"Yes. The half we still have to sort out is the murder of Belinda Carter. It's beginning to look as though they are related. But again we're back to motive. People don't generally do things without a reason. And murdering Belinda Carter at that party means that there's a damned good reason for doing it. Find the reason and we find the killer."

"Plenty of people appear to have had the opportunity. However, I don't think it was anybody at the party. She was lured out of the room by the phone call. See anybody making a call? No. And neither did anyone else. On the other hand, there's a significant weakness in my theory that it was somebody from the outside."

"I'm listening," Melissa said.
"Oh good," I replied. "I'll continue then. Somebody rang her and obviously enticed her into the library. That phone call has to be directly related to her murder. It can't be just a coincidence. Not when you take into account that it wasn't found on or near her body."
"Meaning the killer took it."
"Meaning the killer took it. And not just for a souvenir. But let's take a

step back. Cover old ground so to speak. Did you see Belinda Carter leave?"

She nodded. "But that's because you had been with her"

"And you were keeping an eye on me," I grinned.

"I noticed her leave. Okay!" she snapped.

I composed myself and continued. "If you noticed, others likely noticed. So if somebody else had been gone for a considerable length of time, their absence would also likely have been noticed.

"But let's assume that they decided to take the risk. What would their actions have been? Go to the kitchen and find a suitable knife? Apart from the party goers, Gibson had his two minders lurking around, keeping their eye on things. Our would-be culprit would have been aware of that. That's not taking a risk. That's plain stupidity.

"But let's assume for a moment that our killer was plainly stupid. So they successfully find a suitable weapon and wander from the kitchen and into the library whereupon they ring Mrs Carter, lure her into the library and stab her to death. With just one strike, mind you. Not making certain by stabbing her two or three or more times.

"Stabbed her to death," I repeated. "In my experience, a single stab wound is rarely found outside of a street fight. And only then as a consequence of a spontaneous act of fear or anger.

"But this was premeditated. Go to the kitchen and get a weapon. Lure your intended victim. Stab her and leave. One stab wound. Most people survive a single stab wound. If you want to make sure, you make sure.

"The whole thing feels wrong. Illogical. It doesn't make sense. Killing a fellow guest at a party knowing you're going to end up in the middle of a relatively small list of suspects. Phoning, knowing your phone's going to be looked at as ours were. Risk being seen. Risk the strong possibility of blood spatter all over your clothes. It's all wrong.

"Being stupid wouldn't account for all that risk taking. You'd have to have been partially brain dead to take all those risks. And I don't think that Gibson associates with people like that. He might use them once in awhile. But he wouldn't associate with them. And if, after all I've said it does turn out to be somebody at the party, what did they do with the missing phone. Couldn't have had it on them the police would have found it. So they hid it somewhere?" I shook my head in my most disbelieving way.

"When did you discover her phone missing?" Melissa asked.
"When I went to the body. She did have a phone in her bag, but it was an old one. The one she'd got the call on was a smart phone with a turquoise cover."

"So you think somebody broke in," she said.
"Didn't have to break in. The French Windows in the library were open. But unfortunately, that scenario doesn't fit either. If somebody had planned to kill Belinda Carter at the party, wouldn't they have arrived tooled up? Who would go to the effort of planning a killing and then arriving without a weapon of some sort?"
"Maybe it was spontaneous," she suggested. "A planned meeting that went wrong."
"So somebody creeps from the outside into the library, rings Mrs Carter and says meet me in the library. Whereupon they have a heated argument. The killer then says words to the effect; hang on while I pop to the kitchen to get a knife to kill you with because I've lost my temper with you. I won't be long."

"You're right," she agreed. "Nothing makes sense. So what we're looking for is somebody who wasn't at the party and didn't come in from the outside. Gibson's men fit that description."
"They wouldn't kill somebody and leave the body lying around. No, your summing up is about right. Nobody at the party did, and nobody came in from the outside."

For a second, I almost saw something in my mind. Somebody or something I'd seen at the party. It was gone in an instant. Hopefully, it would come back.

I looked at my watch and saw that it was time for me to get prepared to meet Gibson at his usual afternoon haunt. Last night I had a question for him. Today, I discovered I had an even more important one.

After making arrangements for that evening, and assuring Melissa I wouldn't go anywhere near her in what she called my 'Action Man' outfit, I departed for my room.

Chapter Twenty-Four

On the way to meet Gibson, my mind mulled over many things. Few to do with the case. Walking along the seafront in Hastings on a summer's day was, at times, distracting. My first few days had been exceptionally interesting. Then Melissa showed up and everything changed.

Now one of my partners in fun was dead and the other two virtually ignored me. If I didn't need Melissa's help I would get rid of her. Maybe tomorrow. Meanwhile, I'd be better off averting my eyes from things that I took enormous pleasure in looking at. But better off or not, my eyes went where they went. And the dull, persistent ache I endured was a consequence.

I reached the pub and entered. Déjà vu. Could have been yesterday, or most days come to that. Everything the same. The recent slaying had changed nothing. Same regulars, a couple of grockles, the minders sat in the usual seats and Gibson alone, seated at the end of the bar. I wondered what he got out of it all. That same routine, day in day out. But I've long since learned that people will be people and how they lead their lives is often a mystery to others.

I moved a bar stool a little closer to him and sat down.
"Any news?" I asked, after allowing him to order my usual.
"Police are still wandering around with their white suits on looking serious. I've no idea what they expect to find. No idea."
"Neither do they," I said. "That's why they take so long." I paused. "If you're happy to talk here, I've got a couple of questions for you."
He gestured with both hands. "Perfectly all right, Mr Street. Nobody here to listen. If that were to change our conversation would change. Trust my judgement, Mr Street."

"Of course," I said."Right. Belinda Carter was convinced that her husband was dead. Murdered. Murdered by you, as it happens."

His fat face split into an enormous grin, and his body shook with silent laughter.

"You obviously find the idea amusing."
"Very amusing, Mr Street." He shook his head. "Oh dear, it does seem that you have been taken for a ride, Mr Street."
"How so?" I asked. Yet I was fairly certain I already knew. That's why I needed to re-visit the boat. Last time I was there, I wasn't particularly open minded when I viewed the scene. I likely manipulated the evidence to fit in with a preconceived idea of what had happened. Partly due to my relationship with Belinda Carter and the resulting penile distraction it caused. Tonight would be different.

"If I understand things correctly," he began. "Mrs Carter came to you to find her husband who had disappeared along with his boat."
"And two crew members. Kids who had their whole lives ahead of them."
"Indeed. Indeed. A terrible thing that. Terrible. I know the mother of one. She works for me. She too would like to know what really happened." He put his head to one side and for some reason I was reminded of an owl. He stared at me for a few moments. "Mrs Carter told you that she believed her husband to be the victim of some nefarious plot orchestrated by me. Is that not so?"
"That's about the sum of it."
"No doubt she gave you certain information that led you too me."
I nodded.
He nodded too. Just as well we weren't sitting in the back of a car.

"Did you ever question her veracity, Mr Street? No, I can see from your face that you did not. Tell me, if you would, Mr Street. Did she ever use other means to distract you from questioning her motives?"
"I thought it was down to my overwhelming masculinity."

He laughed, body shaking as usual.

"I suppose it served another purpose as well," I said. "She never showed any sign of mourning. I assumed that it wasn't love that brought her to me. What was important to her was establishing his death in order to get her hands on the insurance or whatever. Doing what she did with me, instigating it, in fact, emphasised that assumption.

"That leads me nicely to my first question."

He was about to reply so I held up a hand to stop an immediate response. I hadn't finished.

"The reason I ask is that I'm having trouble finding a motive for her murder. Life would be a lot easier if I could accept the possibility that Jim Carter was alive and it was he who killed his wife.

"He must have known your house and the layout. Using your kitchen knife would've pointed the finger at somebody at the party. Point the finger at you, maybe. Pretty risky. But if something happened between him and his wife; something very emotional... Well, emotions can easily cloud judgement even in the brightest of people."

Arthur Gibson clapped his hands a couple of times. "Wonderful, Mr Street. A truly amazing theory. Answers everything. Wife killed by disgruntled husband. Well, I do have to admit that it would be more than foolish to rule out such a possibility, but I'm afraid that I must."

"Why?" I asked, feeling somewhat disappointed by his response. I had considered it to be a damned good explanation. Ticked all of the boxes. Assuming Carter was still alive, of course. And to that, I knew I had to keep an open mind.

"Why?" he repeated. "I knew the happy couple very well, Mr Street. And on the surface they did appear to be very happy indeed. Yet, there was always an undercurrent. Something not right. At least, in my view, not right. Yet, at the same time, they appeared to be content with the arrangement."

"Arrangement?" I thought that to be an odd term to use.

"Yes," he nodded. "I will explain. Carter worked for me, Mr Street. True he was a reasonably successful estate agent, but both his and her needs far exceeded any possible income from being a mere estate agent, here in Hastings.

"I always thought that they made lots of money."

"Oh, they do, Mr Street. They do. But the Carters needed more. Much more.

"I bumped into Carter whilst looking for a property. I knew him from years ago. Knew him to be a somewhat dubious character. Weak. But reliable if well supervised. To me, he hadn't changed over the years.

"Obviously, he remembered me. One thing led to another and I began to use him for various little things that needed to be done by somebody who wore a suit, spoke well and looked respectable.

"Then my little diamond enterprise matured fully into being. Now, Mr Street, I know nothing of boats. Nothing at all. Even today I know little. However, it was, at that time, fortuitous that I knew Jim Carter. Somebody very familiar.

"Carter had been into yachting for years. I believe he still maintains a cruiser on the Thames. Used to frequently use it to bring back certain goods and commodities from the continent, I'm led to believe. A business that I was once familiar with. Though my means were far simpler. One of Carter's defects is that he always had the need to complicate the most simplest of things. It made him feel clever, I believe. But in practise it frequently proved to be the opposite."

"Did he import drugs?" I asked.

He shrugged. "Probably. He would certainly have no scruples in that direction. But I have no direct evidence that that was the case. Just rumour.

"To cut this story short, Mr Street, I used Carter to bring in my infrequent packages. While he did that, I spent many an uncomfortable night in another boat, getting in people's way and trying to seem interested in what they were doing. Whatever they thought of my presence they did not say to me and I did not care. They accepted my money. That was enough. The reason for my discomfort was that I needed to be close to Carter. As I said, he needed constant supervision."

"Who supervised his trips to the continent?"
"Exactly, Mr Street. Exactly. You have understood immediately."
"I have?"
"Indeed. Belinda, Mr Street. She was his supervisor. She drove him. He did nothing without her supervision. Nothing. He did nothing without her agreement. She pushed him, Mr Street. Continually pushed him. Without her continual pressing, he would do nothing."
"You seem to be suggesting that the missing diamonds, the missing boat and crew was all Belinda Carter's idea." I hadn't considered that possibility.
"She would have had to approve of it," he said. "If she did not think it up, plan it, she would have had to approve of it. Then she would have had to push him into doing it. Thereafter, she would have had to maintain her supervision. Keep him focused and directed all this time."

"So," I said, "for my idea of him killing her to work, at a rational level, from what you have told me, she would've had to push him into doing it."
He nodded and smiled.
"Best leave that on the back burner," I said. Then I thought of something. "Don't suppose you know where he keeps his cruiser on the Thames. Might be a good place for him to hang out."
"Yes," he agreed, slowly, thoughtfully. "I will make a point of finding out."

"Ok. My next question. What do you know of Tay Wilson?"

I could almost see his mind computing. It was a question he hadn't anticipated. "Tay Wilson," he repeated. "Yes, I can understand why you would have spoken to him. I know him. Indeed I do.

"Very erudite, charming, knowledgeable, friendly, helpful. Those, Mr Street, are his positive attributes. Unfortunately, Tay has a somewhat less than savoury negative side. He is a compulsive gambler, dishonest, disingenuous and totally untrustworthy. As I understand it, everything that he owns is likely to be lost because of debts, unpaid

127

bills.

"His debts, in truth, are not large, but they are many. That is one of the reasons why we chose his boat for the occasional trip. Tay would do anything for money. Anything. However..." he paused, thoughtful again. "I did hear from a fairly reliable source that he recently came into some sort of a windfall. But where he got it from is unknown to me. Neither can I make an educated guess.

"Tell me, Mr Street, curiosity, you understand, have you any idea what he did to merit that windfall?"
I nodded, satisfied. "I think so. I think that he was paid to be a signpost."
"Signpost?" You are being somewhat cryptic, Mr Street, and I am absolutely hopeless at solving cryptic problems."
"He was paid to point me in a certain direction," I told him. Now it was my turn to smile. "If things had gone the way they wanted, it is quite probable that by now you'd be sitting in a cell awaiting trial for a triple homicide." It gave me a great deal of satisfaction telling him that.

He momentarily sat more erect. "That is most interesting. Most interesting. Are you going to elucidate?"
"No. Not right now. I've been given a job. Two jobs to be precise, to find Jim Carter. I'm not going to give you any opportunity of finding him first and wriggling out of paying me."
"Mr Street," he said, grinning. "How could you possibly consider such a thing?"
"Because you've already decided to check out his cruiser yourself. If it's clear, you'll let me know where it is. If it's occupied, my fee won't be coming my way."
"You really are a detective," he chuckled good humouredly.
"I like to think so. Now, about this fee. We haven't discussed it yet."
"Time for another drink," he said. "All this talking has left me rather dry." He stared at me pointedly.
I sighed and reached for my wallet.

Chapter Twenty-Five

We sat in the same spot in the lay-by in Hythe opposite the property supposedly rented by Gibson. Dusk was descending into darkness and we were almost ready to revisit the boathouse.

This visit would be different. I intended to examine the crime scene using my brain and not my prick. In other words, my trust in Belinda Carter's statements had somewhat diminished. This time I would look at the evidence with a relatively open mind. Before, I saw more or less what I expected to see. Which was what Belinda Carter wanted me to see.

"If you know this place is empty," Melissa said. Why are we waiting?" "Neighbours," I told her. "Last thing we want is for somebody to spot a couple of suspicious characters creeping about their neighbour's property and ringing the police. That would take a lot of explaining. And I'm not ready for that."

We waited awhile longer. Finally.
"Time," I told her as I felt in my pocket for the flash light I'd remembered to bring.

Taking the same route as last time, we crept into the boathouse, closing the still unlatched door behind us before we both turned on our torches. I was relieved to see that everything was the same as when we were last here. Though, I suppose I'd have been pretty dumbfounded if anything had changed.

I climbed on board and shone the beam over the two separate blood spatters on the wheelhouse. Then I turned and went to the back of the boat to look at the third deposit of blood. I studied it for a few moments before turning to Melissa.

"Okay," I said to her. "Let's do a re-enactment of sorts. We know that there should have been only Carter, White and Tweedy on board when the boat set off. There is nowhere a third person could have hid. So if they were killed by a hit-man or one of Gibson's cronies, he would have had to board this boat in the dark away from the shore. A small inflatable would have sufficed for that.

"So what I want you to imagine is the two lads standing by the wheelhouse in front of the blood spatter. And Carter at the back of the boat. Come on board threatening me with a gun."
"Why do I have to come on board? If I'm alongside you, why don't I just shoot you from where I am?"
"Exactly. You've got the picture." I shone my torch over the two high velocity blood spatters on the wheelhouse. "Whoever shot those two lads, did from the centre of the deck. If they'd been shot from the side the patterns would've been different. One lot would have been closer to the centre. Maybe a bit on the cabin door frame. The other might have missed the wheelhouse altogether and we would have found it on the side." I shone my torch to where I meant.

"So I shoot Carter first, climb on board and shoot the other two," she suggested.
"Let's run with that. You shoot Carter first and while you're climbing on board he stands still for awhile dripping blood. Maybe he's in shock, can't move. But then he turns his back on the shooter, dropping even more blood whilst moving slowly along the back of the boat.

"Picture the scene," I told her. "You're on the inflatable alongside. Carter, who you've just shot, is for some reason still standing, and with his back to you, dripping blood. Maybe from the entry wound. We can't see any high velocity spatter because there isn't any. It went into the sea.

"The two kids are standing by the wheelhouse."
"Frozen with fear?"
"Possible," I agreed. "But our supposed killer wouldn't know that.

Things are happening quickly, illuminated only by the light in the wheelhouse which probably isn't that bright. The killer needs to take complete control before anybody can act against him. With three on board it's highly likely that that could happen. So they all needed to be subdued quickly with as little fuss as possible. What if one of the kids dived overboard? Lots of variables."

"But they obviously didn't," Melissa said.

"No, they didn't," I agreed. "But our killer wouldn't know that wouldn't happen. We're talking about somebody who's done a lot of planning. The whole scenario must have been thought through. 'What are the kids going to be doing after I've shot Carter and am climbing on board?'

"I'm now beginning to see this whole thing as fake. A set-up. Designed to implicate Arthur Gibson."

"Why?"

"Two million quid. I might explain that later. As I said, it's a frame. A set-up. But it just doesn't work. The blood points to something completely different. If Gibson wanted Carter dead and hired a hit on him, what king of professional would do it at sea knowing he'd also have to get rid of two witnesses? On top of that, we've got the problem of the other boat. Where'd it come from? Especially, where'd it go? This boat was sailed to here. Where's the other one he used to get on board? And bring it here? A place that can be traced back to Gibson. On paper anyway. It's nonsensical." I shook my head.

"I'm ashamed," I admitted to her.

"Ashamed? Why?"

"Because I originally believed the whole thing was possible. Missed or didn't want to see all the contradictory evidence. Twisted or ignored things that were staring me in the face in order to fit things into a preconceived scenario. Want more? I can probably berate myself even more if you want."

"Don't bother. It's not a pretty sight. Not that it ever is."

"Thanks."

"So do you have any idea what really happened?"

"I know exactly what happened. Carter shot the two kids, cut himself deliberately and dripped blood along the back of the boat. Forensics would have discovered that there were three blood donors.

"Carter planned that. Three types of blood, three missing people. Three murders. And the boat being found here on Gibson's property wouldn't have looked too good for Gibson." I climbed off the boat.

"But why?" she asked. "What was the motive?"

"That's simple. Carter ripped Gibson off for two mill of uncut diamonds. Now that's neither an easy or sensible thing to do. But if they could somehow remove or distract Gibson for long enough, they believed they could get away with it."

"They? You said they."

"I know I did. I meant the Carters. The happy couple."

We were in the car driving back to Hastings when Melissa spoke again. She's obviously been thinking. Seeing her confused gave me such a good feeling.

"I don't understand why Arthur Gibson rented that property for Carter to stick the boat in."

"He didn't," I told her. "I'll explain that in a minute."

"Why would they involve you? Why not just leave things? And why did Gibson rent that house? I'm lost."

"Think about it. They needed to get Gibson out of the way as soon as possible. Their 'Plan A' failed, but they needed Gibson out of the way as soon as possible. They didn't want to wait until the house was reclaimed when the rent wasn't paid or the lease ran out. They need the boat found as soon as possible. Waiting would have taken months. Meanwhile, Belinda Carter would have had to play her game. I don't think she could have kept it up for all that time. And don't forget Gibson. At some stage he would've decided to have a word with her. And that idea probably terrified her. That's why she was so nervy when she went to the party."

"So what was their 'Plan A?'?"

"Bringing a boat like the Amy Grey along the canal early in the morning should have drawn attention. Especially after it was announced that such a boat had gone missing probably with the loss of three lives. For some reason that didn't happen."

She fell silent for a few minutes as we drove along an almost deserted road.

"Why not just anonymously ring the police and tell them about it? That would have been quicker and easier than involving you. I mean, they couldn't have known you'd actually find it. And they would have wasted a lot of time and money."

"You're absolutely right," I told her. "It would have been so much simpler to have rang the police and told them that the missing boat was in the boathouse. So much simpler.

"Let me tell you a little story," I said. "A few years ago I met an acquaintance in a pub. A very clever bloke. His job involved serious decision making. He was forever having to solve difficult problems. It was what he did. Well, when I saw him he was in a state of panic. His car was in for repair but he had to get somewhere for a very important meeting. His problem was that the rail timetable didn't work for him. The closest he could get to solving the problem was to get an evening train somewhere and wait on the platform for six hours over night until his connection turned up first thing in the morning. Not an option he wanted to choose. But he had to make that meeting. He was not a happy man. He even thought about getting a cab, but that would have cost him far too much. Apparently, the viability of a helicopter was also considered.

"Just at the point I thought he was about to cut his wrists, I led him over to the window and pointed. On the other side of the road was a car hire company.

"You see, it's often down to psychology. A way of thinking. If you spend your time solving difficult problems, it's often difficult to solve easy ones.

"In the case of the Carters, well, it's almost the same thing. They thought of a clever, complicated plan, and when it came to the end play, that too had to be clever. The simple, easy solution never occurred to them."

"But you might not have found the boat," she said.

"They made sure I spoke to the person who would point me in the right direction. And it's likely that if that didn't work and I didn't follow up that lead, they had something else cooked to direct me there.
"

She still looked unconvinced.

"It still doesn't make a lot of sense to me. Even if what you say is correct. I mean, why would Gibson rent the property for Carter to put his boat in?"

He didn't," I told her.

"But I showed the estate agent his photo, and..." she trailed off.

"Fuck!" she said."

That brought a smile to my face. Perhaps a glimpse of the real Melissa.

"Fuck," she said again. "I hadn't met Gibson or Carter for that matter. I didn't actually point out which was which on the photo. I've just had a playback of the agent tapping his finger on the photo. But he didn't tap on Gibson; he pointed to the other one."

"Thought that might have been what happened. But look on the bright side, if I'd just given you a picture of Carter, we might not have got this far. So that was lucky."

"So now we can go home," she said. "The case has been solved. You've found out what happened to Carter and his crew."

I shook my head. "No. I've solved two murders. But I still have to get Carter. And there's the little problem of Belinda Carter. It would be good for my ego to sort that as well."

"You're going to tell the police about this?"

"I'm thinking on it. My brain is kind of fuzzy right now. Too much overtime thinking. And my earlier afternoon session is beginning to catch up on me. I need the hair of the dog, so to speak."

Chapter Twenty-Six

Thursday 11th June

Tay Wilson. I needed to speak to him again. That's why I was ringing his doorbell mid-morning on the day following my trip to Hythe.

He opened the door looking somewhat dishevelled wearing a dirty old tracksuit. Surprise at seeing me standing there was something he couldn't hide. I also thought I glimpsed a flicker of wariness pass over his features. But it might have been my imagination.

He invited me in with a false smile stuck on his lips. Offered me a cup of coffee or tea, which I accepted. Coffee, black, two sugars. I sat down listening to the clattering coming from the adjoining kitchen. I spent my time looking around the room.

Everything centred around the large screen television which looked fairly new. The furniture didn't look new. The armchair I sat in was well worn. So much so that the ends of the arm were smooth, the original material having been worn away, leaving just the fabric base. The room, as a whole, wasn't exactly dirty, but neither could it be considered clean. If it had had love and attention it hadn't been recent. I hoped the mug he'd used for my coffee had been at least half clean.

"So what can I do for you, Mr Street?" he asked after he'd seated himself down in an equally worn armchair. "Not sure if I can think of any other way to help."
"I just thought I'd pop in to let you know what's happening. Thought you'd like to be kept up to date."
"I'm all ears."
Not quite, I thought, looking at them. Though they were pretty big.
"You've heard about Belinda Carter?"

135

"Belinda?" he frowned.

His expression suddenly became furtive. Something was happening that he hadn't factored in. To me, it was obvious he had something to hide.

I watched him carefully. "She was murdered a couple of nights ago."

Furtiveness changed to fear. "No," he said, breathlessly, eyes wide. "You're kidding me. Murdered? How?"
"Surprised you haven't heard. It was in the nationals. I glanced down at the 'Sporting Life' on his coffee table.
"I don't usually get papers," he said. "Murdered," he shook his head as he tried to absorb the information.
"She was at Arthur Gibson's place, found in the library, stabbed through the heart."

His expression became dynamic and he wriggled uncomfortably as if he wanted to run, to be somewhere else; alone so that he could somehow come to terms with the news. That told me that I was on the right track. He was, or had been, involved.

"Do they know who did it?" he asked. I could tell that he wasn't sure he actually wanted an answer, fearing that it would cause his world, his plans to fall even more apart.
"Not yet," I replied. "She was stabbed with a kitchen knife, so I assume they think somebody at the party did it."
"Party?"
"Gibson was giving a small party. Belinda Carter was one of the guests."
"Right," he breathed, trying to think.

I let him ponder for a few minutes. Then...
"I found the Amy Grey."

More facial dynamism. He could never play poker and hope to win.
"You did?"
I nodded. "Exactly where you said it would be."
"A lucky guess." He tried a smile. It didn't work. Just made him look

ugly.

"Wasn't a guess at all."

Now he looked wary. Body language changed, hands pressed down on the arms of his chair. Almost as if he was on the point of panicking and having a need to escape. He was now out of his depth and he knew it.

"No, it wasn't a guess at all," I repeated. I leant forward, making my expression as serious as I could manage. "Knowledge. You knew where it was."

His mouth opened by no words came out. Panic! That had got the bastard scared.

"Knowledge based upon logical deduction," I said, smiling at him. "You deduced that the only possible place the Amy Grey could be would be under cover. And the only likely local place would be a boathouse in Hythe. You made my job a lot easier." I sat back and relaxed.

He followed suit, panic and fear ebbing away. "Was there any..."
"Evidence?" I finished for him. "Yes, plenty. Enough to prove that Carter, Tim and Dick were killed. Shot. There's three lots of blood. All three, murdered and thrown overboard."
"You've told the police?"
"Doing that when I leave here. Thought I'd let you know first. Seems that Belinda Carter was right. Her husband was killed by Arthur Gibson."
"How... How do you know that?"
"The boathouse is on a property rented by Gibson." I stood up.
"Thought you might like to be updated.
"Right," he said, also standing. "Thanks. It's sort of great news and terrible news. I mean good news that you know who killed them, but bad news..."
"I know exactly what you mean."

We walked together to the front door. I stepped out and turned to him. "I'll keep you informed," I promised. I turned to go, stopped and turned back to him. "I'm not sure if Belinda Carter had had some sort of premonition but when I told her I was going to let you know about finding the boat she gave me a message to give to you."

"Yes?" He looked puzzled.

"She said words to the effect that no matter what, you should hold on to the parcel, or package, or whatever. Haven't a clue what she was talking about and I suppose it doesn't matter now she's dead."

"Okay," he said, slowly, thoughtfully.

"Mean anything to you?" I asked casually as I started to move away. He nodded. "I think so."

"Good," I said with a wave. "See you when I've got an update."

I heard the door close softly behind me.

"That worked," I said to myself out loud, as I strolled contentedly down the hill towards the sea front. A hunch. That's all it had been.

Build up the tension, the fear. Give new information; constantly change the point of attack. Then suddenly release the tension and the fear. Do that and defences tend to get lowered more than is safe. The brain is saying there's nothing to fear here, and doors open. Wilson confirmed my hunch which, in turn, told me how to get Carter.

Now I have to play a complicated and delicate game. I needed the less than legal resources of Arthur Gibson, and the resources of the police. And I needed to keep them apart.

The delicate manipulation I had planned required me to give up certain information to certain parties. But what to give up and what to withhold was the complicated part. The timing was even more delicate.

My thoughtful stroll was interrupted by my phone ringing. I dragged it out of my pocket and looked. It was Arthur Gibson on the other end.

Chapter Twenty-Seven

It felt odd sitting across from Arthur Gibson in the afternoon, at his place, rather than the pub. In the pub I felt more comfortable. But he had insisted that I visit him. I did. He wouldn't give me the reason over the phone. As a policeman, there's one thing you find out very early. If people have the opportunity to be awkward and secretive they will take it.

The forensic team were still at it; kitchen and library still taped off. You could use one word to describe our forensic teams, namely, thorough. Or you could use several. Unnecessarily slow using inappropriate techniques that utilised tick boxes and were not designed to any specific crime scene. This latter description was the one I preferred.

But it was exactly what I had hoped for. Because if they were here at Gibson's, they wouldn't be anywhere else. And I had gathered from Gibson that they intended to continue to be a nuisance for a couple more days. So I had the time to take Melissa on another fishing trip. Though, I suppose, technically she would be taking me. She still had the hire car. Hopefully.

When I had arrived, Gibson was not looking happy and I had yet to find out why.
"What's this all about?" I asked.
"I had a visit this morning," he said. "A certain gentleman. One Chief Inspector McKinley."
"Mackie? From London?" That surprised me. Why would he want to involve himself in Belinda Carter's murder? He was strictly Serious Crime. Unless, of course, it was a different McKinley. "Tall, gaunt,

with a hooked nose?"

Gibson nodded. "You know him."

"Worked with him on and off." Perfect, I thought. Mackie owed me a few. Whether he'd pay up was another matter. "What did he want?"

"To ask me a few questions," he replied. No humour currently on his face. Things must be serious.

"About Belinda Carter?" I asked, frowning, failing to see a relevant connection.

"No. Not about Mrs Carter. He came to see me about Don. He was at the party. Don Prior, my accountant. Your Melissa spent some time with him." He smiled slightly. "He told me at the end of the night that he'd never before had had so much fun at one of my little gatherings. Your Melissa had made him feel good. I must thank her for that. Thank her."

"I don't understand." Not an unfamiliar feeling. But I remembered the fat, little bugger.

"He was murdered last night," Gibson said, voice grim." Shot in the head in his own hallway." He paused to study my expression on hearing the news. If he expected me to look shocked, he wasn't disappointed.

He continued.

"Apparently he opened the door to somebody. Somebody whom he knew. Don was a very careful man. He opened the door to somebody who immediately shot him and left. McKinley said it had all the hallmarks of a professional hit."

"Looks that way," I agreed, mind racing, trying to find a connection between the two murders. Then Gibson suggested one.

"Carter," he said, face angry.

"Why do you think it was Carter?" I asked. "Why kill Prior? Because he was your accountant?"

He slowly shook his heavy head. "Revenge!"

"Revenge?" I wasn't sure what he was getting at. "Revenge for what?"

"For his wife's killing. She was killed at my party. He knows who regularly attends. Same faces every time. He knows, or believes, somebody at the party killed his wife"

"So you think he's about to go through everybody who was at the party thinking that he'll get the killer in the end? That's stretching things a bit far, isn't it?" Seemed a little too farfetched to me.

Gibson leant forward. "You don't know Carter. He was kept in control by Belinda. Underneath his polite voice, his forced sophistication, he was nothing more than a spoilt brat. A spoilt brat. Now he's lost Belinda, he feels lost himself. Her guidance, her control has gone. Somebody has stolen the brat's sweets. So he'll take everybody else's in return. He's lost and out of control. And what do brats do when the feel scared and lost? They lash out."

I still wasn't convinced. Yet Prior was shot. Somebody had shot him. The lads on the boat were shot. Therefore Carter was definitely some sort of socio-path. It was possible. Definitely possible.
"You think he'll come after you?" I asked.

He shrugged. "I doubt it. Not until he's hit easier targets first. Not until he's hurt me."

I thought of something. "So your niece, Tina, is a likely target?"
"Yes. Indeed, Mr Street, indeed. And that is precisely why I sent for you. You continue to astound me with your prescience. Incredible. Absolutely incredible."

He's obviously regained his composure.

"The reason you asked me here is to do with Tina?"
"Indeed," he nodded. His smile had returned. "It will take me two days, Mr Street. Two days to arrange for adequate protection around the clock for her. At the moment, Eddie is staying with her. But I need him back here."
"Eddie?" I queried.
"One of my two shadows. I need him here. Not only that, but although the man is very good at what he does, he is not, by any stretch of the imagination, what one might call, a conversationalist. By this evening, Tina will no doubt be considering poisoning him."

I had caught on. Could I spend a couple of days in the company of the heavily tattooed, punk, Tina and not end up on the wrong side of Gibson? She was pretty, female. Still... I decided to give it a go. At least, I'd be out of Melissa's sight and influence.

"I'll be there tomorrow," I told him.

He seemed satisfied.

"You going to have any comebacks with Prior's murder? I asked him.

"What do you mean? I can prove I was here."

"I didn't mean that. He was your accountant. The police are going to dig into everything. Especially where you're concerned. He'll have records of your transactions and the like."

"All totally above board. Totally above board. The more, how shall I say, difficult figures are not kept in London. They are held safely elsewhere."

I nodded. Understanding.

Now it was time for me to give him information.

"I have a story for you," I began. "First, let me tell you the ending. It ends with you being arrested and perhaps even convicted on three counts of murder that you did not commit." I smiled with satisfaction, but was somewhat deflated by his underwhelming response, which amounted to a slightly raised eyebrow.

"Interesting. Most interesting to say the least. Please enlighten me, Mr Street."

I enlightened him. Told him everything. Everything from Belinda Carter's first visit to my office to my last visit to the Amy Grey.

"Ingenious," he smiled. "Truly ingenious. She was a very devious woman, was Belinda Carter. Even more devious than I had imagined. Very devious indeed." He shook his head. "Two socio-paths together, Mr Street. An explosive combination. Most dangerous to all concerned."

"That's all you've got to say?" His calmness annoyed me.

He shrugged casually. "Their plan had many holes in it, Mr Street. Many holes. No chance of a conviction. Though, nonetheless an enormous inconvenience." He leant forward slightly. "Why do you think they decided on you? A simple phone call to the police would have been enough. The missing boat spotted on the canal."

"We discussed that," I told him.
"We?"
"Melissa and I."
"Ah, the wonderful Melissa. And, tell me, what did you conclude?"
"That they had such a complicated plan that simple solutions were outside of their frame of reference. Complicated plans needed complicated solutions as far as they were concerned. It's called trying to be too clever.

"However, I think that involving me was not in their original planning. They assumed that the boat would have been seen on the canal the morning it went missing. And as soon as the news got out somebody would have reported it. When that didn't happen... Well, that's where I came in."

"Yes," he said. "It is quite likely that your deductions are correct. Quite correct. Life has become rather interesting since I met you, Mr Street. I'm rather glad that I did. I'm reminded somewhat of the old days when I was rather more... Shall we say, adventurous? I do truly believe that things will continue to get even more interesting as we continue along this path that we tread together. They will, of course, eventually settle down again.

"However, Mr Street. We must not lose sight of our ultimate goal. That is, to find Carter and recover my property."
"I've not lost sight. And that neatly leads me to the next thing. Have you got any computer hackers on your payroll?"
"Hackers? Now that is an interesting development. You continue to astound me. But, unfortunately, Mr Street, here I must disappoint you. I am somewhat old fashioned. I currently have no need for computers. No need at all."
"A pity." I would have to find another source.

143

"And this has something to do with finding Carter?" he asked, puzzled.

"It does. But I need somebody to hack into a computer and look at some files I expect will be there."

"And how will that help you find Carter?"

"Mr Gibson," I said, smiling, "you don't expect me to divulge the secrets of detective work."

He gave a short chuckle. Then he became serious again, as though he'd just thought of something. "So you need a computer expert."

I nodded.

"I thought of a possibility. You may well be in luck. I know of none personally, but I believe I know somebody who does."

"You do? Who?" I asked, hopefully.

"You will be seeing her tomorrow. Tina."

Chapter Twenty-Eight

"Are you sure about this?" Melissa asked, as she drove into the St Leonards part of Hastings.

It was late afternoon, the sun was shining and the sky was full of fluffy clouds. Now and then, we heard the distant call of a seagull. We were embarking on a somewhat illegal enterprise.

"I've been there before. Several times," I said. "If there's a nosy neighbour they'd recognise me. In any event, they'd expect a certain amount of traffic if they've heard what had happened. In addition, I do think I might be able to pass for a policeman."

"Yes, but in case you haven't noticed, we're not wearing uniforms." She glanced at me, obviously unconvinced about our little venture. "Won't it be taped up, or guarded?"

"Doubt it. If it is we're buggered. But the forensic team are still at Gibson's. So they've probably left the Carter's place alone. It's not really a crime scene as such. Though there's obviously the chance of evidence being found there.

"Anyway, we're here now. Turn left just passed the Volkswagen," I pointed unnecessarily.

"You want me to go right into the driveway?" she asked, dubiously.

"Into the driveway," I confirmed. "Our disguise is obviousness. Being invisible by being visible."

She shook her head. "You're crazy."

"Thank you."

"We're not going to be invisible when you start smashing down the door."

"I don't need to do that."

We pulled onto a short, gravel drive. The sound of the tyres on the gravel stopped when the car stopped. Melissa looked at me again, hand poised on the ignition key.

I grinned. "You thinking of leaving the engine running so we can make a quick getaway?"

Her expression displayed more than a little contempt, but she did turn off the engine.

There was no sign of any police presence. No tape, no bobby guarding the front door. All was quiet in a quiet neighbourhood. Exactly what I'd hoped for. The house might have contained important evidence. But the forensic team would get first access, because clumsy plods, plodding around would likely introduce contamination. That at least, was the theory.

We walked up to the front door and I extracted from my jacket pocket a handy little tool a dodgy locksmith had 'voluntarily' donated to me. I pushed it into the lock, and pulled a little trigger a couple of times to enable it to figure out what bits should be up, and what bits shouldn't. When I felt everything had slipped into place, I turned it. We went in, closing the door behind us.

"You sure you used to be in the police force," she said. "Seems you're better suited to the other side."

I ignored her. Had bigger things on my mind. It was, to some degree, crunch time. I had no 'Plan B'.

She followed me into the main living room. I knew exactly where to go because I'd noted it last time I had been there. It was on an open bureau, on the far side of the room. A laptop.

I went straight over to it, closed the lid and unplugged it; took the mains plug out of the socket and rolled up the cable. I glanced over the surface that the laptop had stood on. It seemed okay. But just to be certain I picked up a cushion from a nearby armchair and wiped the surface with it. Now, nobody could see that a laptop had been sitting

146

there. Nothing stands out more than a dust free part of an otherwise dusty surface. Just to add to the effect I took a few writing materials from the back of the bureau and scattered then around.

No doubt the police would quickly realise that there was a computer missing. But a bit of confusion helps the cause. And, in any event, I'd be days and miles ahead of them.

"Going to hide the printer?" Melissa said, nodding towards it.

I shrugged. "It's an idea. But just a little too big. This'll have to do. See if you can find a bag to put this in."

She quickly came back from the kitchen and handed me a plastic carrier bag. "All I could find. Have we done now?"

"Not quite," I told her. I slowly turned, taking in the room, trying to put myself in the place of the Carters. Where would I put it? I perceived the usual furniture, suite, sideboard covered in naff ornaments, glass cabinet full of flash glasses, extensive book shelves equally full of, probably unread, books, large screen television. In other words, a living room undistinguishable from pretty much any other. Nothing special about it.

But I was looking for something. Something I was fairly certain would be there in the house. And most likely in that room; easy to get to and close at hand. Unfortunately, my initial scan of the room told me nothing. Nothing stood out. Nothing obvious. It wouldn't be found in a drawer. The Carters were too devious to put it anywhere so obvious. Neither would it be simply under something. Concealed but easily retrievable in a hurry.

"The bookcases," I said to Melissa. "Go through the books, or behind them or between them."

She frowned at me. Though in truth, she'd been doing that ever since we left the hotel.
"Why? What are we looking for?"
"An envelope. A package. Something like that," I told her. "I'll explain

later," I added, seeing the doubt on her face. One thing about Melissa I could be certain of. She had negligible trust where I was concerned.

We set to work, flicking down book to see if there was anything behind them, or between pages. Book after book, shelf after shelf.

"Is this what you're looking for?" Melissa suddenly said, stepping back from the bookcase and pointing.

I went over and looked. Behind some paperbacks was a fat, white package. A few inches thick. I grabbed at it, a huge grin on my face. I split open the package. Twenty pound notes. A few thousand pounds worth. Maybe ten, probably more. I extracted a few notes and gave them to Melissa.
"Here, buy yourself a new chastity belt."

She almost smiled. "Anne Summers."

Pictures flicked through my head. Both enjoyable and painful at the same time. It took a few moments to get rid of them.

"Time to go." I put the package into my inside pocket and began tidying the books.

"Okay," she said, as we were on our way back to the hotel, "how did you know?"
"They were clever planners," I began. "Their psychology meant that they'd try to consider every possible outcome and make plans to counter or allow for each of those outcomes. What would we do if that happened? Or that?

"It's obvious that at least one of the scenarios these ever so clever people would conjure up would require easily got at cash. Ergo, they have a stash. In fact, they have, or had, two. One for her and one for him. Not only that. It's likely they learnt from Gibson. It's natural for those sorts of people; given the business they're in, to deal in cash. Lots of it."
"Why two?" she asked.
"Because they thought complicated. Obviously, because he was

supposed to be dead, he didn't directly have access to this stash so he needed one somewhere else. But if she needed to leg it quickly she'd need it close at hand. So they decided to have two.

"So where is his?"

"His is the bait in the trap," I replied.

"What trap?"

"You will see," I said grinning.

I felt happy. The case was going well. My hunches had paid off and I'd just come into some extra pocket money. I looked at Melissa for a few seconds. That was enough to get things stirring given my current mood. It would really add icing to the cake if... I wondered what style of knickers she wore, or didn't. Was she sitting beside me knickerless?

I put the image out of my head and sat quietly watching the seafront move by.

Chapter Twenty-Nine

Friday 12th June

I had explained to my hostess that she wouldn't be seeing me for a couple of days because I had some business to attend to. She took the information coldly, expressionless. She'd been like that since Melissa had arrived, as had daughter. So the arrival of my so-called personal assistant had turned a good thing into nothing. No idea if she'd told them anything. No idea what she could have told them. Somehow, it seemed fitting that her presence would ruin things for me. She seemed to have that effect. It made me even more determined to sack her when the opportunity arrived.

I'd stuffed a few things into an overnight bag and was waiting outside of the hotel for the car Gibson had promised. Almost to the second of the arranged time, a black Mercedes pulled up and a large, heavily tattooed, tee-shirted individual unfurled himself from the drivers' seat and got out. He looked across at me.
"Your name Street?" he asked, before picking at his teeth with a thumbnail.

"Sometimes," I replied as I approached.

He came round and opened the back door for me and I climbed in, throwing my bag on the seat beside me.

"Seatbelt," he said after he'd started the engine. "Don't want you sliding about, it's distracting."
"Right," I said, complying and wondering what sort of journey I was about to have.

He pulled away from the kerb and into the traffic. "Sorry about the car, mate."

"What's wrong with it?" It seemed fine to me. New, with all the electronics, a large sat nav screen, leather seats. A luxury saloon, in fact.

"No good to drive, mate," he told me. "Journey's going to take a lot longer than I like."

"Right," I said quietly, wondering if I should cross my fingers.

"Blame it on AG," he continued, "this is all I could nick in the time I had. Suppose it'll have to do."

"Right," I said.

"Don't worry about the Bill, mate," he said, catching my eye in the rear-view mirror. "I changed the plates, so we're kosher for the time being."

"Good to know," I replied, wishing I had a cigarette, even though I no longer smoked.

We worked our way out of town heading north on the main road to London. A slow, hilly, single carriageway road. In the back seat I could do little other than study the passing scenery or try to figure out the driver, who's name I didn't know and wasn't sure if I wanted to know.

"What's with the duck tattoo?" I asked him, referring to an almost perfect rendering of a male duck on the side of his neck.

"Saved my life, mate," he told me.

"What? A duck did?" Wasn't sure where this was going. Wish I hadn't said anything.

"Not just one duck, mate, lots of them."

I should have stayed quiet, but I couldn't help myself. "How did ducks save your life?"

"Long story, mate," he began. "Used to have a bit of a problem. Still have really, but thanks to the ducks I've mainly got it under control." He paused. "Well most of the time it is."

"Okay. I've got to hear this. How could ducks solve a problem?"

"Violence, mate," he said shaking his head. "Couldn't help myself. Sort of inner demons it was. The ducks helped me get over it."

151

"Violence? Ducks? Sounds interesting."

"Used to get this urge, you see. A terrible urge. Couldn't control it."

"What sort of urge?" I couldn't even begin to guess where this was going but he had wakened my curiosity.

"There I am, mate. Imagine what it was like. Happily walking down the road when it came over me. Took control."

"What did?" I was getting impatient. That was something I had difficulty controlling.

"Telling you ain't I," he said. "Yeah, well, I used to get the urge, see. Find the nearest pub, going in and finding the biggest, ugliest geezer in the place and going up to him and smashing him in the face."

"Felt like doing that myself," I admitted.

"I'm bloody serious, mate."

"So was I. But carry on."

"Yeah, well. Usually when that happened all hell broke loose. Seems like old grudges leapt to the surface and before you knew it chairs and bottles were flying everywhere." He shook his head as if reliving the memory. "That's when I used to leg it."

"And the ducks stopped that?"

"Yeah. Happened by accident. I was at a bit of a loose end. Bored like. So I popped into my local store and nicked a loaf of bread."

"As one does," I heard myself say.

"Yeah, well. Having got the loaf, I didn't really know what to do with it."

"You could've gone back and nicked some butter," I suggested.

He ignored that. "Wandered around, I did. Pretty aimlessly. Then I found myself in the local park. Nobody there except kids and you can't beat them up.

"Yeah, well. I found myself standing by the pond watching the ducks paddling around. That's when I started feeding them. And that's when it happened mate."

"What happened?" I had to ask.

"Contentment, mate. Felt sort of peaceful. All the fight drained out of me. Felt sort of fresh. Even when a couple of yobs went by, I didn't feel like kicking their heads in. Didn't remember feeling like that before."

"Right..."

"That's how come I've got the duck on my neck, mate."

"I can understand that," I said. And wondered if the day would ever come when a violent arsehole would get sentenced to a term of duck feeding.

"So how do you know Arthur Gibson?" I asked.

"AG? Family friend, mate. He and dad were at school together. Been mates ever since. They used to go out nicking things together. Been the same ever since."

"Sort of family tradition then, nicking things," I said. It was meant to be a joke, but he seemed to take it seriously.

"Bloody right, mate," he said proudly. "Why spend your money when you don't have to. Sort of family motto that."

"Right..." An interesting subject for a police officer to listen to. Even a somewhat dodgy ex-policeman.

"Cupboard full of eggs," he said suddenly.

Duck eggs, I wondered, having no idea where the sudden change of direction was heading.

"Always been like that since I was a kid," he continued.

"You eat a lot of eggs." Half statement, half question.

"That's the problem, innit. Nobody in the family really like eggs."

"I see..." But I didn't. Not in the slightest.

"Superstition, I suppose. It started with eggs and it's still eggs today."

"Right..."

I had a feeling that I was about to receive more information that I shouldn't.

"Mum and Rosa, me eldest sister started it years ago. They're both quite thin. That's how they were when they arrived at the supermarket but they both came out as two big, fat women. With a box of eggs."

"I would have thought they'd have trouble getting away with that," I said.

"No. Nobody looks at what you're doing in a supermarket. Push a trolley around and you're invisible. Most of the cameras are dummies and the others aren't watched by anyone."

"So how long have they been doing that for?" It was a story I had trouble believing. On the other hand, I've heard and experienced stranger ones.

"Years, mate. Been doing it for years they have. Ever since I was a kid."

"And they've never been caught?"

"Once mate," he said. "A few years back. A tin of beans fell out of Rosa's knickers as she was walking out."

I snorted.

"Weren't so bleeding funny at the time, mate," he said. He half turned towards me, which was unnerving as he was overtaking another car at the time.

"What happened?" I managed to ask, once he'd left the overtaken car way behind.

"She was taken into the office and had most of the stuff taken off her."

"Most of it?"

"Yeah. Well. Some of it was well hidden, wasn't it?"

"Suppose it must-have been. What happened next?"

"The bastards rang the Bill. That's when Rosa had her fit. So they had to ring for an ambulance. She was taken to the hospital and put into A & E. Soon as she was left alone, she upped and legged it through the hospital and out into the car park where mum and dad were waiting."

"In a nicked car, I suppose."

"'course," he replied.

The conversation ceased for awhile as he concentrated on his driving. Now we were motoring along a dual carriageway heading rapidly towards the M25, the London Orbital. We slid onto that road at a 120mph. Fortunately, the motorway was relatively quiet. And with judicious use of all the lanes, undertaking and overtaking we reached the Dartford Crossing in several minutes. At that point he had to slow down.

"We'll be there shortly," he said. Make sure you take care of Teenypops; I'm quite fond of her. Would have looked after her myself

154

but AG wouldn't have it."
"She'll be okay," I said. Teenypops?

The traffic was now heavy; constant stopping and starting but we eventually reached our destination and pulled into the car park of a small but smart looking block of flats. He turned the engine off. "Let's go."

We went.

Chapter Thirty

The address was 17 Carsbrock Mansions. First floor flat facing the main road. Directly opposite was a side road. Petrol station on one corner, convenience store on the other. All on a busy main road.

The duck tattooed guy rang the bell and we were buzzed in. In that short communication I learned that duck tattoo was Roy and Tina still sounded like Tina, voice undisguised by the tinny intercom.

We went through the hallway, postal boxes on one side, notice board pinned full of bits of paper on the other. Directly ahead was a lift. Beside it a flight of stairs. Roy opted for the lift.

Exiting on the first floor I found myself on a narrowish corridor. To the left, at the end, was a fire door. A lit 'Fire Exit' sign above it. To the right was a windowed wall.

Number 17 was midway down. We stopped outside and Roy rapped his knuckles on the door.

"It's me," he said loudly, face close to the door.

A door that had double locks. Good. That made it more difficult for somebody to get in. Though I wasn't complacent. I've seen such security easily by-passed. Just lever out the whole door frame from the wall. But I didn't think that means of entry would be attempted. It's really a two man job. I doubted if Carter had the tools or the knowledge. And it wasn't exactly the quietest means of entry. Moreover, the building looked fairly new enough for the builders to have been aware of that security risk. One that can be easily avoided by the expediency of sticking a couple of bolts through the door frame and into the wall.

We were let in by Eddie, and what I saw wasn't anything like I expected. Though, in truth, I hadn't much idea what to expect. I hadn't given it a lot of thought. However, if I had expected something it wasn't what I saw. At the party, Tina had been a punk. So walls adorned with outlandish posters, dirt and untidiness wouldn't have been a surprise. Especially to me who had no idea of the life-style of punks.

However, the only untidy area was around the large desk flanked by two, tall overflowing bookcases. The rest of the room was clean, neat and conventionally furnished with leather three piece suite and central, glass topped coffee table. The latter lacking the designer magazines or trendy books that one often sees in people's homes.

Tina was seated, like a pixie, cross legged on one of the armchairs. She was wearing a grey, halter neck top, tiny green, but loose fitting shorts. She might just have got out of bed, because they looked a lot like sleep-ware.

To my left, Eddie had returned to where he'd obviously been before he roused himself to open the door. Seated at a small, four seater, glass dining table, playing patience. Letting us in seemed to be the full extent of his interest.

And there was somebody else seated at Tina's untidy desk. He was young, unshaven, round faced with long untidy hair. He wore the regulation t-shirt with an unreadable, washed out slogan on, jeans and white trainers. His face seemed to be set in a perpetual grin. Either that or he was in so much pain it was making him grimace.

"You okay?" Roy asked Tina.
"Fine," she said. "For a prisoner, that is."
"Prisoner?" Roy queried.
"Yeah," she flicked a thumb towards Eddie. "He wouldn't let me go anywhere."

Eddie continued to turn his cards, three at a time.

"Are you going to keep me a prisoner too?" Tina said, looking at me. I shrugged. "We'll talk about it later."

Roy strode across the room and he and the guy at the desk slapped their palms together. "How you doing, dude?" Roy asked.
"Winning," the dude said. "Et tu?"
"Usual," was Roy's reply. "Anyway, got to be somewhere else. See you at Jasmine's?"
"Expect it," Dude said to his back.

Roy stopped in front of Tina. "Be cool," he instructed.
"I'll be cool." Her mouth and eyes smiled up at Roy.

Roy nodded and walked up to Eddie. "You ready?"

Eddie scooped up his cards, put them in a box and pocketed it. Roy tossed him the car keys. Eddie caught them smoothly even though he hadn't been looking in Roy's direction. I decided that Eddie was somewhat more than he seemed. Not just a big, bulky stiff. Now I wasn't so sure I could take him and his partner. Wasn't even certain I could take him on his own.

We were looking at each other whilst those thoughts were passing through my mind. And something happened. Perhaps brought on by a subtle change in body language, or maybe something else. But we both seemed to relax with each other.

Roy stopped on his way out and stared at me for a few moments as if trying to work me out. "Make sure you take good care of her."
"She'll be okay." I couldn't think of many scenarios where she wouldn't be. Not with me beside her.
"Good," he said. To Eddie. "Let's go."

Eddie nodded to me as he followed Roy out of the door. The nod was the equivalent of getting a goodbye hug from most other people.

The door closed behind them.

I turned to Tina "Seems that I'm going to be your babysitter for the next couple of days."

"Seems you are. Uncle rang me last night. Said you had a need for a computer genius." She pointed to the guy at the desk. That's Tony. He's your genius. Tony, this is Al."

I nodded. Shaking hands somehow didn't seem appropriate. And I couldn't see myself doing a high five. He must have felt the same way, he just nodded back.

"What do you need?" he asked.

"I'll tell you," I said as I picked up my bag, unzipped it and extracted the laptop. I took it over to him. "What I need is all the banking and credit card details I think you're going to find on this." I handed him the laptop.

"No problem," he said as he put it down on the desk. "I take it you know the name of the card-holder."

"There's two. Probably. Jim and Belinda Carter."

"You don't happen to know their dates of birth?"

I shook my head. "Haven't a clue. Do you need them?"

"Not really. Though they might have been useful. But if I do need then I'll track them down. Live in Hastings do they?"

I nodded. "They had an estate agency there. You might be able to get something from Companies House."

"Good thinking... So tell me Al, what exactly do you want from their accounts? You need to know how much money they've got or something?"

"No. I'm not really much interested in how much they've got."

"You want to spend some of it, maybe?" he smiled at me.

"You can do that?" I was momentarily distracted by the idea.

He simply shrugged. "Such things have been known to happen."

"Thanks for the offer. But no. What I ultimately want is for all their cards to be cancelled."

He looked thoughtful for a moment. "Denying access to their resources. Wouldn't stop them from going into their bank and withdrawing if they had some other form of identity."

"I doubt if he'll go into his bank and make a withdrawal because he's dead."

"But he can still use his credit cards," he laughed. "Now that sounds like a good way to be dead."

"He can use his wife's cards in ATM's," I told him. "But he can hardly disguise himself as his wife and go into a bank."

"His wife doesn't mind her dead husband using up her credit, then?"

"No," I told him. "She's dead too."

"Too much, too much," Tony said, holding up his arms. He looked at Tina, who was standing beside me. "Told you there must be some truth behind all those stories about zombies."

"That's why Al's here," she told him.

"To protect you from zombies," he grinned.

"More or less."

"Okay," he raised his hands again. "I don't think I need to know any more. Right Al, you want me to find and stop all their credit and bank cards."

"Yes," I answered. "Exactly. But I probably want them kept going until I leave here."

"When will that be?"

"A couple of days," Tina replied for me.

"Okay, we'll worry about the timing later. But first, Al, there's a few ground rules."

"I'm listening."

"Firstly, I don't like being asked how I'm doing things. Secondly, don't ask me how I'm doing. And finally don't ask me when I'll be done. If you break any of those rules, I'll pack up my gear and bugger off." He turned to Tina. "And my fourth rule is don't ask me if I want a coffee or a beer. If I want one, I'll say." He looked at the both of us. "Understand?"

"Understood," I said. Tina repeated it.

"Now what I'd really like," he said, "is for you two to bugger off for a couple of hours and let me get on with things. I don't like working with somebody looking over my shoulder either physically or metaphorically."

"Suits me," Tina said, looking me in the eye as if challenging me to disagree. "You up for it? Or are you going to keep me stuck in here too?"

I considered the situation. "You got Tony's mobile?"
"Of course."

"Tony," I said. "We'll bugger off for a couple of hours, but before we return we'll ring to make sure you haven't had any visitors."
"Cool."

"And I'll go and get changed. "Tina practically skipped into what must have been her bedroom.

Too young, I told myself. Maria, the landlady's daughter was younger, another part said. But that was different, the first part replied. Not all that different, the second part argued. Hey, a third part intervened, what happened to all her tattoos?

Chapter Thirty-One

While Tina was changing into whatever, I stood at a distance and watched as Tony extracted equipment and cables from the bag at his feet. He proceeded to plug them together. I was tempted to ask him what he was doing and what his gear was for. But it was only a little temptation. I knew it would wind him up. But I needed results so I resisted. In any event, I wouldn't have understood a thing he said anyway. Computers were not my scene. I know the basics of a few programs and I can type using more than two fingers but attempting to delve more deeply into computing, for some reason, made my head go tilt.

"I'm ready."

I turned and saw Tina standing beside me. Her short, dark hair was brushed neatly and she wore only a minimal amount of make-up. Even her clothes were reasonably sober. Dark green, tight fitting, long sleeved top, black leather mini skirt, black tights and matching high heeled shoes. She looked nothing like the punk that I met at Gibson's party.

"I can see," I said. "Where do you want to take me?"
"Anywhere. I just need to get out of this place for awhile. Let's go to my local. It's as good as anywhere. Quite civilised in fact."
"Lead on."
"Will I be safe?" she asked, looking up with a mischievous smile on her face.
"From what?"
She shrugged.
"Eddie seemed to think that it wasn't safe for me to go out."
"You're probably in more danger here than outside. It's daylight and you're on a slow, busy main road. Hardly the ideal conditions for a

drive-by shooting. Here, in this building, it's quite and private."
"Okay. Let's go."
"Is it far? The pub."
"Few hundred yards. Shouldn't tire you too much." She turned to Tony. "Popping out Tony."
"I gathered that," he said without turning." Enjoy."

We left the flat.
"Stairs or lift?" she asked.
"Lift."
"Saving your energy?"

I chose to ignore that. The lift would be safer. If Carter had been on his way up, he wouldn't recognise me when the lift door opened. That would bring about the ending of this case a lot quicker than I expected.

But, unfortunately, the lift was free of Carters when it arrived.

I had a pleasant stroll to the pub. Walking alongside Tina felt comfortable. We didn't speak. Didn't have to speak. Pleasant, comfortable and strange. Most people I have had cause to accompany fell into one of two categories. Those you'd prefer to be walking one or two paces behind, those you feel that you need to chatter to in order to distract for one reason or another.

Her local pub was The Prince Blucher. Small with frosted glass windows. However, its main feature was its hanging baskets. The whole building was festooned with multicoloured flowers. It looked so incongruous situated in a rather staid residential street with its three bedroom terraced houses with their drab, practical virtually non-existent front gardens.

The pub's interior was equally quaint. Dimly lit, clean and with a barmaid who looked more like a barmaid than a bar-person. One who actually greeted as though really pleased to see you.
Unlike many, who for whatever reason, chose to work behind a bar and typically treated customers as simply people who came in and therefore ruined an otherwise half decent job.

We ordered our drinks and retired to a small, round table at the back of the pub. I sat across from Tina facing the door. I felt pretty confident that we were unlikely to be disturbed. But from experience, I was fully aware that confidence was no excuse for complacency.

Apart from the process of entering and ordering the drinks, neither of us had spoken since leaving the apartment block. Now she sat looking at me, head cocked slightly to one side, eyes narrowed making for a quizzical expression. It was as though she was having trouble deciding what sort of animal I was.

"You look as though you have a question," I said.
"Are you a violent man?"

That was unexpected. Wasn't sure how to respond.
"Not in the same way as your friend, Roy."

She frowned as though she had trouble understanding.
"Roy? What does he have to do with it? And why do you think he's violent? Did he do anything?"
"Not when he was with me," I replied, answering the last question first. "But he told me the story of the ducks."
"Excuse me?" That came after she almost choked on the sip of red wine she'd just sipped.
"He told me about how feeding the ducks saved his life."

She stared at me, face twitching slightly.

"Hence the duck tattoo on his neck," I added.

Inside, I began to feel a little uneasy. A bit like climbing down a ladder in the dark into a pit, fearing what was in it, and knowing it would not be good.

"And you're a detective," she smiled.
I nodded, wondering where she was taking things.
"And Uncle sent you to look after me?"
I nodded again.

She sat back into her chair heavily and sighed loudly. "Then it must be me."

"What must be you?"

"It doesn't matter. I'll tell you later." She stared at me for a few seconds. "You're a detective."

"Private these days."

"But you were in the police force."

"Eighteen years, since I was a kid just old enough to join."

"But you're no longer a real policeman. Well, that just goes to confirm what I already thought about the state of the British police force."

"What does?"

"The fact that you lasted for eighteen years."

I took a large sip from my glass. Soon I'd need another pint and probably a few more after that. I couldn't think of anything to say. I think I'd reached the bottom of the ladder and was fighting for survival deep in the pit.

"Let me show you something." She delved into her hand bag and extracted her smart-phone. With a few presses and swipes she found what she had been looking for. She handed the phone across to me. "Look."

I took it from her and looked. A photo of Roy. Head and shoulders. And neck. Tattoo free neck. I handed the phone back and she put it back into her bag.

"So the duck thing was recent," I said. And wished I hadn't.

"It's a running joke," she laughed. "Uncle abhors tattoos. So whenever any of us are due to meet him we stick on the most outlandish or silly temporary tattoos that we can find. Though he never says anything. So we have never found out whether he notices that every time we see him the tattoos are different. But we carry on because it's good fun."

"So you really don't have any tattoos."

She smiled, eyes sparkling. "One. One little one. A small apple with a bite taken out of it."

"Right." My mind had gone numb I needed to know something but I was scared to ask. But I had to. So I did.

"So Roy doesn't come from a family of thieves?

Her eyes sparkled even more brightly. "He told you that? Wonderful. Wonderful." She clapped her hands together and laughed, though it was more of a tinkle than a laugh. A lovely sound.

But I felt so small that I felt as though I'd have to reach up for my glass on the table. I reached up and took the empty glass in my hand and stood. "Another?" I asked, looking up at her over the rim of the table.

She looked into her half full glass, thought for a moment. "Yes, I think I will."

I went to the bar, hoping that I wouldn't accidentally get trodden on.

Ever see a cartoon where the character is trying to escape a situation in some sort of panic? Running into one thing then another in a desperate attempt to flee from the situation; tripping into things, knocking them over on top of him, but never actually getting anywhere? Well, that's a fair description of what was going on in my head as I stood waiting at the bar to be served.

I got the drinks, returned and sat back down. Somebody had turned the lights out in my head because I could no longer visualise the cartoon character. But I still felt the echoes of his increasingly clumsy and futile attempts to escape into some semblance of acceptable reality.

"Tell me," she began. "If they didn't get rid of you for being useless, why did you leave the police?"

"A few reasons."

"Such as?"

"It's a long story."

She smiled across at me as she sat, both elbows on the table cupping her wine glass in both hands. "Are you about to rush off somewhere?"

"Never been too strong on morality," I said. "But I've always had a sense of justice. That's probably why I picked the police and not the army. And it beat working in a factory or an office.

"I soon found out that being a policeman has bugger all to do with justice. All policing is concerned about is the law. Well you've got good laws, bad laws, stupid laws, ineffective laws and even missing laws. But being a policeman meant that all laws were equal. Justice is left to others. And the sickening thing is, was, I soon also realised that those great purveyors of justice, judges, were more concerned with property than person.

"If you robbed a train of a couple of million, you'd get thirty-five years. If you cold bloodedly killed a couple of people, you might get fifteen. British Justice for you.

"So I quickly became disillusioned with the whole business. Nicking violent scum-bags who as a so-called punishment, were put on probation because a judge thought that the victim's scarring wasn't all that disfiguring and it would be wrong to deprive the scum-bag of its liberty because it was his first offence, and he had promised not to do it again.

"So, as I said, policing has nothing to do with justice. The task of the policeman or woman is simply to uphold the law. No more, no less. Just wasn't good enough for me."

She put her glass down. "So you left because you were disillusioned and not too keen on judges."
I shook my head and tried to smile, uncertain whether or not I had succeeded; smiling at that moment was difficult. Old wounds had opened.
"I left because I had little choice in the matter."
"Ah, now we're getting somewhere."
"We'd get there quicker if you stopped interrupting."
"I will stay quiet," she said, placing a finger across her lips.

"Right. There were a few things over the years. Raids where we expected to find a lot of cash, but found nothing or little. Things like that, if you get my drift."
She nodded. "I think so. Do you mean when you said, 'we expected to find a lot of cash', 'they expected to find a lot of cash'?"
"Something like that."

"So they found out that you were helping yourself and sacked you."

"They suspected. But they couldn't prove anything. I wasn't exactly flavour of the month, but, believe it or not, I was bloody good at what I did. So I survived. That is, until..."

"Until what? Whoops. Sorry."

"Until I chased a child murdering paedo onto a roof. He was leaving his flat just as we were closing in to arrest him, and he legged it up onto the roof of his apartment block. I chased him with a couple of uniforms.

"When I caught up with him he was standing on the edge threatening to jump. I approached him and tried to talk him down from the narrow parapet he was standing on. I'm sure I had succeeded because he moved his arm for me to take his hand. Well, just as I reached out to take it, he somehow stumbled and fell. He screeched the whole seven stories down.

"That, at least, is how I described it to the enquiry. Unfortunately, the two uniforms who'd came onto the roof with me, described something ever so slightly different."

Tina smiled broadly; half stood, leant over the table and planted a soft, wet kiss on the end of my nose.

"What was that for?"

She shrugged. "Not sure. Perhaps to thank you for telling me." She paused thoughtfully. "How did you feel about it? Afterwards, I mean."

"About what?"

"The guy falling off the building."

"Honestly?"

"Honestly."

"I enjoyed the arsehole scream. Probably like the kids he killed had screamed. It wasn't within the law but it was justice."

"Well, Mr Street," she said. "I think I know you a lot better now.

"The name is Al."

"I know Al. It's a rotten name for you. Doesn't suit you at all."

"I have to live with it. Kind of got used to it you know."

"I refuse to call you Al. How about Cul? Yes, Cul." She laughed. "Cul

168

de Sac. It's a sort of street."

"Very funny."

"I liked it. But if I can't call you Cul, what can I call you?"

"Do you like making the simplest of things difficult?"

"Most assuredly. Most assuredly."

"Don't start speaking like that!"

"Like what?" she frowned.

"Like your bloody uncle."

"Oh dear. I did sound like him, didn't I?"

"Indeed you did. Indeed you did."

We laughed together.

"Another?" I asked holding up a freshly emptied glass.

"Why not? I think I'm in the mood for getting tiddly." She handed me an empty glass. She still had some in another glass which she proceeded to drink as I walked away.

As I stood once again waiting at the bar I realised I no longer had the chaos raging in my head. I was feeling... Feeling ineffably ineffable. Put another way, I had an indescribable feeling about something I could not describe. And underneath those feelings and foggy thoughts I could sense a tinge of worry, maybe even fear.

I returned with the drinks. She wore a half smile on her face as if she knew something that I didn't. She raised her glass. "To you."

We touched glasses.

"To you," I repeated.

Her smile broadened. "To us."

We touched glasses.

My mouth wouldn't function. I suddenly, badly needed a pee.

Returning to Tina I sat down wishing I could empty my head as easily as I had emptied my bladder. I forced myself to speak, trying hard to appear merely conversational.

"What do you do? Assuming you do something, that is."

"I'm a post-grad. Forensic Psychology, in case you were about to ask."

"Any particular area?" I knew a bit about forensic psychology. Some of it was useful, good; some obvious; some innovative.

"Profiling. I'm researching into what makes a good profiler."

"And what does make a good profiler?"

"Haven't got the answer yet," she smiled. "Is profiling just about ticking boxes based upon precedence or is there also an intuitive component? If so, how important is it?"

"And is there?"

She shrugged. "I'll let you know when I find out."

"What does Uncle Arthur think about you studying the subject you've chosen?"

"He thinks it's wonderful. I mean, he's paying for it. He thinks it's wonderfully ironic considering that most of his income is based upon... Well, you know, shall we say irregular revenues."

"That's one way of putting it.

She suddenly developed a frown. "I remember asking you a question ages ago. I'm not sure you answered."

"What question was that?"

"Are you a violent man? I mean, apart from pushing people off the top of buildings." The frown became a grin.

"Not especially," I said. "And the incident on top of the building, well, it's as I've already explained, the consequence of him tripping over his own feet and falling."

"In the same way as some people ram their noses into the fists of others, I suppose."

"In answer to your question. I can be, have been, and probably will be in the future, violent when the situation calls for it."

"And what sort of situations cause you to become violent?"

"Off the top of my head, I can only think of two. When it's the only way to take control of what's going on." There I stopped, trying to find a way to describe the second situation.

"Well?" she asked after she had obviously decided my pause had taken too long. "What is situation number two?"

"When the urge gets too great to resist."

"You lose your temper?"

I shook my head. "The exact opposite. Sometimes an inner calm comes over me. Time seems to stop. At that point I either have to walk away or act."

"Seems complicated."

"Not really. So why do you have this need to know about my violent tendencies?"

"They are part of you. I need to learn about you." The mischievous grin again, letting me know that she knew things that I didn't. "But there is no rush," she added. "I can take my time."

"I'll be going the day after tomorrow," I reminded her.

"You won't be going far because you'll be leaving something behind."

"What?" What would I be leaving behind? Once again I felt a tinge of fear. I looked across at her smiling face, the sparkling eyes and the fear began to well up.

"Another?" I managed to say after downing my pint.

Chapter Thirty-Two

Time passed, and in the street-lamp illuminated darkness, we headed back to Tina's apartment. The traffic on the main road had lightened, though it was still relatively heavy. Although I had consumed a fair amount of alcohol, I managed to stay alert. At least, that's what I told myself.

We entered the flat and found Tony still there. I had completely forgotten him. He was sat at the desk, feet up on it and was reading a book. He looked up at us as we entered, slammed the book shut and took his feet off the desk. Swivelling the chair, he turned to face us.
"Welcome home," he said, in a not unsarcastic tone of voice.
"You didn't have to stay," Tina countered as she threw herself down into an armchair. "Did you do it?"
"Finished about an hour after you left," he replied drily.
"You should have rang me." She looked up at me. "Told you he was a genius."

Wasn't sure she had, but I didn't really care. The fight to stay alert on our walk home was beginning to have its affect in a most negative way.

"Do you want to know what I've found?" Tony asked me.
I nodded, and then shook my head. "Yes. No." My words reflected my head movement. "Can it wait until the morning?"

Tony thought for a few moments, deciding. "I suppose. But I've got things to do later on. So I'll be over earlyish."
"Not too early," Tina groaned.
"I don't do too early," Tony said. "Tennish?"
"If you have to," Tina sighed and stretched. As she did, her already short skirt rode up even more over her thighs. She saw me looking and glanced down at herself, then looked at me, a small smile playing on

172

her face. But she made no attempt to pull down the hem of her skirt. Instead her smile grew. "You can look as much as you want. But you are going to have to earn the privilege to touch."

"Think it's time I was going," Tony said suddenly, standing up and getting his things together in a hurry.

After the goodbyes, he scooted through the front door. I followed after him and slid the security lock into place. Then I turned to Tina who was still sat back in the big armchair, hands behind her head, shapely legs stretched out. I was convinced she'd eased her skirt up even more. For now, I could just about see a trace of white knickers. And she still wore that smile which intimated she knew something I didn't.

"Keep looking," she said. "Keep wondering."

I said nothing.

"Are you hungry?" she asked, ever so slightly opening her thighs as she spoke.
"Haven't thought about it." Not food, anyway.
"Well I am. What do you fancy?" Her eyes sparkled.
I shrugged. Probably sulkily. I felt like a little boy who'd been taken to a sweet shop then told he couldn't have any.
"Curry?" she suggested.
"Why not."
"Are you sulking?" she asked, whilst suppressing obvious laughter.
"I don't do sulking." I hoped I'd lowered my voice to say that.
Anyway, I hoped something along those lines.
"I think you are sulking. I'll tell you what. Forget the curry. Let's go to bed instead."
"Sounds like a good idea to me." It certainly did. Things were looking a lot brighter. I felt a stirring which didn't stop.
She climbed out of the armchair. "Wait here. I'll go and get things ready."
"Right."

As she went into the bedroom, I took my jacket off, undid my tie and started to undo the buttons on my shirt. It wasn't easy; my hands were shaking a little. I resisted the temptation to just simply tear of my shirt and the rest of my clothes.

She returned from the bedroom. In her arms she carried a duvet and a pillow which she tossed onto the settee. She gave me a little wave before turning back to the bedroom. Closing the door with a loud and definitive bang.

For several moments I stood motionless staring at the closed door. An insurmountable barrier that prevented me from fulfilling a desperate need. I tried to will it to reopen, but the door stayed shut. And I knew that I'd been consigned to the settee, to spend the night alone.

Eventually, I laid back on the settee, head on the pillow and feet overhanging an arm as I stared up at the ceiling. I told myself that it was good the way things had turned out. She was too young. Or I was too old. Didn't feel old. Wondered if she felt young. I was on a job and had to stay professional. But that hadn't bothered me in the past. Didn't mention to Tina other discretions that had upset a few of my superiors when I was still on the force.

If I could get rid of Melissa for a few days, there was mother and daughter back at the hotel.

A single guy, no matter how successful, spends more time sleeping on his own than he spends with company. That's part of the reason why the company part, when it happens, is often so good. Nevertheless, sleeping alone tends to be the norm. You get used to it. Never give it any consideration.

Those thoughts, and similar, percolated through my mind for seemingly hours, as I lay alone in the dark, feeling quite sorry for myself. But one of my last thoughts before I fled into sleep was would the curry have helped the deep hunger I felt.

Chapter Thirty-Three

The aroma of bacon frying. I opened my eyes, orientated myself. I hadn't been dreaming. Somewhere, somebody not far away, was frying bacon. I pulled the duvet from myself, swung stiff legs, and stood up. Bare footed, wearing only my underpants, I padded across the light grey carpet in search of the source of the mouth watering smell.

Being a detective, I soon found it. I stood in the kitchen doorway and stared at Tina. She was standing with her back to me wearing only a T-shirt that barely covered her backside. I had this terrible urge to go up to her, put my arms around her and gently kiss her neck.

Weird. Usually, my urge would have been somewhat different; lift her T-shirt, push myself against her as I hardened, one hand caressing a boob and the other venturing between her legs all groping fingers.

I resisted both temptations. Though my pants were quickly tightening.

She must have sensed my presence in the doorway. She turned and looked at me as I stood there clad only in briefs that were now threatening not to hold me in. For several moments our eyes locked, then she broke the mutual gaze and I saw her eyes drift slowly down my body where they rested for awhile on the growing bulge between my legs. She just smiled, shook her head and turned back to her bacon. Not a word had been spoken.

Suddenly, I felt embarrassed. At least, I think it was embarrassment. In any event. It wasn't a feeling that I was familiar with.

"How do you like your eggs? She asked without turning.
"Cooked." I couldn't think of anything else to say. At that moment I

couldn't even be sure of what an egg was. My head, once again, was full of chaos. Urges, feelings, reason, logic, self-preservation, and a desperate need for a wee, all competed with each other. I turned and rapidly headed for the bathroom, uncertain as to whether my head or my bladder would explode first.

We sat opposite each other across the small, two seater, breakfast table. I had quickly dressed, she was still wearing her loose fitting, shapeless T-shirt. My head had stopped boiling and was now quietly simmering.

As she ate her, egg, bacon and tomatoes she would occasionally pause and look over at me with her half smile and her knowing expression. The latter caused me discomfort, so I almost obsessively concentrated on the rapidly diminishing content of my plate.

Then she broke the silence. "Have you any suggestions as to how we should spend the day?"

I glanced at my watch. "Tony should be here soon. Hadn't thought about anything else."

We had both finished eating. She stood and leant over the table to pick up my plate. As she did, the front of her T-shirt fell open and I could see down the low neck. Beautiful dark nipples. I wish I hadn't looked. My head started to boil again.

She straightened, holding the plates, and looked down at me. Those eyes.
"Did you enjoy that?"
"Enjoy what? The breakfast? It was great. Thank you."

She sighed and shook her head. "I told you, you would have to earn it. Look all you like." She took the plates and cutlery to the sink and rinsed them before dropping them into the bowl in the sink. She turned back to me looking thoughtful.

"What?" I asked.
"I'm just wondering."

"Wondering what?"

"Wondering how long it will take you to realise. What with you being such a clever detective."

"Realise what?"

"Realise how you feel."

"Feel about what?"

She shook her head before striding to her bedroom and before slamming the door behind her, she turned and said, "Me!"

As I sat staring at the closed door, I realised that my mouth was hanging open. I closed it. What did she mean, how I felt about her? 'Oh fuck,' I thought, just before a mental circuit breaker clicked in.

I heard Tina's phone ring faintly in her bedroom and I got up to put the finishing touched on getting dressed, like tying my shoe laces. I was surprised I remembered how, given my current mental state. It was a state I needed to get rid of quickly. Tony was due to arrive shortly and I needed my wits about me. Or what was left of them. At least he would bring with him the badly needed distraction.

I immediately got my distraction. But it wasn't what I'd expected. Tina came out of the bedroom, dressed but somewhat unkempt. Her expression told me instantly that the call she'd received had not been a happy one.

"That was Uncle on the phone. He..." She hesitated as though looking for the right words, or maybe to fully absorb the news she'd just received. "There's been another shooting."

That got my attention. "Who? Somebody from the party?"

"Yes, I mean no. Did you meet Bill Crane?"

I scanned my memory. "Tattoos, broken nose, soft hands. Something to do with diamonds?"

She nodded. "But it wasn't him. It was his son. Pretty little Rich. Fourteen years old. Yesterday evening, while we were in the pub. He went to answer the door and got shot in the hallway."

"Killed?"

"No. apparently he's going to be okay. He was shot in the shoulder." She stared at me as if I could explain what had gone on. "Why the shoulder?"

I tried. "The killer or shooter was probably after the father. Started to pull the trigger as the door opened; realised it wasn't his target and altered his aim.
"Why didn't he just not shoot?"
"Probably because it was more instinctive to, and easier to turn the gun than to release the trigger. Turning the gun away from a non-target was instinctive, without thought. Pulling the trigger was deliberate and premeditated."

She sat down. "This is scary. I'm glad you are here. It's all become real."

I smiled. "I'm glad I'm here too."

My distraction didn't last long. I needed to hold her. To tell her...

The doorbell went. Hopefully, Tony had arrived to save me.

Tina crossed the room and picked up the handset. She listened and then pressed the buzzer to let her visitor in the outside door. "It's Tony."

She began to go to the door.

"Wait!"
She stopped and turned.
"Don't open it," I ordered.
"But..."
"Tony buzzed you. But will it be Tony outside your door?"

Her almond eyes widened as she understood. She backed away from the door, scared.

I put a hand on her shoulder and smiled down at her. "You'll be okay. I'm here."
She nodded. "But will you be okay?"

I smiled again, cupped her chin in my hand and raised her head, bent and gave her a peck on her soft lips. It was the second time in seconds that her eyes widened, but she didn't protest. But I wished I hadn't done it. For some reason it made me feel vulnerable. Not a feeling I've experienced much in the past. Though my action seemed to make her relax a little. So it wasn't all bad. I pointed to the living room and she obediently retreated.

There was a knock on the door. As I slid back the security bolt and reached for the lock, I put my hand into my trousers' pocket and extracted 'Sue', my pet name for my spring loaded baton.

I opened the door, staying behind it. I didn't like using the spy hole they put in doors. Never fancied a bullet through my eye.

Tony walked in. I slid 'Sue' back into my pocket.

"Morning," Tony said. "Not too early am I?"
"Just in time," I said as I closed the door behind him.

After the 'hellos' and the 'you okay's', Tony seated himself at the desk while Tina went to the kitchen to make the coffees.

"Okay," Tony said. "What exactly do you want?"
"You hacked the computer and got the bank details."
"Yeah. But I wouldn't exactly call it hacking. The Carters treated security like most people. They've got several credit cards and a couple of bank accounts. That means several passwords and user names etc. Only in their case, they only used one password each. Usernames were slightly different but they didn't put up much of a fight.

"So what do you do to make sure you don't forget your usernames or passwords? Well you write them down somewhere. Now you can either do that on bits of paper or you can put them on your computer in a text file. The Carters opted for the latter. Very good of them. It made my life easier.

"All I had to do was find the text file, or two text files, in this case.

They contained everything I needed to know. Each credit card was itemised complete with all the info needed. So yeah, I think I've got what you need."

I think I understood all that.

"Can you check for recent movements, withdrawals? More likely to have been on her cards. He's supposed to be dead."

Tony turned to the Carter's laptop, still open on Tina's desk. I sat down nearby and waited almost patiently. Tina came in with a tray full of coffee.

"Okay," Tony eventually said after a long series of tapping. "There's been a series of withdrawals over the past several weeks on various cards in the name of Belinda Carter. The last one was only yesterday. Three hundred quid taken out of a Sainsbury's ATM in Ilford."
"The one before?" I needed to know the regularity.

He turned back to the screen. "Four days ago."

A few mouse clicks later. "Four days before that. On another card. Still Belinda Carter's. Still three hundred quid. That time an ATM in Barking." He continued to delve. "Four days before that, another three hundred. You want more?"

So he got through three hundred every three or four days. Yesterday was Friday. So his next withdrawal should be Monday. Though tomorrow's a possibility.

"Can you stop the cards?" I asked.
"Easy. I just have to click on the lost or stolen tab for each card and the cards will be cancelled instantly. The Carters will automatically be sent new ones. Though don't suppose it'll do them a lot of good, hey. But I thought you guys followed the money, as it were. Figure out a pattern and sit in wait for them to turn up."

"You've sort of got things right with regard to what I've got planned. However, I'm not the police any more. I can't exactly take him down in a Sainsbury's car park and not go unnoticed. But I have another way of getting him. If things go right."

"What's that then?" Tony was curious.

He'd been helpful and it would cost me nothing to tell him.

"A trap. What do you do if you've got no money? But you know you can get your hands on some fairly easily?"

He shrugged. "Go and get it, I suppose."

"That's the trap."

"I understand. I think. So you want me to stop the cards?"

I nodded.

"Both? I mean both his and hers?"

I nodded.

"Consider it done."

I relaxed in the armchair, taking a sip of coffee that Tina had given me before going to the bathroom where she'd been, for what seemed like, hours. As I watched Tony moving a mouse around and tapping away at the keyboard, Tina emerged from the bathroom, wordlessly passed me by and went into the bedroom.

"It's done," Tony told me, swivelling to face me. "Does this mean I'm completely done and I can bugger off?"

"A couple more things. Have there been any payments to hotels? Things like that?"

He shook his head. "None. That was one of the first things I checked. Thought you might want to know that. What I can tell you is a couple of months ago he hired a car. Paid a few hundred quid down so he must have rented it for a month or two at least. He used one of his own cards for that. If he's still got the car, he's been paying cash for it."

"You just answered my next question." I managed a friendly smile. Probably didn't quite come off. Smiling had never come easy for me. Especially when I was sober.

After yelling goodbye to Tina and getting a faint response from the bedroom, with a nod to me, Tony departed.

A thought entered my head. Tina lived in Ilford. Carter was in Ilford yesterday. A few days ago, he drew money from an ATM in Barking.

At that convenient moment, Tina emerged from the bedroom. I looked up into her sparkling, almond eyes and almost forgot what I was about to ask. "Do you happen to know where Bill Crane lives?"
"Yes. I've got his address in my book. Somewhere in Barking, if I remember correctly. Why?"

Chapter Thirty-Four

So Carter moves into the Barking area of London, evidenced by the money withdrawal. Spends a couple of days casing the Crane home. Satisfied, he strikes. Okay, he cocked up with respect to his target, but he still made his point. Gibson still likely felt the pain. Others get to feel fear.

Yesterday, he moves up the road to Ilford. Tina lives in Ilford. Now there might be others from the party who also live in Ilford, but that's irrelevant. Even if there are other potential targets in Ilford, it's likely that Tina is next on the list. Female. Easy. She is also close to Gibson and a bullet in the head would certainly hurt him badly.

It wouldn't do her any good either. Neither would it make my day. An image I drove from my mind as soon as it had arrived. But I had to do something. I wasn't about to passively wait around while Carter was out there somewhere, waiting to pounce. Especially since this was supposed to be my last day protecting her. I had no doubts that if I called Gibson and told him I intended to stay he wouldn't grumble too much. But I couldn't. I had other plans that couldn't be postponed.

So Tina had to be kept safe without me being around. I had no idea who Gibson was arranging to take over from me. I doubted if it would be Eddie or his partner. Gibson needed them close at hand. Whoever he had chosen would probably be competent enough. But they weren't me.

It seemed I had two choices. Not mutually exclusive but they could be. I decided on the first of them. Something I had planned to do anyway. Since Belinda Carter got herself stabbed to death and Gibson employed me to get Carter and the diamonds, then the killing of Prior, followed by the shooting of Crane's teenage son, added to the two previous murders of the lads on the boat, meant the Carter was too dangerous, too nasty to remain free.

I had an equation to solve. I wanted Carter off the streets. To go down one way or another. If my trap worked, I'd get him. If I got him, Gibson would likely get his diamonds back and I would get paid something or other, if I was lucky.

But if the trap didn't work, I didn't have a 'Plan B'. Not yet, anyway. So far, Carter had killed at least three people. All innocent as far as I could tell. Maybe he killed his wife for some reason. That would make four. And one attempted. So we're up to five possibles with more to come. That couldn't be allowed to continue. I had to do something. It was perhaps time I had a chat with my old buddy, DI McKinley, Mackie.

Tina asked me if I wanted a coffee. I nodded, only half aware of the offer. She had sat quietly while those thoughts had been running through my head. Maybe she had intuited that it wasn't a good idea to disrupt my train of thought. I was thankful for that.

She returned with the coffees as I ran things through my mind one last time. I needed to be certain that what I was about to do was, in fact, the right thing to do. I decided that it was.

I took out my phone, pleasantly surprised to see that the battery hadn't gone flat. A situation I frequently experience. Slipping through my contacts I found Mackie and rang his number. I didn't care about Tina listening in. She'd only hear half the conversation anyway.

The phone rang a few times, and then it was answered.
"Hang on for a minute."

I hung on.

A couple of minutes passed. I figured Mackie had seen who was calling and had gone somewhere discrete to take the call.

"Street. What the hell do you want?"

"Glad to see you've not removed me from your contacts."
"An oversight. What do you want? You're bad news. If you bugger around I'll hang up."

I smiled inside. Mackie was never one to beat about the bush.
"I've heard you're involved in the Prior killing."
Hesitation. The response told me I'd guessed right.
"What of it?"
"And the Crane shooting last night."
Longer hesitation. "That hasn't come through to me yet. What's that got to do with Prior? More to the point, what's it got to do with you?"
"They're connected. And I'm currently sat across a coffee table from the next potential victim."

Tina's eyes narrowed slightly when I said that, but the coffee cup in her hand never wavered.

"Talk," Mackie ordered.
"I am. We need to meet up. And we need to do it today."
"Give me just one good reason to meet with you. You're persona non grata."
"I can give you the name of the killer."
Hesitation.
"Where do you want to meet? And when?"

"One thing," I told him. "Before we meet, do a bit of homework. A fishing boat went missing a few months back off the coast at Hastings. Check out the police report, it will give you some background. You're going to need it."

I then told him to meet me at The Prince Blucher, Tina's local. He knew it. There were few pubs in London that Mackie didn't know.

I always found that carrying out such business worked better when both parties had a pint in front of them.

I put my phone away and looked across at Tina. She was sitting quietly, cradling her coffee cup in both hands, wearing a thoughtful expression.

"Did you get that?" I asked her.

She put her cup down and sat back. "You think I'm going to be the next victim?"

"You're not going to be a victim, full stop. But you may well be the next target."

She smiled, a little wistfully I thought. "How are you going to look after me if you go back to Hastings tomorrow?"

"Your uncle is seeing to that."

"I'd prefer it to be you."

"So would I. But I've got things to do."

"More important than looking after me?" She tried to look sad and hurt but she couldn't keep it up. Instead, she laughed. "I'm sorry. I couldn't help myself. The look on your face..." She laughed even more loudly.

After a brief struggle with a few unrecognised emotions, I managed to refrain from reacting. "I'd prefer it if you waited before mentioning this afternoon's meeting to your uncle. He might not approve."

"I won't say a word. How long will you be gone?"

"You're coming with me. I'm not leaving you on your own."

I think she looked relieved, but it was hard to tell. She could shut off all clues to what she was thinking whenever she wanted.

The journey to the pub was slightly tentative. I didn't expect Carter to try anything in broad daylight. But I considered him to be an amateur who found himself in a situation where all rationality had fled. He was likely to be a time-bomb waiting to explode. Probably becoming increasingly desperate and therefore increasingly reckless. His plans thwarted he was lashing out like a spoilt narcissistic child and spoilt children are quite happy to hurt themselves if they can make a point.

Trouble with that theory which was the whole basis of figuring out Carter's motivation and thereby predicting future behaviour, was if he was seeking revenge over the killing of his wife, the driving force behind him and their plans, who actually did kill her? And why?

That would be a problem for another day. Getting Carter before he could do any more harm was my priority. Hence the meet with

Mackie.

He arrived at the pub shortly after Tina and I had seated ourselves down with our drinks. He entered, scanned the bar, spotted me and went to order himself a drink. He looked exactly how I remembered him. If he'd been any different it would have been a surprise. Hardly any time had passed since we last met. Yet, there's a tendency to exaggerate time and to expect change, as if one's absence would surely have some sort of bad effect on another.

Yes, just how I remembered. Dark hair flattened by gel. Smart, pin striped charcoal suit with colour matched shirt and tie. He had, what can only be described as an oblong face. All features carefully placed asymmetrically like a badly sketched wanted poster. One that was probably sketched by a five year old.

He came over and sat; carefully, as he always sat, pulling at the legs of his trousers to prevent the creases at the knees for being ruined, and bolt upright in case his jacket got a crease in it. He looked at me, and then stared at Tina for a few seconds before turning his badly drawn features back to me.

"Tina..." I began. Only to be interrupted by her.
"I'm Street's fiancée," she told Mackie, a big smile on her face.

What could I do? What could I say? Where could I run to?

Mackie nodded.
"Why am I here?" he asked me.
"To receive a lot of information. Did you check up on the missing boat?"
"Yes. Badly investigated. But I don't see the connection. But having received the report I admit to seeing a connection between the Prior killing and the Crane shooting. The reason I never got to hear of it sooner was that because of the victim's age the locals assumed it was gang related."
"No doubt you disabused them of that."
He almost smiled.
"That I did. You know that being seen with you might result in me

being investigated, so I hope that what you have for me is worth the potential trouble."

"It is," I assured him.

"And in return, what do you want? You're not doing this as a concerned citizen."

"Tina here, is likely to be the next target. I want her protected. A full team on it, not some half bored uniform."

He turned his attention to Tina, who responded with an expression of total innocence. She would make a good actress. She could convey more with her eyes than most can with words.

He turned back to me and nodded. "Done. Talk."

"I was approached by one, Belinda Carter," I began. "She wanted me to find out what had happened to her missing husband. I took the case in good faith."

I then proceeded to outline most of what had then happened; omitting Arthur Gibson's central involvement and the missing uncut diamonds. But, unfortunately, he had to be mentioned in other areas. I also failed to mention the stopping of Carter's credit cards and the trap I had set.

"I hear what you say," Mackie said. "But there's one to two things you haven't made clear. Firstly, what possible motive could Belinda Carter have for employing you to find her dead husband?"

"She knew he was still alive. That's the whole point. They expected the Amy Grey, the boat, would be seen in the canal in the early hours. When the news of the missing boat was released they expected that its presence on the canal would be reported. And then found.

"When that didn't happen they needed to try something else. So I was employed. Belinda Carter made a point of giving me the name of Tay Wilson as being somebody who might be able to help. He was obviously fed with the information that would lead me to the boathouse."

"I'll need his address," Mackie said. "He might be able to help pin tracking this Carter down."

"I can tell you where he drinks and point him out to you."
"That will have to do. Carry on."

"We found the Amy Grey in the suggested boathouse. There'd been no attempt to destroy the evidence. That was suspicious. There had to have been a reason for that. Looking more closely at the blood evidence, the high velocity spatter, it was obvious two people had been shot with a high calibre firearm. But the third blood evidence was different. No high velocity there. Just simple gravity drops. Looked to me as if somebody had cut themselves and allowed the blood to drip, moving slowly around, spreading it to make it look as bad as possible.

"I figured that Carter had killed the two lads, threw them overboard, took the boat to the boathouse, cut himself, spread the blood around a little then disappeared."

"Making it look as somebody had killed all three of them."
"Exactly," I nodded.

"All sounds logical. You've done a good job." Mackie paused, clasped his hands together and leant slightly forward. "Now tell me why... Why they, the Carters developed this very complicated plan."
"Money. It has to be money. Life insurance? Maybe they were being investigated for some sort of fraud to do with their Estate Agency. Tax maybe. They decided to leg it and needed the money. Who knows? That's for you to find out, isn't it?"

"Yes, and we will. Have no doubts about that. Have you worked out how Belinda Carter's murder fits into your theoretical scenario?"
"My first idea... In fact my only idea so far was Carter. But that doesn't fit with the revenge killings. Unless... Unless he did kill her. Can't handle it and needs to blame others. If there hadn't been a party he wouldn't have killed her there, so it's the fault of people at the party. That sort of thing. However, if it wasn't him who killed her, then somebody else did and whoever that person was, well, that deprived him of not only a partner, but the opportunity to get his hands on the money from whatever scam they had devised.

"That's a lot of motive for revenge. He might not know who actually did the killing but he knows it must have been somebody at Gibson's party. If he gets them all, he gets the killer. Then he'll likely go for Gibson himself. Even if it means dying in the attempt. Because, by then, he'll likely be a lot crazier and out of control than he is now."

"I owe you a drink," he said, standing. He stared down at me. "I never doubted that you were good at your job, Street. But some of your methods were questionable. What are you having?"

He returned with the drinks, sat and pulled at his trousers. "Do you have any photos of Carter?"

I got out the Gibson and Carter photo and handed it across.

"This will possibly help confirm your suspicions about the Crane shooting. Hopefully, he'll be able to recognise his assailant." He looked at the picture for a few more seconds. "Seems to be good friends with Arthur Gibson. Any connection I need to know about?"

"AG is my uncle," Tina told him. I didn't know whether her intervention was simply the offer of a simple explanation or if she was deliberately running interference. Being the niece of Gibson, I suspected the latter. Maybe that's why I hadn't warned her about mentioning Carter's computer and Tony's involvement, subconsciously realising that she didn't need to be told. Intuitively knowing she was on the ball.

"A family affair then." Mackie s tone was somewhat sarcastic. "An uncle and a fiancée. And a likely victim. You seem to have a complicated life Miss..."
"Wise," she informed him (and me).
He nodded. "Well, let us hope you have an appropriate name. But get me up to speed here, if you will. Ex-detective Street gets a job and goes to Hastings. Part of his investigation involved Arthur Gibson. Street ends up at Mr Gibson's party, where his employer gets murdered. After which, Mr Gibson, your uncle, sends him here to look after you, where he turns out to be your fiancée. And all this happens in a couple of weeks?"
"Incredible, isn't it." She reached out across the table and took one of

my hands in both of hers. "I can hardly believe it myself." She looked into my eyes. "How about you, Street. Do you find it incredible too?"

"I can hardly believe it myself."

"But these things do happen," she said to Mackie.

"Why do you call him Street?"

"That's simple. I don't like his name Al. And I refuse to utter the longer version. And I can't go through life addressing him as Mr Street, can I. He won't accept any suggestions I make for any other names. So I might as well call him Street." She suddenly giggled and squeezed my hand tightly. "I wonder what you will call me when we're married." She giggled again.

I had a really strong and terrible need to be somewhere else.

"Back to business," Mackie said. "When are you returning to Hastings?"

"Tomorrow. Gibson is arranging for Tina to have protection. I would imagine they'll be inside with her all the time. I don't know who or what this protection is, so my confidence is limited. That's why I wanted you involved. You now know what Carter looks like. You should be able to intercept him before he gets into Tina's block."

"Stop!" Tina interrupted. "I forgot to tell you, Street. I've arranged with Uncle to go to Hastings with you. I'll stay with him. Maybe, if I ask him nicely, he'll let you stay too. I'll be perfectly safe there" She gave me a big smile and squeezed my hand again. "Anyway, in Hastings I'll be able to keep an eye on you and that Melissa character. I don't trust her."

"She stole the T's," I muttered.

Chapter Thirty-Five

Mackie told us he was going to get the names and addresses of all those who attended the party and was going to put surveillance on all of them. And that included Tina's address, even though she wasn't going to be there. Then he took his leave.

After he'd gone we sat across the table and watched each other in silence. I attempted to review what I'd told Mackie, and other aspects of the case, because while I was doing that I could avoid reviewing, or even thinking about other things that had been said. Unfortunately, the time of silence soon passed and Tina had other ideas about what I chose to, or not to, think about. As I saw her expression slowly change, I knew I was about to endure more of her mischievous malice.

"You took it well," she said. "Your expression barely changed. But I suppose that was to be expected. You do tend to avoid showing what you feel. Assuming, that is, you do actually feel."
"What exactly are you talking about?" A futile attempt to delay or to avoid.
She smiled broadly. "You didn't deny being betrothed."
"Didn't admit to it either."
"But I'm sure that as far as your friend Mackie is concerned, your silence simply confirmed the fact."
"He's not my friend, and it's not a fact. Why the hell did you come out with a thing like that?"
She shrugged, her smile never waning. "It felt right. You needed some sort of prompt."
"Prompt?"
"Yes prompt. It's time you started to open up to your inner feelings."
"Inner feelings?" I sounded like a parrot. "What inner feelings? I know what I feel."
"Do you? Do you know what you feel about me?"

"You're a good kid."
"Ha! Is that all? All you can say?"
"What else is there to say?"

Her smile disappeared. It had been fading for awhile as our words had progressed. Now it was gone completely. She glared at me. Though I wasn't certain she was all that serious in reality.

"Okay," she said, "if you want to play it that way, I'll just have to up the stakes."
"Haven't got a clue what you're talking about."
"You will have soon enough. Now go and get me another drink. I feel like getting pissed. Especially as this is going to be our last night together... She eyed me, expecting, or hoping, for a reaction. She got none.

I collected the empty glasses and retreated to the sanctuary of the bar. Where did she get her ideas from, I asked myself. I'd done nothing. Said nothing to suggest that I was any way in love with her. Or had I? No. Looking at thighs or peeking down a T-shirt doesn't amount to a declaration of love. Neither does perfectly natural lusting.

What did I actually feel about her? Nothing. That is, nothing comes to mind. I could feel nothing. About her, about anything. It was as if my head had entered into an emotion free zone. And that was a fact that was scary if you think about it. Why should I switch off my feelings? Was I, in fact, hiding something? Not only from her, but also from myself.

I returned with the drinks and put them down before sitting.

"Woody," she said.
I think I frowned. If I didn't I should have.
"A new name suggestion," she grinned. "Fits your wooden face."
"If you say so." I wasn't going to let her wind me up.
"Woody Street. It's got a ring to it" She thought for a second or two.
"Though Woody Avenue sounds even better.
"Look. You can call me what you like."
"And now your humour has left you. Oh dear. Have I upset you in

193

some way?"

I leant across the table, intent on being serious. Putting a stop to all the innuendoes and talk about feelings and love, marriage and whatever. "Listen," I began. "This has to stop Tina. I know you're doing it to pass the time. Maybe because deep down you're scared of what's going on. Maybe it's just boredom; being unable to lead a normal life. But this is just temporary. It'll be done with. Over in a day or two. So let it rest. Your uncle sent me here to look after you. I'm doing that. Tomorrow it ends."

She got out of her chair and moved to sit in the one next to mine. She leant towards me.
"Do you enjoy oral sex?" she whispered in my ear. I could feel her warm breath on me.

I pulled my head away. And got myself under control. That hadn't been expected.
"Haven't you been listening?"
"I heard. But you haven't answered my question."
"What question?" She had a way of making me panic.
"You know what question. Would you like me to repeat it loudly? Or would you prefer me to explain in great detail what oral sex is all about. Just in case you have doubts?"
"No. I mean, no need. Yes."
She nodded. "So do I."
"And? Well? Why change the subject?"
She leant towards me again. I could feel her breath on my neck. "I just wondered how good it would be to have your head between my legs and your tongue on me. Have you wondered too?"

My lips had gone dry. I took a large swig from my glass as I fought to control the images.

"Well?" she asked.
"You're an attractive girl. And I'm a normal bloke"
"So your answer is yes. It's such a pity that you're just here to protect me and tomorrow it will all come to an end without you having had the chance to taste me, or I the chance to slide you into my mouth."

The sparkle in her eyes reached a new intensity. I felt many things at that moment. Angry at her winding me up. Helpless. Trying to rid myself of the pictures she had painted in my head. I eventually succeeded in regaining control. Or some semblance of control.

"Things are what they are," I said, as stoically as I could.

"And they will be what they will be."

"True. Can we change the subject?"

"The bulge in your pants looks promising," she grinned.

"Time! Enough!" If she carried on I might have screamed and ran away.

"Okay," she held up her hands. "I agree. Enough is enough. I shall put all thoughts of sitting astride you and galloping, away. What do you want to talk about?"

"Anything." My voice creaked.

"Pardon? I didn't catch that."

I cleared my throat. "Anything. What do you want to talk about?"

Her response was one of her enormous mischievous grins. I needed to do something about my tactics. Everything I attempted seemed to have the opposite effect of what I wanted.

"How about you telling me who you think killed the slapper," she suggested.

"Slapper? Do you mean Belinda Carter? 'An obvious slapper.' Melissa's description. Melissa? Something else to put to one side. Maybe I ought to think about becoming a monk or hermit or something.

"Of course I mean Belinda Carter."

"Why'd you call her a slapper?"

"Because she was. Her reputation was that if she could buy something with her pussy she would. Then she could save her money for her old age."

I couldn't help but laugh. "Not a bad attitude if you think about it."

Tina screwed up her face. It made her look cute. "Not if the bills she paid were the milkman, baker and candlestick make and anybody else she owed money to."

"So you're saying that she wasn't just a slapper, she was a cheap slapper." I was glad she hadn't added detective to her list.

"You said it."

"How do you know all that?"

"Got to see her a few times when I stayed down with Uncle. He always had something to say about her when she left"

"Are you saying that it was her, shall we say, lifestyle that had something to do with her murder?"

"How would I know?"

"No enemies that you knew of?"

"I'd imagine there'd be a lot of wives and girlfriends who would be willing to queue up to stick a knife in her if they thought they could get away with it. But I don't have any names for you. Uncle would know better."

"But they would have to know she was at the party. This really leaves us with the wives or partners who were there."

She thought. "Four, I think. Yes, four. Jennie Crane, Alison Maybury, Lisa Douglas and Davina Davenport. And me, of course. But I'm not yet a wife and if I was I wouldn't have to worry about the likes of Belinda Carter... Would I? On the other hand, I might have other reasons for wanting her out of the way. Maybe I'm secretly lusting over Jim Carter."

I ignored that latter part.

"You and I, we were talking together, just before she was killed," I reminded her.

"We were talking together when she was found. That's not quite the same thing."

"Still, I'm not going to include you in my list of subjects."

"Why not? I had a motive."

"Which was?"

"That disgusting, cloying perfume she was wearing. Cheap Bordello juice. Any self-respecting woman would kill another for wearing that, for bringing their sex into disrepute."

"I take it, that you weren't too keen on her."

She laughed. "Not a lot, no. And her fat, smarmy husband I probably disliked even more."

"Tell me about him."

196

"Sort of guy who, when he speaks to a woman, tends to invade their personal space. A groper who uses his eyes and body language instead of his hands. I always got the impression that because he allowed his wife to be a slapper; he had, somehow, to try to emulate her. But he, being so smarmy and singularly unattractive, wasn't very good at it,"

"I didn't know you could be so..."

"Catty?" she intervened.

I nodded. It was a good a word as any.

"Part drink, part frustration... Part anger," she explained. "But I'll get over it."

I thought it would be a good idea not to delve into her current feelings so I continued on the same path.

"The four other women at the party. Tell me about them."

"Jennie..." She paused, gathering her thoughts. "Pleasant. Likes a laugh and the occasional drink. Bill and she are very close. I don't think Bill liked Belinda very much. As far as I could see, he tried to avoid her. Most people seemed to. I can't see Jennie having a reason to kill her."

"Perhaps Bill Crane avoided her in public in order to cover up a private relationship with her."

Tina screwed up her face. "You could say that about anybody. Implying that because somebody seems not to like somebody it means they're covering something up. Maybe my obvious dislike for Belinda was because I'm really covering up a secret lesbian affair I had with her."

"Are you?" I smiled. Once again avoiding pictures in my head.

"What? Having a lesbian affair." She gave me one of her smiles. "Not with Belinda Carter. No."

"So who is next on the list of our female party-goers?"

"Lisa Douglas. Married to Brian. He owns a haulage company. Specialises in continental haulage, so I understand. Can't see him having had anything to do with our slapper... Never talks about anything other than his business." She raised a hand to stop and expected interruption. "So, from your weird outlook, his apparent interest in business is obviously a cover up for something else."

I ignored that.
"Who's next?"

"Alison Maybury. Now she's interesting. Don't know if you remember her from the party. Long black hair, beautiful face, but somewhat large. Though that doesn't stop her from wearing tight fitting low cut dresses which she fills admirably. If you'd seen her you'd remember her."

I shook my head. "Don't remember seeing her. Didn't really have a chance to mingle. But why do you say she's interesting?"
"Well... You know I'm enjoying this. Gossiping. Most pleasant. Every woman should do it."
"Thought all women did."
"Yes, okay. But back to Alison. Her husband's tiny compared to her. The joke is that he used to be a big, strong man but Alison's needs have slowly drained him over the years. It's rumoured that Alison is one of those women who needs it two or three times a night, every night, and more at the weekends.
"He's a lucky man," I said, trying to imagine what such a relationship would be like.
"You think so? It might be alright for a week or two, but they've been together for years... Anyway, I don't think Fred would have the energy to entertain another woman."

"Which brings us to?"
Davina Davenport. Now she certainly isn't a suspect."
"For why?"
"For why? Davina is your ultimate snob. Loaded. Partly inherited, partly because her husband, Martin, owns a chain of convenience stores. Davina's the sort, who, if offended, would simply make a phone call and allow one of her impoverished relatives sort it for her. She'd simply call and forget. She has too many other things to worry about than, to her, such detritus as Belinda Carter. Her husband Martin is also a snob and wouldn't consider Belinda Carter as at all suitable."

That says a lot for me, I suppose.

"Interesting people," I said. And they were. At some stage, I decided, I'd sit back and try to figure out what all these disparate people had in common with Arthur Gibson...

However, I didn't feel as though I'd made any progress whatsoever in trying to figure out who killed Belinda Carter. It seemed that there was nobody at the party who had any apparent motive for getting rid of her. And, apart from her husband, I'd heard of nobody from the outside that knew the layout of the house and had a reason to kill her.

Though it did seem that Jim Carter thought somebody at the party had done it. But what did he know? His targets so far had only two things in common. They were at the party and they worked for Gibson. And here, I assume that Gibson's interest in diamonds and Crane's profession were not mere coincidence.

So was he going through the list as people came to mind? It was a list that existed in his head because they were always the same faces at Gibson's parties. Did it really matter if there was or wasn't a pattern? No. He would continue until he believed he'd got the one who killed his wife. Probably leaving Gibson himself to last.

And I shouldn't forget that as far as Carter is aware, nobody knows he's alive. By now Wilson would have told him that I found the boat, seen the blood and had come to the obvious conclusion. He probably bought papers every day expecting to hear about the finding of the boat.

"When are you taking me home?" Tina asked.
"When I've had another drink."
"Good. Then I might insist on another after that. I'm still feeling somewhat grumpy. A few more and it'll all pass me by."
"You're too big to carry home."
"We'll worry about that later. Why are you still here and not at the bar? Go."

Chapter Thirty-Six

Into Sunday 14th June

We got back without incident. Both decided that we couldn't be bothered with eating, even though I was starving. We'd had enough to drink and decided to call it a night. Though I had no confidence, I did hold a little hope that I'd end up sleeping in a bed.

Wordlessly, Tina disappeared into her bedroom. I presumed to get the duvet for my make-shift bed on the sofa. Though my hope increased slightly when she seemed to take a little longer than she had the previous night. I began to strip in readiness for anything that might come my way, duvet or Tina.
Wearing only my underpants I retired to the bathroom to rid myself of several pints that had accumulated.

When I came out I found Tina waiting, holding the duvet and pillow in front of her. I noticed she was barefoot. Her load covered her from neck to knees.

She smiled at me. Alcohol had not diminished the sparkle in her eyes. She threw the duvet and pillow onto the sofa. She still wore that sweet, now innocent smile. And a tiny thong. I froze. Became a gawking statue. She just stood there smiling. I just stood and stared. Stared at the almost naked, miniature, perfectly built goddess. A corny description but I couldn't think of anything better.

Her eyes drifted downwards and her smile broadened, her eyes sparkled even more. A smile that threatened to turn into laughter. I looked down, following her gaze and found myself poking out of the top of my underpants. I quickly made an attempt to cover myself, though I really wanted to do the exact opposite. The result reminded me of a tent.

Without a word, she turned and walked away, two cheeks rotating in slow motion, a visual symphony of round, smooth, creamy flesh. And a small tattoo, an apple with a bite taken out of it. Never before had I craved so much to just take one gentle bite of an apple.

"That's not fair," I called after her.
"Sweet dreams," was her response as she slammed the door behind her.

I looked down at myself and the only thing that came to mind at that moment was that I was glad I'd already used the bathroom. If I had to go then, I could've only done it by standing on my head.

I sorted out the duvet, turned out the light and lay down; hoping that I wouldn't dream of Tina, wishing that I did.

In the early hours of the morning I woke up. My brain must have been processing during the night as I slept. Now it was completely clear. Belinda Carter's murder was an act of spontaneity not premeditation. Whoever had rang her must've been surprised at her being there and lured her into the library. Maybe just to talk to her for some unknown, at the moment, reason. Then... A confrontation that went wrong? Probably.

Therefore, the police can easily find her killer by checking her phone records. They didn't need the missing phone to do that. Just the number, assuming she had a contract and her phone was registered. And that the killer's phone was also registered. But the police might not be looking. She had two phones. They'd have checked the one in her handbag. But it wouldn't have registered any incoming call at the right time. That would've confused them. One solution to that problem they may have adopted, was that she was only pretending to have received a call. I'm the only one, because I was with her at the time, who could confirm that she did indeed receive a call. I heard it ring. It wasn't loud, so it's likely nobody else heard it. But they haven't asked me.

So do I tell them? If I did, it would mean forgetting about the murder and concentrating only on getting Carter. On the other hand, for me to find the killer and hand him or her over to the police would be most satisfying.

I awoke a few hours later to the familiar aroma of bacon frying. I still remembered my revelation from earlier, but now I had to face the day. Thankfully, the last day under the spell of Tina. That, at least, is what I told myself. Back to Hastings. Back to Melissa. Why does life have to be so complicated when it came to women?

I enjoyed solving crimes. When it came to working out women I had no chance. Things either flowed or they didn't. Trouble with me was that I tended to spend a lot of time trying to force things to flow uphill.

I sat up, hoping, strangely, that she was wearing more than just a smile. There's only so much a man can take before cracking and begging. And I was fully cognisant of the moral behind the Meatloaf song, 'Love by the dashboard light.' And I didn't want to end up 'praying for the end of time.'

I dug the last of my clean clothes out of my overnight bag and put them on. The clothes might have been clean, but I felt grubby. Grubby and hungry. Since I'd been staying, looking after Tina, I'd barely eaten anything apart from breakfast. Alcohol can have that affect.

Now I was ready to face my hostess. Well, sort of ready.

Fortunately, or unfortunately, when I saw her in the kitchen she too was fully dressed. She glanced over her shoulder as I entered but said nothing. The table was laid with a pot of tea and the usual bits so I took a seat and waited to be fed.

"We're being picked up in an hour," Tina said.
"Back to Hastings," I said, unnecessarily.
"At least you'll have a bed to lie in."
"True." Wasn't sure if she was just making conversation or her comment had some underlying innuendo.

During breakfast we said little. I found myself avoiding looking at her. Scared that if I did, I'd recapture the memory of her strolling jauntily into her bedroom. And I didn't want my head to go down that path.

We left the breakfast table. She to wash up and me to make a phone call.

I rang Melissa, got through the usual sarcasms and gave her some instructions. She took them reluctantly, but at least she took them.

The trap was set.

I spent the next three quarter's of an hour busying myself by getting my things together and then sitting in silence whilst Tina was in her bedroom. The atmosphere between us had become both strained and strange. For some reason, I felt decidedly uncomfortable. I had no idea how she was feeling or how she was thinking. Don't think I looked into her eyes once that morning.

Though when we did say the occasional word she seemed her usual jolly self. So I suppose anything I felt was brought about by my own, currently dysfunctional, internal processes. But at least it would all soon be over. I'd probably see her at Gibson's, but there I would have other things to think of and other people would be around.

Yet, it had been interesting. She had been interesting. And if the situation had been different... Who knows?"

The door buzzer buzzed. Tina answered it.
"He's here," she told me as she put down the receiver. "We're to go down."

I stood up and got my bag. "You've decided not to be a punk today," I said, trying to lighten the atmosphere I knew I'd made.
"Too much on my mind. Come on." She hefted a large bag onto her shoulder.
"I'll go first," I said. Just because we were leaving it didn't mean that the danger had passed or had lessened,

Roy was stood by a big, black Chrysler, boot lid open. He took Tina's bag, put it in the boot and shut it. I figured he expected me to keep my smaller bag with me.

Tina got in the front seat next to Roy; I climbed into the back feeling a little, actually a lot, hurt that she should choose to sit next to Roy and not me. We moved off and I sat back. Then I noticed Roy's neck. He had a tattoo of Bugs Bunny on it.

"I suppose rabbits save your life," I said to him. I saw him look back at me in the rear-view mirror.

"Too true, mate. Did Tina tell you about it?"
"No. Was just a lucky guess on my part, I suppose."
"I'll tell you about it after I've worked my way through this crap traffic.

As we manoeuvred through the streets of London, Tina and Roy became increasingly voluble; laughing and joking together; talking about mutual friends; sharing gossip.

I sat back staring at Roy's neck and contemplating breaking it.

The journey took two hours. It was two hours of hell. I never said a word. They never said a word to me until we pulled up outside of the hotel.

"See you, mate," Roy said with a friendly wave after I'd dragged myself out of the car with my bag.
"Might see you at Uncle's," Tina said without really looking at me.

I overcame the desire to slam the door shut and shut as calmly and as gently as I could. I half lifted a hand to wave goodbye but neither of them bothered to look at me. The last I saw of Tina as they drove off, was her looking at Roy and laughing.

Chapter Thirty-Seven

Back in my hotel room I sat on my bed and fought to take back control of my thoughts. Dispelling the negative, replacing it with the positive. I think that I was eventually successful, even my ache had faded. I proceeded to become professional again. I decided on a quick shower that I really needed. Then I would go and meet up with Melissa.

She was exactly where I had told her to be. And her positioning couldn't have been any better. Parked opposite a road junction which she could use if she needed to make a quick u-turn.

She was seated in the hire car a few doors along from Tay Wilson's house. She looked bored and angry. But then, she looked angry most of the time. Especially when I was around. So that didn't bother me. If she hadn't had had some sort of negative expression on her face I would have figured that she was on some sort of happy drug.

I got in beside her.
"You okay?"

A stupid question. She was never okay. Except, maybe, when she was in the company of little, fat, bald, middle-aged men.

She just turned her head and glared at me. "How long do we have to do this for? More importantly, why are we doing it? How do you know he's going to turn up? It might be days. Weeks."
"Want to throw in a few more questions before I explain?"

Cold stare. Pursed lips.

"Okay. Carter's in deep shit. He no longer has access to any money. I'm sure he's got a stack in there." I pointed to Wilson's place. "I mentioned a package to him last time I saw him. He didn't deny it. That confirmed what I thought. The Carters of this world, complicated planners, have to think of everything. That would include what would we do if we needed to get away quick and couldn't get to a bank. Answer. Hide some money somewhere. Some at home for her. Some for him somewhere else. Here. I've told you this.

"He last drew out three hundred quid a few days ago. He pays cash for everything. Even his hotel or wherever he's staying. There's no record of any hotel payment on his card statements. He's not going to be able to pay for his hire car. That was on his statement. So he's broke.

"Where else can he get money from? His house, where one stash was kept is now, for obvious reasons, out of bounds for him. So the only place he can get cash from, that he needs, is here."

"And we sit and wait?"
"We sit and wait."
"What then?"
"We follow him. Find out where he's laying low..."
"And tell the police."

I sighed loudly and demonstratively. I tended to do that at times. It's my way of telling somebody that they're being exceptionally stupid. "No. We do not call the police. If I wanted that outcome, why are we sitting here? It would be a lot easier to tell them now and let them do the waiting.

"We're tasked with finding Carter and enabling Gibson to get back his diamonds."
"Aren't you getting yourself...? Getting me involved in something rather bad?"

I looked at her hard, or tried to.
"These days, in case you've maybe forgotten I'm a private detective and you're my worthy assistant. I'm no longer a policeman. I no longer have to comply with the letter of the law."
"From what I understand, you didn't when you were a policeman."

I ignored the last bit. Though there was a lot of truth in the statement. "Look, I'm going to find out where Carter is hiding and let Gibson know. What he does is up to him. Carter has killed at least three people and shot a lad in the shoulder. Could easily have killed him too.

"I don't honestly care what Gibson does to him. So now I'm giving you a choice. You in or out?"
"How much is my bonus?"

I grinned at her. Language I could understand.
"Five grand." I'd take it out of Belinda Carter's stash.
"Ten. I saw what you got from the Carter's house."
"Seven and a half."
She looked at me hard as she made up her mind. "Okay. On one condition. If you're right about there being another stash here. I get half."
That caused me to raise my eyebrows. Clever bitch. I considered quickly. "Done. But no more whingeing."

We sat back in silence and waited.

Time passed.

"I need to use the toilet," Melissa said with a pained expression.

It fitted. Women always need to use the toilet and they always tell you with a pained expression on their faces.
"Pub few hundred yards down the hill," I told her.
"I know where it is." She moved to open the door. "I won't..."

I held up a hand to silence her. My phone was vibrating and ringing. I took it out and looked. Gibson.

"What?" The call was unexpected.
"Mr Street. I need you and your assistant here at my place now."

He seemed quite unlike his normal self.

"I'm in the middle of something," I told him.

"Drop it immediately."

"It's to do with Carter. I'm expecting him to turn up any minute. You want him don't you? If I leave now, the whole thing might go down the pan."

"I need you here right now, Mr Street. And I need your assistant as well."

"But..."

"Mr Street. This is to do with Carter. Something very bad has happened."

"What can be so bad that we can throw away the opportunity of getting the bastard?"

"Tina, Mr Street. Tina."

"What about her?" I heard the sudden strain that appeared in my voice.

"She's been kidnapped, Mr Street. Taken in my own driveway."

My response wasn't immediate. Then...

"Have you told the police?" I wasn't thinking straight and I knew it. Had to fight down the panic. Stay cool.

"Get here as quickly as you can, Mr Street. As quickly as you can. And you must bring your assistant Melissa with you. She is needed. Needed."

"We're on our way. Be with you shortly."

Her still partially open door slammed shut and the engine started.

I hung up and turned to Melissa. "Gibson's as quick as you can."

She pulled quickly away from the kerb.

No questions. She must have heard everything and was waiting for my decision.

"If I piss my pants I'll hate you forever."

"Didn't know you wore them," I said.

"I don't."

We tore through and out of Hastings.

Chapter Thirty-Eight

When Melissa eventually returned, now secure in the fact she wasn't about to piss her non-existent pants and thereby leaving an embarrassing puddle on the ground, there were six of us in Gibson's library. Gibson and myself, Melissa, Roy and his two minders.

Roy was seated away from us, on an upright wooden chair, bent over, elbows on thighs, head in hands, looking decidedly miserable. Melissa and I sat in front of Gibson's desk, he in his big leather chair behind it. Eddie and Toby slowly prowled around.

There was little sign of Gibson's usual benign expression. Instead I could see a terrible hardness in his eyes. He reminded me of the rolling, growing dark clouds of a brewing thunderstorm. And pacing around were his two bolts of lightning waiting to strike. A heavy atmosphere full of bad portent.

"How'd it happen?" I asked as soon as Melissa had sat.
"Wilfulness. Wilfulness on the part of Tina. I shouldn't have allowed it but I did. She insisted and her wishes are not easy for me to resist."
"Tell me about it," I muttered to myself.
"She insisted that any danger to her had been left behind in London. She managed to convince me that she'd be perfectly safe here in Hastings. I let her go. I let her have her trip into town that she insisted on. Roy took her. They didn't get further than the gate. The gate."

Gibson never used one word when he could use twenty.
"So what happened?"
"Roy can't remember. He has no memory of it. Or so he says." He glanced over at Roy. His expression wasn't amiable. "The boy said that he woke up on the side of the drive. The Chrysler and Tina gone. He then managed to stagger back here." He glanced at Roy again.

"Fortunately, for all concerned I succeeded in my effort to restrain myself when I discovered what had happened."
"I saw the Chrysler parked outside."

"Yes. It was retrieved." He picked up his phone that was laying on his desk, brought it to life and handed to me. "This message came through about an hour after Roy got back here. About an hour after Tina went missing. That's when I decided I needed your services Mr Street. Your services and those of your good assistant sat beside you."

I took the phone from him and read the message.

'You'll find the car parked on the verge a couple of hundred metres away. Get it. You'll need it.

If you want to see your little niece in one piece again you will do everything EXACTLY as I tell you.

This is the deal. £500,000 in exchange for your precious little girl.

Pay that, and you can have her back and the diamonds as well.

I know you have the money. You taught me the importance of having a stash hidden away.

She is currently unharmed She will not be that way by the end of the night if you fail to comply with the following. EXACTLY!

At 10 o'clock park the Chrysler on the seafront facing west. Towards Bexhill.
Attach your phone to the car's blue-tooth and await instructions.

The car MUST be driven by a woman. I don't care who. Use your cook if you have to. And she MUST have with her the money.

You must instruct her to leave the phone on call after she receives the first instruction because further instructions will be ongoing.

If there is any sign of the Chrysler being followed the transaction will be aborted and so will Tina. SLOWLY!

10 o'clock. £500,000'

I handed the phone to Melissa and watched her face as she began to
read it. Her expression never changed. I turned back to Gibson.
"Do you have the money?"
He nodded towards the aluminium case by the side of the desk.

Wish I had half a mill in petty cash.

"I take it you want Melissa to make the drop."
"Yes. If she is willing."

She nodded as she continued reading.
Although I hated her and would have got enormous pleasure out of her
pissing her non-existent pants, I did realise that there was something
special about her. She had more than just balls.

"Are you planning on just going along with what he wants and
following his instructions?" I asked.
He shrugged his heavy shoulders. "I am open to suggestions, Mr
Street. Especially from one such as yourself."

"Our main concern," I said, "is getting Tina back unharmed. We can't
be certain that'll happen if we just follow Carter's instructions. The
man is unstable. I doubt very much that he'll let her go. Don't forget
that the man is out for revenge for the killing of his wife. He probably
blames you for that. It was your party. Therefore you're responsible.
Big prize. Half a million, the diamonds and the pain he can give you
by murdering Tina."
"We assume, of course that she's still alive," breathed Gibson.
"Yes, we will assume that. We have to assume that. What Carter did
was opportunistic. He must've been here for another reason. Probably
to see how easy it would be to get at you. He didn't know that Tina
would be around or that she would be leaving at the time she did.

"Judging by everything I've heard about Carter, he is very clever. Too
clever, in fact. He has a tendency to over complicate by thinking he

211

can allow for every eventuality. Also he hasn't had a lot of time to think things through. Therefore there's likely to be holes in his planning."

I sat back and took a deep breath, noting that I had everybody's attention. Even Melissa's who'd finished reading the message.

"We've got to find the holes," I continued. "But before that, let's jump ahead. What does he intend to do when he's got the money? What's his exit plan? He's not going to sit around. He's going to be gone as quickly as possible. How? Hastings is close to Dover and the ferry. It's close to Folkstone and Le Shuttle. It's close to Gatwick."
"Is that important?" Melissa interrupted.
"Very important. If he decided on the boat or the train, he'll use his car. If it's a plane he opts for the car becomes a nuisance. It has to be parked etc. If it's a plane he'll likely get a cab.

"The ferry and train are easy. He'll have no trouble getting a suitcase full of money out of the country. The plane is different. You're going to raise a few eyebrows if you try to take it as hand luggage. But spreading it out and mixing it with clothes in a suitcase destined for the hold would work. The x-ray machines wouldn't pick it up as being a security risk.

"So what would he go for?" I paused. Probably for effect. "If he thinks the police are likely to be after him, he'll want to use his car as little as possible."
"Why should he think the police are after him?" Gibson asked.
"Because I stopped all of his bank and credit cards. I wanted to drive him out of his nest. His comfort zone. But he doesn't know it was me. So who else would do it? Only the police. But back to his exit strategy. He's pictured himself getting the money. Holding it. Having it. He's probably also pictured himself poodling along the motorway towards Dover docks with a suitcase of money, then seeing the blue flashing lights in his rear-view mirror. I'm certain he'll go for the airport. Driven there in a cab.

"So now let's turn to the instructions. And we'd better get a move on. Time's running out. We'll get back to the importance of the cab later.

Now he's likely to be waiting on the seafront for Melissa to arrive in the Chrysler. A car he can easily pick out. It's a car you can't really miss. He'll be waiting for a tail. He'll give Melissa her instructions making sure she stays online to give further instructions. On line, he can also hear if she speaks to anybody on another phone.

"He'll sit and wait until he's certain she isn't being tailed, nobody pulls out behind her to follow at a distance. He won't move until he's sure. But he can't leave it too long because he has to know where she is in order to direct her to the next stage. Even so we can't risk a tail. We won't know where he is, what he can see.

"Now, he might easily spot an obvious tail. But he's unlikely to spot a different sort of tail. This is a tail with a difference. Instead of following, it will be leading.

"This is what I suggest. When Melissa gets her instructions she'll pull out to follow them. As she drives along the front she'll flash her headlights and a car will pull out in front of her. It'll carry straight on in every situation including roundabouts, until she flashes her lights again. One flash means turn left. Two flashes, turn right. Easy."

"As this is going on, the first car will be in contact with a second that'll be a long way back. The purpose of the second car is carrying the backup. To be there when needed. Does everybody follow? If we go for this, everybody is involved. We're all needed to make it work."

I looked around at everybody in turn. They all looked at Arthur Gibson.

He simply stared at me. Obviously thinking. Weighing the pros and cons. seeing if he had other options.

"It seems that you have done this sort of thing before, Mr Street. I seems to me to be a most admirable plan. Admirable.... If it works."
"I was a DI remember," I told him. "Organising things like this was part of the job."
"Were you very successful with respect to outcome, Mr Street?" He managed a half smile.

"Most of the time. Can get a bit complicated in London. Cars cutting in, traffic lights, pedestrians. Lots of things to go wrong. It's a lot quieter here in Hastings, less chance of unexpected problems."

"And if something does go wrong?"

"Then it's down to Melissa to deliver the parcel, or maybe get creative. Something has to be done."

I looked at Melissa who turned her head to me, appearing completely unfazed. But I could never be certain I was reading her correctly.

Gibson made up his mind. He nodded slowly, as if coming to an agreement with himself.

"We'll do what Mr Street suggests. Mr Street, please get this affair on the road, so to speak. We have but forty-five minutes to get things arranged.

"Melissa. You will be well rewarded for your effort. Please do not take any unnecessary risks. And thank you."

She just smiled and stood up.

It was time to get moving.

Chapter Thirty-Nine

Dusk was turning quickly to night, the glow in the night sky to the west was fading and the many of street lights were on as we pulled into a parking space on the seafront. Fortunately, there were plenty of other spaces behind us. Melissa was going to park in the first one she found. That way she was certain to have parked behind us.

It was 9.40. Melissa wouldn't be arriving for another quarter of an hour. I got out of the car leaving Roy behind the wheel. I wasn't at all sure about him. He seemed to be in some sort of manic-depressive state. One minute he's be almost ranting about his desire for revenge, the next he'd sink into morose silence. I wondered if he was concussed and whether it would get better before it got worse. I hoped that I wouldn't have to find out.

I strolled over the wide pavement and went and stood by the railings. The sea was at low tide, calm and placid. The exact opposite to how I felt. The occasional seagull notified the world of its presence, but generally even they seemed subdued. Traffic was light, pedestrians few. At least on this side of the road. On the other side, illuminated by amusement arcades, cafés, restaurants and bars, it was somewhat busier. It was that time when the town began to wake up as the night people emerged.

I turned my back to the sea and looked to the east, waiting to see the distinctive shape of the Chrysler appear. I had instructed Melissa to turn her lights off the moment she parked and to turn them on immediately she began to get her instructions.

What I didn't tell her or Gibson was that kidnappers frequently set things up as a dummy run. To see if their instructions are being carried out. I didn't think Carter would do that. He hadn't had time to plan that

215

deeply. And for him, time was of the essence. Moreover, he considered himself to be far too clever to need a rehearsal.

On schedule, a big, black Chrysler pulled into the kerb a few hundred yards away. Its lights went off even before it came to a halt. I stood waiting. Hoping some idiot didn't pull in front of it blocking my view of its lights. Though I guessed that Melissa would have taken that into consideration when she parked and left a gap not big enough for anybody to park in.

I knew that Gibson, Eddie and Toby were now waiting in that part of Hastings known as Rock-n-Ore just off the sea front. They would be following on behind once we were well clear.

A few minutes later, the Chrysler's headlamps came back on. Melissa was receiving her instructions. I sauntered casually back to the car, got in and cursed loudly. Roy sat with his head back, mouth open and snoring. Concussion.

I yelled at him and shook him violently. He woke up, obviously uncertain as to his whereabouts, but he was at the wheel of a car. That helped. Instinct.

"Can you do this?" I shouted at him.
"Do it?" he frowned as if trying to get fried senses together. "Do it?" He nodded. Must have remembered. He started the engine; put the car into gear whilst peering into his wing mirror. "Here she comes; I'd recognise those headlamps anywhere." He pulled out in front of Melissa and proceeded along the seafront. Through two sets of traffic lights. As we approached the third, Melissa flashed her lights twice.

"Right at the lights," I told Roy.
"I saw it."

I dialled Gibson.

"Tell them we're turning onto the Old London Road. The A21. Seems like we're heading out of town."

I relayed the information to Gibson. Glanced sideways at Roy. He seemed to have recovered somewhat. But I was expecting an imminent relapse. Concussion can be most unpredictable.

We continued for about a mile before we stopped at a fairly complicated, at least to me, light controlled junction. To the left was signposted 'Battle'. London was straight on. The lights behind didn't flash, so we proceeded straight on. The Chrysler followed.

Eventually buildings became hedges and trees as we left the town and moved into the countryside. Behind us, Melissa followed. The traffic was light, but nonetheless there were several cars immediately behind her. Any one of them could have been Carter... Or maybe he had been bluffing and he was waiting somewhere. But that was illogical. He would have had to be there; somewhere behind otherwise he couldn't give precise instructions to Melissa.

On we went. Soon we reached a large roundabout. Left to Battle, right to London. On time, Melissa flashed twice.

"Did you see that?" I asked Roy.
"Towards London. Still on the A21."

"At the roundabout carry on towards London," I told Gibson.

We continued for about a mile or two when Melissa flashed once.

"I got it," Roy said. "Left into Robertsbridge." He paused for a moment. "There's a pub by the station. I think they do accommodation."
"I doubt if Carter would have dragged Tina through a pub."
"I hadn't finished, Had I. Half a mile or so passed the station there's a small motel. Rumoured to be one of those places that rents its rooms by the hour if needed. No questions asked. Half a dozen posh sheds beside a caravan park."
"Now that sounds good."

We turned down the road to Robertsbridge. The Chrysler followed.

"Robertsbridge," I told Gibson.

We went round a few bends, came around another, saw lights ahead as we entered the village. We passed by the station.

The Chrysler came round the bend behind us and immediately flashed its lights twice. It pulled into the station. We had already gone by.

"Melissa has pulled into Robertsbridge railway station," I told Gibson. "We'd already gone by. We're going to have to turn around and go back."
"We're about four minutes behind you."
"Any sign of Carter?" I asked.
"Just red lights."

Roy pulled onto the side of the road and stopped. "What now?"

I thought for a moment, and then spoke into the phone. "Watch out for Melissa coming back your way." A couple of cars went by us. The Chrysler wasn't one of them. "It's time to take a gamble."
"I sincerely hope you know what you are doing Mr Street."
"So do I."

I turned to Roy. "Show me this motel."
He pulled back onto the road. "It's right on the next bend. A car that just went by signalled to turn in. At least, I think that's where the motel is. It's been years since... There it is. Just as I remember." Headlights lit up the sign.
"Take us in." To Gibson. "We're heading into the Galaxy Motel. It's just passed the station on the other side of the road.

We turned up a hedge lined driveway, passed a green sign with gold lettering which listed some of the virtues of the motel's luxury chalets. Continued until we came into sight of the motel's buildings. There were several large detached chalets, a small car park with a few cars. Some of the chalets had cars parked directly outside. A busy little place. Judging by the ratio of the number of cars to the number of lights showing in the chalet windows that there were two cars to each chalet. It was an ideal place for clandestine meetings; out of the way

218

but easily accessible.

The closest chalet had an illuminated sign outside saying, 'Reception.' I told Roy to pull up outside. I gave him my phone and told him to keep Gibson updated if anything happened while I was gone.

I entered the Reception and walked up to the unoccupied desk and banged my hand down on the bell shaped ringer. An item that seemed to be a statutory requirement in hotels and motels.

Eventually, somebody came through a door behind the counter. He was old, wizened with a worn out expression which notified that he'd seen it all before, heard it all before, so there was no point in giving him a lot of bollocks.

He moved so slowly that if you just happened to glance in his direction you would have sworn he was stationary. Perhaps it was some sort of marketing ploy to make a frustrated guest waiting to get his kit off even more frustrated by the slowness such that when things do happen the tension had grown to such an extent that he doesn't last very long, thereby freeing up the room sooner.

All that passed through my mind as he progressed towards me. He eventually reached the counter, and stood head slightly to one side as if waiting to hear what nonsensical reason I was going to give for wanting one of his luxury chalets for a couple of hours.

I surprised him. Or I should have done. I took out my fake police ID. Never used to be fake. At least, not before I lost it. He didn't bat an eyelid. Just stood there.

I showed him the, now rather worn, photo of Gibson and Carter... I pointed at Carter. "Is he staying here?"
"Four." Expression not changing. An effort even to move his lips. He turned away to head back from whence he came.
"There might be a slight disturbance," I called after him. "Nothing to worry about."

He gave a slight shrug but that was it. Seen it all before. Heard it all before.

I left the Reception pleased and relieved that my gamble, my guess had paid off. I got into the car beside Roy.

"About time," he said. "Melissa just pulled into the car park. She flashed her lights, got out and went into that hut over there after it turned its lights out and on again." He pointed to one of the chalets.

I took back my phone checked that it was still connected. "Did you overhear that?" I asked Gibson.

"Partly. We're almost at the motel."

"Good. But stay by the entrance to the driveway. Don't come any further. If I've worked things out correctly, there should be a cab arriving shortly. Stop it. Find out what the cabby's instructions are and carry them out yourselves. See you soon."

"Wait," Gibson said. "What are your intentions Mr Street? We do not want anything to go wrong at this stage."

"No we don't. I'm playing this by ear from now. I'll do what is necessary." I hung up and turned the phone off before putting it away. I didn't want it ringing at an inopportune moment.

I patted Roy on the shoulder and grinned. "A little job, for you. If Carter should come out of the chalet alone and get into a car. Wreck it."

"Oh yes. That'll be fun." He rubbed his hands together.

Chapter Forty

I walked as much as I could in the shadows towards the chalet that Roy had said Melissa had gone into. There was light behind the drawn curtains, but the curtains themselves never moved. Carter, fortunately, wasn't being too paranoid. Probably too intent on his just received fortune, the case full of banknotes. Enough to distract most people.

I reached the door, put my ear to it, and listened. I heard movement inside, a shuffling sound. Then...

"When you've finished packing, are you going to let Arthur Gibson know where we are?" Melissa, but barely audible.

Male laughter. Humourless. "Oh yes, I'll tell him alright. I'll really enjoy telling him."

That didn't sound too promising. But Melissa's words told me two things. Tina was there and still alive.

"What do you mean by that?" Melissa, concerned.
"What I mean is when arsehole Gibson finds your pretty bodies I'll be on a beach sunning myself."
"What about the deal?"
"Deal?"
"Yes, you've got your money. Why do us harm?"
"Why not?" Carter laughed again, "I haven't a clue who you are, darling, but I guess you're close to the fat bastard in some way. That's reason enough. As for the little bitch beside you... Well, he's terribly fond of her. Probably almost as fond of her as he is of his precious diamonds. So he's about to have a bad day. Unfortunately for you two, well... your day's going to be even worse. Now shut the fuck up before I kick your face in and let me get on with this."

I took a step back from the door and looked it over. No need for an external door to be a fire door so it was likely to be as flimsy as it looked. The door frame was probably pine. The chalet was built with pine. Pine splits easily.

I knew that time was running out for the two girls. I had to act. I took Sue out of my pocket. I extended it with a satisfying metallic 'thwack'. I turned my back on the door, took a couple of deep breaths, relaxed, then lashed out with a mule kick, foot aimed as close to the lock as I could manage.

The door burst open. I turned and took in the scene as I rushed in. The central part of my vision was focused on Carter as he scrambled from the foot of the bed to the pistol that lay on a bedside table. He reached it slightly before I reached him. His fingers encircled the pistol's grip and he began to lift it from the table. That's when Sue encountered his wrist. The result was a pleasingly, sickening crack as bone shattered and the gun fell to the floor.

And Carter screamed like a little girl. A sound that faded into a grunt when Sue kissed the side of his head. His legs simply gave way and he collapsed in a heap, half sitting, back propped up by the side of the bed, head drooping, tiny drops of blood beginning to ooze from the red weal that was already darkening.

It had all happened in slow motion. Then time accelerated back to normal and I was able to look around.

Tina tied with plastic ties to a wooden chair, back to recent proceedings. I glimpsed duct tape across her mouth as she tried to turn to see what was going on.

Melissa was on the floor, wrists tied in the same way to the same chair that held Tina's wrists and ankles.

On the bed was a large open suitcase. Carter had been in the process of distributing banknotes among clothes. Gibson's aluminium case was now half empty.

Then I caught sight of a fat white packet lying on the pillow. I picked it up and split it open. I felt myself grinning as I split up the contents and deposited the notes in various pockets. I looked down at Melissa, still grinning.

"Ten," she said. "And cut me free."

Tina grunted something through her taped mouth.

I bent and cut Melissa's ties with my pocket knife. She had been closest and the easiest to free. Going round the chair to Tina. The bruise on her eye wasn't too bad. As she looked up at me I couldn't read the expression in her eyes.

"This might hurt," I told her as my fingers picked at the edge of the tape before gripping it and tearing it away.

She spluttered and glared at me. I could read that expression.
"You enjoyed that."

I simply smiled as I bent down to cut her free.

Finished I stood up. She sat on the chair rubbing her wrists before making an effort to stand. I reached out to steady her but she batted my hand away.
"It's good to see you're okay," I said.
"It took you long enough," was her response.
"A few hours," I pointed out.
"Yeah, and pocketing the money on the bed was more important than seeing if I was alright."
"I could see you were," I protested.
"I can see what your priorities are too."
"That's not fair. I didn't..."

"Will you two shut up," Melissa shouted. "You sound like an old married couple. Don't you think you should do something about that thing?" She pointed at Carter.

"You're right," I said and took out my phone. An unnecessary act because no sooner had I got it out of my pocket when Eddie stormed into the chalet, sweeping it with a small semi-automatic. He was followed by the Abram's tank, Gibson. He entered the room at a speed that belied his bulk. Then stopped so suddenly that Toby immediately behind him had to take evasive action to avoid a collision.

Gibson ignored everything and everybody except for Tina. He went over to her and picked her up as easily as I could pick up a rag doll.

He stood there holding her and looking into her face as if to determine what she was thinking and feeling. I hoped he had better luck than I did.

He put her down and turned away. Neither had said a word to each other. Odd.

"Door," Gibson said to Toby who promptly pushed the door closed. Gibson then turned to me.
"It is good that your rather impromptu actions have turned out well, Mr Street. Please tell me why you chose not to wait."
"He was planning on killing us," Melissa said.

Gibson looked at her, and then nodded. He visibly relaxed and his smile returned. He tapped me on the shoulder. "All is well that ends well, Mr Street. Well done. Well done indeed. In the morning Mr Street, in the morning, you must pay me a visit. You have earned your fee. Earned it well, I might add."

At the back of the room Tina made a disparaging noise. Everybody turned to her. "Just clearing my throat," she said, staring directly at me.

Gibson clapped his hands twice. "Time to move on. Mr Street, would you kindly take Tina home. Melissa, you must accompany Mr Street in the morning. I owe you a debt. Yes, a debt I must repay."

He turned his back on us and looked down at Carter. He was obviously finished with us.

Melissa filed out of the chalet followed by Tina and then me. Before pulling the door shut, I turned back to Gibson. "Be gentle with him. He seems to have a broken wrist."

Gibson looked over his shoulder to me. His face wore a huge smile.

I pulled the door closed and went over to Roy in the car. He was still sat in the driver's seat; head back, mouth open, snoring.

I opened his door and shook him awake.

"Time to tell me about the rabbit that saved your life."

Chapter Forty-One

Monday 14th June

Got back to the hotel the following morning with Melissa. I had with me a wad of money. As did Melissa. Not as much as me, I think. But enough. Especially if you add on the thousands she'd manipulated out of me. But all in all it had been a fantastically profitable case. Gibson, if he had any faults, which he obviously did, well, they were neither a lack of appreciation nor generosity. He paid what he felt he owed and did it seemingly happily. Maybe that was the secret of his success. Maybe generosity breeds loyalty.

I never asked him what he had done with Carter. People like Gibson have their own rules and if you join in their game you're expected to abide by those rules, or suffer the consequences. Carter obviously got his red card.

I learnt that Tina had gone back to London with Roy. If she'd left a message for me it hadn't been relayed. Something I'm sure Gibson would have done.

So I had all this money. I could actually afford to take it easy for a few years. Do nothing. Potter around. Take low paid but interesting jobs. I should've been happy, content. Apart from the money I'd succeeded in doing what I set out to do. I should've been satisfied. All that sort of stuff. But I wasn't. Not at all.

I felt empty. Something missing. Sparkling eyes; knowing smile; deep, deep feelings. If only...

I took a deep breath, and continued to pack my banknotes away among my dirty clothes. I needed a distraction. Miss Marple. I'd update her on the case and say good bye. One more night in Hastings and then back home. Think I might miss the place. Maybe come back one day to retire here.

I found her sat in her usual seat facing the window, and reading a newspaper which she folded and put on her lap as soon as she saw me. She actually looked pleased.

"It's sorted. The case is over," I told her when I'd taken the other window seat. "I'm off home tomorrow. Thought I'd update you. You did seem interested."
"Oh yes. Most interested. Do tell."

I did. Leaving out certain bits, I outlined the whole Carter case.

"How exciting it must have been. Terribly dangerous too, Your Melissa must be so very brave."
I nodded. "I suppose she must be."

She leant forward. "I hope you don't think I'm too critical, but the case isn't really entirely over, is it. You can't be wholly satisfied with the outcome."
"You mean with respect to Tina? No. I'm not a bit satisfied. But I've got to forget that. It's past. It's over. Over before it began."
"I don't think so Al," she smiled. "But it wasn't your Tina I was speaking about."
"She isn't mine."

She waved a dismissive hand.
"I'm actually talking about Belinda Carter. You say that you are convinced that her husband did not plant the knife into her. Well then... Who did?"
"The police checked everybody's phone at the party. Nobody at the party had called her to entice her into the library. She was killed with a kitchen knife taken from the kitchen. That points to somebody in the house. An intruder would have been spotted. Almost definitely. Eddie and Toby, Arthur Gibson's body guards, are most efficient at what they do. And it is difficult to imagine a scenario where somebody comes in from the outside and has to go to the kitchen to get a weapon.

"So we're left with a conundrum. Somebody at the party did it, but nobody at the party could have done. Or, as far as I can tell, had any reason to do it. Nobody rang her. Nobody was seen leaving the room after she went into the library."

Miss Turnbull stared at me for awhile then nodded to herself. "Was it not Sherlock Holmes who said words to the effect that if you eliminate the impossible the answer lies in what is left? However improbable?"
"Probably," I replied. "But if we eliminate the impossible we don't have much left in the way of the improbable. Toby and Eddie? Not even worth considering."
"Think," she said. "Think back to the night of the party. Who was at the party but not at the party?"

I thought. I ran the whole thing through my mind, from my arrival to entering the library and seeing Belinda Carter lying on the floor with a knife sticking out of her chest.

Then I looked at Miss Turnbull and smiled. It was all so obvious. But why? I had to find out.

"You've thought of something. I can tell," she said.
"Yes. Thanks to you. I know who killed Belinda Carter. But I'm not sure why yet. I have to find out."
"Who do you believe did it?" She sounded most eager to know.

I leant over and whispered a name in her ear.

Chapter Forty-Two

I rang the doorbell and waited. She opened the door and looked at me. She tried to stay calm, but I saw her face drop a little. "I've been expecting you. Or somebody like you. You'd better come in."

She stepped aside and I entered and went into her tidy sitting room.

"Do we have time for a cup of tea?"
I smiled at her.
"I hope you've got some chocolate biscuits."
She found a smile in return.
"I can do you rich tea. You'd better sit down."

I sat and waited while she fussed in the kitchen. I didn't have to wait long. She came in with a tray that she put down on the coffee table and then she seated herself opposite me in a large comfy looking armchair that dwarfed her diminutive size.

"I've been dreading this day," she said. "Dreading it."
"I don't like Mondays either," I said.

She looked at me oddly. "You have come about..."
"About you killing Belinda Carter? Yes, that's why I'm here."

She nodded. Crestfallen. Hope vanquished.

Well, there was no point in beating around the bush.

"Why?" I asked. "Why did you kill her?"
"I didn't really mean to. I don't think I did. I only put the knife in my bag to protect myself. That woman could be very aggressive, you know."

I didn't but I nodded anyway.

"I don't really care how you did it. I want to know why. Why did you confront her in the library?"

She picked her teacup up and took a sip. Momentarily her depressed appearance disappeared to be replaced with one of anger. "You can probably guess how I felt when the Amy Grey went missing."

I nodded.

"Three gone, including my son. Gone without any explanation. Tim, Dick and Mr Carter. But I got through it, Mr Street. I still had something to live for. A daughter and two wonderful grandchildren. As horrible as it was, I had to continue.

"Well, one day, a few weeks after Tim's disappearance, I was in Hythe with my grandchildren. We'd just been on a trip on the little steam train to Dymchurch. The children loved it.

"We were on the way back to the car when I saw her. Belinda Carter. I thought it odd that we should both be in Hythe at the same time on the same day. Well, I hurried towards her with the children in tow. I wanted to know if she'd heard anything. Had any news.

"Well, before I could reach her, she went into a café. Now, I don't like to spread gossip. I hate that sort of thing, but Belinda did have a... Well, reputation. And the last thing I wanted to do was to intrude on..."
"A secret assignation."
"Yes, yes. One of those. Well, I looked into the window before going in, just to make sure." She took another sip and then with a shaky hand, she put the cup down, "That's when I saw him. Sitting there with her. Sitting there. Alive." She shook her head as she relived the memory.

"I couldn't believe it," she continued. "If he was alive, then..."
"Jim Carter, you're talking about?"
"Yes. Him. Alive. Well, I didn't know what to do. I was torn you see. Torn. I wanted to rush in to talk to him. I had a thousand questions. But I also had the children. They had to come first.

"Well, I got myself together and managed to get the children home safely. Then I came back here to think. To try to figure out what to do.

"I decided to go to the police. They would know. So I went and told them. Well, they nodded and wrote things down. Smiled a lot and told me they'd be in touch. But they never did.

"Well, so a few days later I went back. They told me that they'd spoken to Mrs Carter and she hadn't been to Hythe that day. It was a simple case of mistaken identity, they said. It often happens when people are stressed, and rubbish like that.

"Well, I went home determined to do something about it. I tried ringing her. I tried following her, calling on her but she wouldn't answer the phone to me, wouldn't answer her door... She always managed to avoid me."

She emptied her cup and I followed suit.

"Then I saw her arrive at Mr Gibson's little party. You were there. We talked for a few moments."
"I remember," I said.
"Well, I went back inside before she saw me. I was flustered. Went into the kitchen. Somewhere to think. To work out what to do. I think it was when I was pacing up and down that I picked up the knife.

"I decided, you see, to get her alone to have it out with her. I rang her. I thought she might have difficulty in not answering her phone with people around. Well, she did answer. Maybe she had seen me by the door and was worried that I might speak to her in front of everybody.

"Well, at first she refused to meet me so I threatened to come into the party room to speak to her there. Mr Gibson is most understanding and I'm sure he wouldn't have minded if I had. But I thought private was best. Anyway, she agreed to meet with me in the library.

"I was waiting for her when she arrived. I did try to get her to tell me what had happened but she just shouted at me calling me names, using

231

language I'd never heard a woman use. She came towards me and threatened to strangle me if I didn't keep my stupid mouth to myself. Those were the words she used.

"I think that's when I got the knife out of my bag. Well, she either didn't see it or didn't care. She just kept coming, hands outstretched. She grabbed my throat and I sort of tried to push her away with the knife. Instead, well, I was shocked. The knife just slid into her.

"That's how it happened," she finished.

"There were no prints on the knife. And you took the phone," I said.

She gave a weak smile. "I watch a lot of forensic stuff on television."

"Now it's over," I told her.
"What happens next? I feel so bad. Terrible. It was a terrible thing I did. Part of me wants to go to the police. But the children... What will they think? They wouldn't understand. They..."
"Next?" I interrupted. "Two things." I stared at her hard. They way she was thinking wasn't at all helpful. "Firstly, I need a promise from you."
"Yes?"
"Wait a second. Before I extract that from you. There are things you need to know."
"Yes?"

I told her a story. As they say in the films, a few names and places were changed to protect certain people's identities, and diamonds were replaced with life insurance. But there was a strong element of truth in what she heard from me.

"So you see," I said when I'd finished. "There's no need to feel any guilt about what happened to Belinda Carter. She thought up the whole scam. She was the one mainly responsible for what happened to Tim. She got what she deserved. She got justice."

She dabbed at her teary eyes.

"Now, about this promise..."

She stared at me through what must have been blurred vision.

"I want you to promise me that you will not tell another living person about any of this. But if, at any time, you do wish to unburden yourself, speak to Arthur Gibson. Understand?"

She looked a little confused. "But..."
"A promise," I insisted.
"Yes, but..."
"A promise!"
She nodded. "Okay. I promise. What... What's the second thing?" Her voice uncertain.
"Another cup of tea," I smiled.

"But the police?"
"Bugger the police. Bugger the law. In this case justice prevails."

Chapter Forty-Three

Future days.

Back in London I felt restless. Excitement over. Nothing promising on the horizon. Not sure if I could have coped if there had been. Spent time in the office in a zombie like state, listening to Melissa rattling away on the keyboard. She had enough money. Why didn't she bugger off and leave me to feel sorry for myself alone?

Occasionally, I heard the phone ring in the outer office, but no call came through to me. And I got bored with reading old newspapers. I said before. I should've felt satisfied. Content even. But I didn't. A deep pocket full of pennies; highly successful completion of case. Two cases even. But the words successful and complete just didn't seem to fit.

Okay, I admit it. I was depressed. Down. Probably because the high I had got from the chase was just too high. Now it was over I was left with a strong feeling of emptiness. Something missing. I was so bad I'd even stopped mentally stripping Melissa and contemplating the fact that she wasn't wearing any knickers.

Drinking didn't help much, but it did pass the time.

So my life consisted of getting up sometime in the morning, trudging to the office where I was greeted by Melissa's disapproving expression. We barely spoke. I didn't care, I had nothing to say.

When the office got too much I sneaked out and went to the local pub where I sat at the bar and watched other people laugh. Every bugger seemed to think that something or other was funny. It got to me a lot

Then, one afternoon, as I sat at the bar watching the bubbles float to the top of my San Miguel, I got a phone call. It was Notso.

"What?" I said, reluctantly accepting the call. The effort in doing so was immense.

"The bloke who went missing in the fishing boat. Carter. Jim Carter."

"What about him?" I had no idea what was coming next. I struggled to bring my brain into gear.

"He's been found. Seems like he decided to jump off Beachy Head. Probably all got too much for him. Case now closed. Thought you'd like to know."

"Cheers."

"Don't know what to make of it all to be honest. Why'd he kill the kids and then pretend to be dead? Why'd he kill his wife and those people in London?"

"Doubt if we'll ever know," I said. "Some sort of scam that went badly wrong, maybe. That's why he killed himself."

"What do you mean?"

In my mind's eye I could picture his face screwed up as he tried to work things out.

"I mean he went around killing all those people for no reason in the end. Realised what he'd done and in a fit of sanity couldn't handle it anymore."

On the other end of the phone there was a temporary silence. The cogs and gears in Notso's head were trying to interrelate. "Yeah. Could be," he said slowly. "You did me favour getting me involved."

"No problem. Glad to do you a service."

"Just thought I'd let you know. Maybe do something for you sometime."

"Thanks. It's a pity I couldn't make any progress, but there you go."

"Shit happens."

"Doesn't it just."

"We'll talk again. No wait. One more thing. Funny little coincidence. Remember a character called Tay Wilson. Bloke who was part owner of the Amy Grey. Well, he was killed the other day. Hit and run. No witnesses. Odd the way things happen."

"Isn't it. Speak soon." I hung up.

Gibson had remembered.

So Gibson had taken Carter on a sightseeing trip to Beachy Head and convinced him he could fly. Fitting end. Now all the loose ends were wrapped up. Now it was history.

They say that if you want a bus in London you can wait an age and then several come along together. Phone calls can be the same.

This time it was Mackie.

"We found Carter," he said.
"You have? Good. He won't be killing anybody again."
"Ever. Looks like he was thrown off Beachy Head." Mackie's view was different to that of Notso.
"Sure he didn't jump?"
"I know he didn't jump. But don't worry. The locals think it was suicide. That's enabled them to wrap everything up. The killing of his wife, the kids on the boat and Prior and the Crane shooting."
"And you've gone along with it?" That was a surprise.
"There are times when it's better to go with the flow. This is one of them."
"Justice prevails?"
"If you say so."
"Any reason you're telling me this?"
"Two reasons. The first is to return the favour of you putting us onto him in the first place. The second is to let you know that I know you know a lot more about the whole case than you're telling."
"Thanks for the first." I said "With regards to the second, not got a clue what you're talking about."
"Watch yourself, Street," he said before hanging up.
"All loose ends tied up then," I said to the phone.

Immediately, with the phone still in my hand the third bus came along.

I looked at the incoming call. Arthur Gibson. What did he want?

"Mr Gibson."

236

"Mr Street."

"Good. We're still talking then. Is this about Beachy Head? Everybody wants to tell me about Beachy Head."

I heard him chuckling. "So you've heard? Excellent. Excellent."

"Okay, so if it's nothing to do with that, why are you ringing me?"

Was it something to do with Tina? I found myself hoping.

He chuckled again. I could picture his whole body shaking. "Still impatient, Mr Street. Still impatient. It is always good to know that people do not easily change. Makes one's predictions so much simpler."

"It hasn't been that long since we last spoke. What sort of change did you expect?"

"None at all. None at all. Am I right in saying that you are seated somewhere in a bar?"

"How do you know that?" I looked around expecting to see a face I knew.

"The background noise, Mr Street. Tell me, are you very busy?"

"Not very."

"Good. Good. Excellent in fact. Now, Mr Street, are you in possession of a passport?"

"Yes. Why?"

"Excellent."

I had no idea where things were going. And I was more wary than curious.

"Mr Street. Knowledge of your abilities have not been confined to those within the walls of my humble home."

"Very humble."

"Indeed. Indeed. But one has to make do the best one can."

"Yeah. One does. What is this all about?"

"I have, or rather, somebody I know, has a job for you Mr Street."

"And I need a passport?"

"You do. You do."

"What is this job?"

"Ah... For reasons that I guarantee will eventually become obvious, I'm afraid I cannot answer that question. However, I have been told to advise you Mr Street, that this job is not without a certain risk."

"I can handle risk." Bring it on. In my present mood, the more risk the better.

"Indeed you can, Mr Street. And handle it admirably, if you don't mind me saying."

"Let me get this straight. You, or a mate of yours has got a job for me that's risky. And I won't find out what it is until I fly off somewhere? I presume I'll be flying. So going with the flow, I suppose I'm not going to find out what I'm going to get paid or offered to take a job for an unknown person in an unknown place."

"Mr Street, you have said it so succinctly. Hit the nail on the head, so to speak."

"Not a lot of incentive, is there?"

"Indeed. Indeed. That is why I have taken a certain liberty."

"Which is?"

"I have young Roy heading towards you as we speak."

"He doesn't know where I am."

"No. but if you tell me, I can relay that information to him."

"Okay. Why is he coming?"

"To deliver a small package. An envelope to be precise."

"Containing?"

"An aeroplane ticket, Mr Street. A ticket from Gatwick to Barcelona. If my usually excellent memory serves me correctly, you will be flying at ten fifteen tomorrow morning."

"And I'm supposed to go without knowing what I'm being offered to go."

"Mr Street, do you agree that the last little thing you did for me was well rewarded."

"Very well," I admitted.

"Then trust me, Mr Street, when I tell you that the potential reward for this, shall we say, little expedition, could be, in many respects, far greater."

I took a deep breath and made up my mind. "Okay. I trust you... So what am I supposed to do when I get to Barcelona? Am I going to be met by someone?"

"Roy will have all your instructions with him. Now please tell me how young Roy can find you."

I told him. In reality, a risky, dangerous job was just what I needed.

238

"I really must go, Mr Street. Like always, speaking to you has been most enjoyable. But it is time I ventured into my kitchen to see Mrs White. She does have this nasty habit of mislaying kitchen knives." He hung up.

I finally finished laughing quite awhile later. And after giving the finger to all those customers who were staring at me, I ordered another pint.

Chapter Forty-Four

Future days plus one.

Barcelona was hot. Bloody hot. And I was wearing a suit and tie. My destination was a seaside resort called Calella. My instructions that told me how to get there, informed me that I had a choice of bus, train or cab. I didn't fancy the first two so I opted for a cab. I had the pennies, so what the hell.

Took me awhile to explain where I wanted to go. The cab driver looked a little dubious and wrote down for me how much it would cost. I showed him my wad of euros and he seemed happy enough, and off to Calella we went.

The journey took just under an hour. Mostly on motorways, then off the motorway and onto a coastal road. Passing through the usual Spanish seaside resorts along the way. Hotels, bars, restaurants; white buildings; old traditional buildings; flanking mountains and winding roads marked the journey.

The driver had put the address of the villa I had shown him into his sat nav, and he had found it easily. It was just above the resort. A town about the size of Hastings, I guessed. Though I had no real idea. We drove up a steep hill flanked by a large hotel when my driver spotted the sign and entered the even steeper driveway and finally stopped outside the white clad, single storey building. He got out and took my suitcase out of the boot and put it down. I paid and he left.

I stood there alone and examined the villa. I supposed it to be typically Spanish. White. Clean, with numerous baskets with flowers in full bloom. The quietness was deafening. What was I getting myself into? Too late for second thoughts. I was committed. What was I going to find? Some middle-aged crony of Gibson? Fat, wrinkled covered in bling?

I approached the heavy, ornate front door and banged on it with the hefty, lion faced knocker, hearing it echo through the villa.

A few seconds later the door opened. A dark haired, dark eyed, middle-aged woman stood and looked me up and down. I felt as though I was being appraised. *'Fresh enough? Suitable for roasting or frying?'* I took my racing imagination back under control.

She was wearing some sort of uniform so I took her to be some sort of maid. Finally she nodded to herself. I'd obviously passed whatever it was I had to pass. "Señor Street?" She pronounced it something like 'Estrayate', but I got the gist.

She snatched the suitcase from my hand and grabbing the sleeve of my jacket. She pretty much dragged me in. She behaved as if she expected me to escape. I stood and stared at her, a bemused expression on my face. She rolled her eyes and pointed, shaking her finger as she did. I looked towards where her finger indicated and saw the open doors to the patio. I looked back at her; she rolled her eyes once again and nodded. "Si. Si," she waved the back of her hand telling me to go to the patio. I was learning Spanish quickly.

Outside I could see the edge of an inviting swimming pool. It was so hot outside, the pool looked even more inviting. Tentatively, I moved towards the open patio doors. Glancing back at the some sort of maid, I saw her carrying a cardigan towards the front door and without hesitating, she was through it and gone.

No witnesses to whatever. And I didn't have Sue with me.

I stopped. A yard away from being outside. Outside there was only silence except for the gentle hum of the air conditioning unit. As silent outside as it was inside. Maybe there was nobody there. A huge practical joke?

Quiet. Ominous. Inside cool. Outside it would be hot.

I still couldn't guess what I was about to find. Well, there was only one way to find out.

I got it together and stepped out onto the balcony. Into the heat. Into...

A figure laying on a sun-bed. A tiny tattoo. An apple with a bite taken out of it.

A small. Pretty face turned to look at me.
"Make yourself useful," she said. "Rub some lotion into me. It's on the table. And I don't think you're dressed appropriately."
I didn't bring a swimsuit."

I so much loved the way her nose wrinkled when she grinned................

This not the end...

Coming Soon

To Be Published Later In 2016

Calm Justice

By

Colin Lodder

(An Al Street Novel)

Read The First Chapter Now...

Chapter 1

A goldfish, a dog and a murder.

A typical day in the office. I was sat at my desk playing billiards with three marbles that I'd found somewhere. Can't say I was feeling content, but I was at ease. Since my last case, money wasn't an issue, wouldn't be for awhile. That enabled me to do pretty much what I wanted. Generally, that was to turn up sometime in the morning, do nothing, then sneak out to my local bar lunchtime.

My personal assistant, Melissa didn't much approve. But Melissa didn't approve full stop. Of anything. As I sat carefully flicking marbles, she was in the outer office tapping away on the computer. I'd known her for what seemed an epoch and whenever she's in my outer office she sits and types. But what she types I have no idea. She certainly doesn't do anything for me. I don't need typing done. Never have.

I've tried sacking her, but she ignores me and turns up the next day anyway. So now I just look upon her as being some sort of infirmity that one has to live with. However, it is an infirmity worth looking at. Only wished it kept me awake at night, but it, or she, doesn't.

Tall, with fluffy blonde hair, deep blue eyes a beautiful body and face, and lips that could keep a man happy for hours. And all day she sits outside typing without any knickers on. At least, I have reason to believe she doesn't wear any. There is no outline visible through her tight fitting skirts, and in any event, she told me she doesn't.

Something I try not to think about. Makes me dribble.

But they say all good things come to an end. Who says it and why is something I've never discovered, but it does have some truth in it. And my game of billiards came to an end. It was initially annoying. I was on a good break.

It ended when Melissa burst in slamming the door closed behind her. She never did anything sedately where I was concerned. She glared at me, looked down at my marbles that were on my desk, rolled her eyes and shook her head.

"There's a woman to see you."

That was a surprise. Didn't do a lot in the way of advertising. I think that Melissa put some ads in somewhere, but she never told me about them.

"What does she want?"

"To see you."

"I worked that out for myself. I am a detective you know."

"She wouldn't say why. Says it's confidential."

"What's she like?"

"See for yourself."

She turned and walked away. I'm sure the way she moved her behind was done deliberately to wind me up. And it always worked.

My potential client entered and Melissa closed the door behind her. She approached my desk slowly clutching her handbag with two hands as though she thought I might suddenly jump up and grab it. Middle-aged, dowdy and drab with big powerful glasses that made the eyes behind them seem enormous.

Her expression was one of uncertainty, but behind that you could see a seriousness that implied that nobody in the history of mankind had ever had to deal with a problem such as hers. Not the sort of person to greet with a smile. Nobody should dare to smile in her company. Such an act would be an insult to the gravity of the situation.

So attempting to emulate her expression, I beckoned her to take one of the two wooden, rickety seats in front of my desk. Clutching her handbag even more tightly, she complied, whilst looking pointedly at the four books that made up my billiard table.

I ignored her stare, leaving them in place.
"I'm Al Street," I told her. Thought I'd get that out of the way. Had trouble in the past because of the missing 'T's' on the sign on my outer door.

She nodded, big eyes staring out.

"How can I help?"

Her mouth opened and closed a few times but no words came out. What with the mouth and glasses, she reminded me of a goldfish. Seemed to get a lot of animals come to see me, one way or another. Eventually, the words found their way to the surface.
"Murder. I'm reporting a murder. I need help. Nobody believes me."

That came as a surprise.
"Murder? Have you told the police?"
"Yes. But they won't believe me. They say there is no evidence. There's nothing they can do. I want you to find the evidence."
"Okay. I can possibly do that. Tell me what happened."
"Chloe. She was murdered, poisoned by them next door. They've been making my life hell ever since they moved there. Flowers having their heads off, rubbish all over my garden, music through the night. I've complained to the police, to the council, but nobody will do anything. Nobody."

"But Chloe was the last straw. The last straw. Now I really am desperate."

"You say Chloe was murdered. Poisoned," I said. "How do you know she was poisoned? Wouldn't an autopsy have shown poison in the system?"
"She never had an autopsy. She was too old they said. Natural causes they said."

This was looking promising.
No autopsy? Even though poison was a possibility? That didn't sound

right to me.

"What happened?"

"She'd been out in the garden. When she came in, she just looked at me with her sad eyes and just died. There on the kitchen floor with her tongue hanging out."

"Right," I said. Something felt wrong... Collapsing on the kitchen floor after doing gardening. Being old. Maybe she just exerted herself too much. Where did the poisoning come in?

"So why do you think she was poisoned. Maybe she did too much in the garden."

"She didn't do anything in the garden. She hadn't dug a hole in years. Just liked to feel the sun and the air."

"Good to know she'd given up digging holes. So how old was she?"

"Coming on nineteen. Had her since she was tiny. Such a wonderful companion over all those years."

"Chloe was a dog?" Not again! This isn't the first time a bloody dog has caused me problems. "So your dog was poisoned by your next door neighbours."

She nodded. "Yes. Yes, that's what I've been saying."

My first instinct was decline the invitation to solve the mystery of the poisoned dog and get back to my billiards. Then I had a better idea. Revenge! I succeeded in keeping a straight face as I ran it through my mind.

"Well, Mrs..."

"Radcliffe. Dora Radcliffe. And I live at..."

"Well Mrs Radcliffe," I interrupted. "You've certainly come to the right place. I have the perfect investigator for you. She's an expert on dogs and poisons. And one of the most competent under-cover operatives that I have ever met. I have no doubt that she'll get to the bottom of this."

"Oh... So you won't personally be taking this case?"

"Of course I will. But most of the fact finding will be done by my operative. I hope that will be okay. It's how we always run things here. Always use the right person for the right job is our motto."

She nodded, seemingly accepting the wisdom of my words.

I stood up.

"Come with me," I said. "You've already met Melissa. She brought you in here. Busy typing out the report on the serial killer she recently apprehended. Will be in all the papers soon. You are very lucky to be getting her. Before solving her last case she was over in America helping the FBI. Sometimes I wonder why she works for me." Well, the last part was true enough so it makes the rest okay too.

I led her out of the office. Melissa had stopped typing and her computer screen showed bubbles floating around. She was either psychic or she had my office tapped. Nobody could react that quickly.

"Melissa, my dear," I said smiling down at her. "Mrs Radcliffe has an assignment right up your alley. It brings together all of your vast expertise."

I strode across the office and got a chair from the optimistic waiting area and brought it and put it down beside Melissa's desk. "Take a seat, Mrs Radcliffe. Tell Melissa everything you told me. Everything. She will want to know every detail."

She sat. "How much..." she began, eyes flickering from Melissa to me. "The fee?" I waved a dismissive hand. "Melissa will sort that out with you."

After giving Melissa a huge smile I practically skipped back to my office. If Melissa's eyes had been lasers I'd have lost the back of my head.

Now that is what can be called a satisfactory conclusion.

I sat down again and studied my marbles.

And the phone rang.

Melissa.

"I have your Mrs Turnbull on the line. She wishes to speak to you."
That caused my eyebrows to lift.
"It's Miss," I said.
"Pardon?"
"Miss Turnbull, not Mrs."
"Whatever. Do you want to talk to her or not?"
"Put her through."

Miss Turnbull. Met her in Hastings, as did Melissa. Gave me words of wisdom when I was stuck on a case. I thought about her as Miss Marple. Had the same sort of logic. Never thought I'd hear from her again.

"Miss Turnbull," I said. "It's good to hear from you. And a most pleasant surprise."
"You're much too kind, Mr Street."
"I don't remember giving you my number. How did you find me? But more importantly what can I do for you?"
"The young lady at the Prince Albert Hotel in Hastings kindly let me have it. I hope you don't mind."
"Not at all."
"Are you terribly busy Mr Street?"
"Not terribly," I replied eyeing my marbles.
"I'm so pleased to hear that. You see, I do believe I have a case that you would be very interested in."
"Really? Tell me about it."
"It's a murder, you see."
"A murder? Nothing to do with a dog is it?"

A long pause.
"Sometimes you say the oddest of things Mr Street."
Tell me about it.
"Please continue."

"I am staying with a very old school friend of mine down in the New Forest. A place called Wych Elm in New Minton. This is quite an involved story Mr Street."
"I'm listening."

249

"The house, Wych Elm, is owned by my dear friend, Lady Maegan Coates-Braden and her brother, Colonel Bradley Braden. They both have children living there."

"With different partners?"

"Your sense of humour does take some getting used to, you know."

"Even I have trouble with it. Sorry."

"It makes you who you are, Mr Street. But I will continue if I may.

"Two weeks ago, Mr Street, there was a tragedy in the household. Lady Maegan's eldest son, Taylor was found murdered in the potting shed near the lake. In the last few days, young Barton, Colonel Braden's son has been arrested for the murder.

"The thing is, Mr Street, nobody here believes that he could have possibly done it. Such a thing would be so out of character. I've known him all his life. He was a good boy, mischievous, of course, and had an eye for the ladies but no more than any other boy. He joined the army as soon as he could and is now an officer. And, dare I say, an officer and a gentleman. I do not feel that he would be capable of such a crude murder."

"Crude?"

"Yes, Mr Street. A garden fork plunged into Taylor's back."

"That is crude. You say that..."

"Barton."

"Barton has been arrested. There must be good evidence for that to happen."

"His bloody hand-print on the garden fork and he was seen coming out of the potting shed about the time of the murder."

"So what does he have to say about it?"

"Nothing. Absolutely nothing. This, of course, makes his situation all the graver."

"By nothing, you mean..."

"Exactly that, Mr Street. Absolutely nothing. The police suggest that given his previous good character, his out of character action has made him feel so guilty that he refuses to defend himself. Apparently, even his solicitor can get nothing from him. He simply refuses to talk."

"And you would like me to come down to the New Forest and find the real killer?"

"Oh, would you Mr Street. Maegan does want to find the murderer of her son, but even she is most unconvinced when it comes to Barton being accused. And Colonel Bradley does not enjoy his son's reputation being damaged in such a way.

"They are both wealthy people Mr Street, so they will be able to afford your fee. After mentioning you. And what you managed to do in Hastings, they are both terribly keen to get you here to help them. There is a place for you here to stay."

"Are there any local pubs nearby?"

"Yes. In the village. Quite a short walk away from the grounds. The Freebooter. And they do, I believe, accommodation."

"Good. I prefer to stay in a pub. There'll be times to get away and be on my own."

"Oh. So you've decided to come. How marvellous."

"I'll be there Miss Turnbull. Maybe we could work on this together."

"That would be fun. Though that's rather naughty of me to say so."

"Very naughty. Give me all the details and I will be down tomorrow. We'll worry about a fee later."

Printed in Great Britain
by Amazon